EFFULGENCE

Pawani Sinha

INDIA • SINGAPORE • MALAYSIA

ISBN 979-8-89277-947-0

To all the suppressed desires burning the ventricles of your heart. Set them free.

PLAYLIST

House of cards by BTS

Beach House by Chainsmokers

With You by Jimin and Ha Sungwoon

Always on my mind by Willie Nelson

24/7 by Kehlani

Mikrokosmos by BTS

Sober by Demi Lovato

Save my soul by JoJo

Afterglow by Ed Sheeran

Bookstore girl by Charlie Burg

Chamber of reflection by Marco DeMarco

Breakeven by The Script

The one by Kodaline

Feelings by Lauv

TRIGGER WARNING

Contains themes of physical violence and manipulation.

Avoid those chapters if you experience slightest discomfort.

CHAPTERS

Chapter 1	Vellichor	11
Chapter 2	Belamour	23
Chapter 3	Resplendence	37
Chapter 4	Lacuna	53
Chapter 5	Redamancy	81
Chapter 6	Novalunosis	95
Chapter 7	Selcouth	106
Chapter 8	Heliophilia	115
Chapter 9	Quiddity	130
Chapter 10	Moed	148
Chapter 11	Tacenda	154
Chapter 12	Onsra	187
Chapter 13	Absquatulate	215
Chapter 14	Cingulomania	251
Chapter 15	Aubade	257

Epilogue: Cwtch 273

Chapter 1

VELLICHOR

"I am so sorry, Jatin. I would not be able to make it to the party at your house today. I hope you understand." Vihaan whispered feebly to his partner and friend, whose kind eyes dimmed due to sadness, but it was just for a fleeting moment, before he replied, "It is okay, dear. I understand. But please, do take care of yourself." Jatin said while rubbing a palm over his shoulder, and for a moment, Vihaan silently thanked God for gifting him with such a great friend, but then, he was reminded that it was the same God who had also put a terrible curse into his life, like poison coursing through veins. No matter how hard you might try to remove it, the traces linger forever, reminding you of its undesirable and painful presence.

Ridding himself of such thoughts, Vihaan hugged Jatin, packed the necessary items off his table, and headed toward the exit door.

Once outside, he took a deep breath, smelling the classic Delhi air, and unlocked his car. Settling inside, but not yet revving the engine, he called his father, who picked up after two rings. His voice was laced with panic. "Vihaan, are you fine? What happened, dear? I am coming right away. Do not move ab-" "Dad, I am fine. Why do you panic so much? It isn't good for your health, and you know that." A pause. "I just wanted to inform you that I might be a bit late, and no, I am not going to a hospital. I just want to walk about for some time, nothing much. Inform mom that I will be back home in about an hour, and that she should not worry." Vihaan said, before his father could bombard him with more questions. He heard his father sigh, after which, the older man resumed, "I know that we might seem a bit too concerned and protective about you, son, but that is how parents are. That is how the people who love you wholeheartedly are. Now, enjoy your time, and come back soon. Bye." Vihaan greeted him back, before disconnecting the call.

He started his car, and instead of driving toward Vasant Vihar, where he lived with his parents, in a house that oozed affluence, he steered toward Connaught Place. He did not know why he was going there. He had no particular intention in mind. He just drove to the first place he could think of. Listening to some offbeat music, he didn't realize the twenty minutes it took for him to reach the area. He drove around quite a bit, silently taking in the scenery. He saw men and women pass by, talking to each other, hand in hand. He saw children smiling in the arms of their parents, fidgeting and giggling, as if no tension in the world would ever attack them in all its brutality. He softly grinned and got out of the car.

Strolling around, he was lost in his thoughts, and suddenly, a very dispiriting memory rushed through the doors of his mind. The miserable conversation he had had with his doctor the last day, who was cautious of his words, but still has to tell the truth to him, nonetheless.

"Vihaan, how are you? Hope you are doing well. If you are free, can we please talk for a bit?" Dr. Nitin sounded hesitant yet desperate.

"Sure, Dr. Nitin. I am assuming it is not something which will make me elated but go on about it. I might as well listen to it." Vihaan sounded despondent yet obliged to the request.

"Oh God, no, it is nothing like that, Vihaan. I had just ringed you up to ask if you are feeling well. Can't a well-wisher do that?"

A faint chuckle resounded. "Of course they can. I just wish I could stop feeling this constant heaviness and dullness throughout my chest."

"This is the matter regarding which I have called you." Dr. Nitin took a deep breath. "Vihaan, the tumor in your lung is benign, as you know. Therefore, it has not grown, or as we like to say, metastasized. And as I remember from our previous encounters, I have informed you a couple of times at least that this tumor does not require any specific treatment of therapy. Most of the time, benign tumors of the lung are not complicated at all. They are not even symptomatic. But, as you are feeling dull, I am of the opinion that it might be due to the medications."

"I know so doctor. I am aware that the condition isn't life threatening, but I surely do also know that sometimes, I feel a definitive shortness of breath that lasts for about twenty minutes or so, and then, the pain spreads over to the whole chest. Moreover, I have coughed up blood a few times, as you

know. The pain isn't really the problem, it is the fact that I know there is something unnatural and unwanted inside me. I just want to get rid of it."

Dr. Nitin sighed, "Do you remember how we diagnosed your tumor?"

"Yeah. I remember. That day is something I would remember as lifesaving and despondent, all in one. I had been suffering from pneumonia. It was terrible. When you had finally ordered a chest x-ray for clearer visualization, we all had been shocked by the results. Apart from the growth of pneumonia, I had a small whitish mass around the margins of my right lung. That was how we found it."

"Exactly. If you hadn't had pneumonia, we probably wouldn't have ever discovered the tumor. I know a person who had the tumor for seven years and had never as much as shown signs of breathlessness, to point out the possibility of a tumor. I am glad you got diagnosed early. As a doctor, it is my duty to help you make an informed decision, but if the removal of the tumor is what you want, then it shall happen. I hope you know that the tumor is present in the upper lobe of your right lung."

Vihaan sighed, and spoke in a tired voice, "I know. And I think I want it to be removed. But still, the issue that irritates me is that I know I want it, but the mere thought of a scalpel over my chest is dreadful enough to mess up my thoughts. In my heart, I know this is what I want, but the protective settings are interfering with me making a solid decision."

"It is a huge step. And that is why you are supposed to be scared. Now, if you want a removal, I suggest you go for a

lung lobectomy, which is a surgical procedure where an entire lobe of your lung is removed. The procedure includes a few small incisions. We also remove the lymph nodes, in order to rule out the chances of further complications."

Silence prevailed for a full minute. Then, Vihaan's low voice passed into the doctor's ears, "I think it would work out for me. I want it to. But the issue again zeros in on my fear. Fear of the uncertainty of the surgery. What if I don't make it?"

"You will, Vihaan. I believe in you. The procedure as well as your condition isn't life threatening. Of course, the surgery has its risks, but we can't let you slip away like that. Moreover, we all have taken the biggest menace, which is to be born into this world. All the others are puny in front of it. Remember, life is the risk we must take because the fulfillment of our desire's rests on the brink of indecision and courage. But I know the mental distress a person goes through at the thought of being on the operation table, and I strongly suggest you talk about it with your parents."

Finally, Vihaan asked, more like drawled, "Do you think, if I take the risk, my life will get any better?"

To this, the doctor smiled and replied, "Vihaan, I don't know. I am no sage; I can't predict things. But I can say one thing for sure. If you are willing to take the risk, the view from the other side, it's spectacular and spellbinding. That's all I have got to say. Take care and convey my regards to your parents."

"I will, Dr. Nitin. Thanks a lot for always being my guiding light through this condition."

"Anything for my favorite patient." Dr. Nitin chuckled, before the line was cut.

The young man thanked him, and after disconnecting the call, buried his face in the palms of his hands. He did not know what to do, and he certainly did not want his parents to fret over his health. They were rich, no doubt, but if anything, he had learned that money can in no way compensate for your health.

For the time being, he decided to keep that thought in the back of his head and moved on with his work.

Now that he thought of it, he felt the urge to inform his parents. They were always there for him, and although they had the tendency to hype the issues concerning his health, he knew how much they cared for him, and that made him immensely content. He promised himself to break the news to his parents and walked ahead.

After a few minutes, he walked past a lane, gleaming with fairy lights, the cobblestone pavement adding to the soft aura that the street emanated. There were a few houses and some stores lined perfectly, which seemed to pronounce the already abundant comfort the atmosphere buzzed with. In the middle, stood a large one storied building, with honeysuckle vines creeping over it in a delicate fashion, whose walls were tinted with a light damask shade. It instantly drew him toward itself, almost as if a magnetic pull was causing him to walk over.

As he stood in front of it, he read the name of the building- 'Café Athena.' "Impressive name," he thought. He did not know a lot about Greek mythology, but he was sure Athena was the Olympian goddess of wisdom and war. He stood there for a moment, taking in the aesthetic details of the café, and finally, opened the door.

It was as if another world thrived there, unbeknownst to the one outside. The aroma of various flavors of coffee floated serenely inside the room, which was lit with yellow LEDs, creating an atmosphere of warmth. Innumerable books were neatly arranged from top to bottom on three walls, leaving only one of them actually visible. The room opened into another, smaller one, also stacked with impressive volumes. The main desk was small, and numerous pairs of tables and chairs were arranged in the center of the room. Another door, near the main desk, opened somewhere inside.

When he walked inside a bit further, he saw a boy, in his late teenage years, emerge from behind the counter. Vihaan greeted him, and asked, "Hello, what is this café? It is unlike any I have ever seen. Is it actually a library converted to serve as a part time café?" The boy smiled toothily, and said, his voice laced with excitement, "Hello sir. My name is Ritul, and I work here. As far as this place goes, yes this is a library, as well as a café. It is what my boss calls a bookstore café. It is quite unique, to be honest, and everybody who loves books, coffee, or a pleasant time in general, is welcome here."

Vihaan was genuinely amused. It was surely a new concept to him, and it felt comforting. He walked toward one of the shelves, and picking out a book, read the title- 'New People by Danzy Senna.' Upon opening the cover, his eyes caught something drawn intricately on the first page. He recognized it to be a dartboard, with an arrow struck in the middle of it. For a few seconds, he stood there, admiring the little piece of artwork. Then, he took the book with him to a table, and sat down. That was then he saw the small menu card placed at the far corner, with the café's name written in bold letters. Tempted, he put the book aside and picked it up, starting to read the various flavors of coffee available at the place.

As his eyes scanned through the numerous names, he passed various types of drinks available, all the types of coffee he knew the names of, and more. Espresso, macchiato, cappuccino, flat white, mocha, and others came by, but finally, he settled for a plain Americano.

"Um... Ritul? Can I have a cup of Americano?" he asked, not sure where the boy was. After a few minutes, he finally spotted him behind the counter, crouched on his knees, cleaning the dust off the corners. Hesitantly, he called out to him again, a bit louder this time. The young lad immediately shot up from the cramped space and looked at Vihaan with questioning eyes. "Can I have a cup of Americano?" the older male asked again. This time, Ritul nodded, the smile returning to his face. "One Americano coming up, sir." He said in a singsong voice, and rushed inside, past the door near the desk.

Vihaan sat back in his seat again and picked up the book. Scanning the pages, he took a general overview of the book. It seemed interesting to him. But when he flipped over to the front page again, his gaze got stuck on the peculiar drawing of a bullseye imprinted there. Admiring it, he turned the book around to read about the author. As his eyes were racing through the words, he heard the door to the room near the counter open. He looked up, expecting to see Ritul emerge from it, holding a cup in his hands, the toothy smile plastered on his face.

Instead, his eyes landed on someone who most definitely was not a boy in his late teenage years. She was holding a cup in her hands, while in the other, she held a porcelain plate full of peanut butter cookies. Before he could notice a lot, she stood in front of him, placing the plate and cup on the table. "I am sorry if you had to wait for quite some time to receive the order. It's just that I was a little stuck up today. I do hope you enjoy your experience, sir." She said in a soft voice. She was about to turn and leave, when her eyes landed on the book kept on the table. A fleeting look of surprise, and then one of happiness crossed her features, as she promptly asked, "You chose this book from the numerous ones here?" Vihaan, who was lost in thoughts, came back to earth in an instant, and looking at the title kept next to him, smiled, and responded in the affirmative. The lady smiled, "Not many people choose this book from the shelves. They usually go with The Alchemist, The Perks of Being a Wallflower, those sorts to read. They are all amazing books, but I prefer some lesser-known titles too. Hope you like it." Before she could go, Vihaan asked, "If you don't mind, can you sit with me for a while? Maybe tell me more about the book?" The woman was quite amazed, but obliged to sit down, nevertheless.

With a sweet smile on her face, she suggested, "If we are going to discuss the book, we might as well get to know each other a bit, right?" With a clear of her throat, she continued, "So, what's your name?" Vihaan was a tiny bit surprised, but the great wave of joy soon overcame it. Breathing in, he poured out some essential information about his own self.

"So, let's do this. People call me Vihaan Sharma. I don't have a job as cool as you, but I have managed to complete my degree and now work as a civil engineer."

Freya nodded, a peaceful smile on her lips. "How about you?" he asked.

"Let's do this properly." She laced her fingers together. "Hello, Vihaan. I am Freya Gupta. Your common café owner. And trust me, handling an engineering job is much less stressful, since you don't have the burden of managing a whole place. But I like it here. The books, the coffee, all of it just makes it worth the effort."

Vihaan gave her a small nod in response, before proceeding to ask, "What gave you the idea of opening the café in the first place?"

A spark of amusement flashed in Freya's eyes. It was as if she had been waiting to be asked the question. "I love being able to be the source of someone's happy moments. Seeing people come here, solely to enjoy some warm coffee or to unwind with a classic book makes my day."

"That is quite interesting of you. I mean, you meet quite a lot of civil engineers, but it isn't every day that you meet a person with degrees in sociology and market research that has decided to open up a bookstore café. It's my pleasure to meet you. So, how is this book, 'New People by Danzy Senna?'" Vihaan asked.

Freya laughed a little, and smiling, she explained, "Based in the seventies, it is a heartbreaking yet darkly humorous book, if taken in the right sense. It beautifully delves into the topics of identity and race, making you wonder deeply at times, how much we have evolved in the course of time. The lead characters, Maria and Khalil are both quite interesting, and I suggest you give this book a read." Deep in thought, Vihaan leaned back in his chair, and after a few seconds, agreed on reading the novel.

One glance at the clock, and Vihaan got up, realizing it was already half past eight, and that he had to reach home as soon as possible. Before he could utter a single word, Freya offered, "You can keep the book, Mr. Sharma. Return it when you come around another time."

'*Another time.*' Vihaan thought. She hoped he would come again. But then again, why wouldn't he? He had discovered another world hiding behind those glass doors, safely tucked away from the world. The aura that the café emanated seemed to calm down his senses. Therefore, without hesitation, he said, "Sure, and please, don't call me Mr. Sharma. I like Vihaan better when outside of work. Moreover, I prefer people who are interested in me to call me by my first name. I hope you don't have a problem with it. Do you, Freya?" He smiled, and that made the lady smile too. "None at all. Okay, then Vihaan, see you soon. Take care." With that, Freya went inside the room again, and Vihaan left the café, filling his lungs with the scent of coffee for one last time.

Content, he walked toward his car, and started the engine, driving toward home. But nearing the place, he realized that he was required to break the news about his health condition to his parents, which he did not want to do, because he was well aware of how panic stricken and fearful, they might get. Nevertheless, he prayed to God to not let them get too much of a shock and stopped at the large ebony doors of his home.

Chapter 2
BELAMOUR

"Son, are you sure that you want such a major procedure to be done upon your body?" Mr. Gautam Sharma, Vihaan's father distressed, hands turning clammy from the mere thought of his son being sprawled on the operation table. Bleak agony and despair were written all over his pale face.

Vihaan tried to reason with him that it was a good, solid step in order to solidify his healing, but the older man wouldn't listen. It was when Vihaan began to run thin on his patience, that his mother, Mrs. Vidya Sharma intervened, trying to cool down the matter. "You are unnecessarily blowing the matter out of proportion, Gautam. Dr. Shah is exceptionally skilled at his job. He has been trying his best to treat our son, and we know that. He even detected the tumor at a preliminary stage, which is quite rare. Also, thinking of it, we should be thankful to God that the mass is benign and not growing. But think of all the times our son must've had to cough up blood. It's terrifying for me. I suggest you should calm down and then think about the steps to be taken further." She said matter-of-factly, as Mr. Sharma tried to compose himself.

Vihaan mouthed a 'thank you' to his mother, and she returned it with a smile. After a few moments of complete silence, Mr. Sharma sighed, and getting up from the sofa, held his son by the shoulders, "Well Vihaan, I hope you understand my concern, dear. You are my only child, and I would die if anything happened to you. I curse myself every day for letting this disease plague you. And now, I can't even seem to find the cure or do anything else about it. I know you might think I panic unnecessarily at times, but that is just my apprehension. I know Dr. Shah is impeccable at his work. Also, I am sorry for this outburst. I should have been more rational about the whole situation. I genuinely apologize."

Silent tears escaped Vihaan's eyes. He hugged his father, and felt the warmth and comfort radiate from him. Mr. Sharma hugged him back, and the mediator of the lot, Mrs. Sharma joined her family, all the worries pushed to the back of her mind.

After a few seconds, they separated, and Mrs. Sharma announced, "Come on, both of you, dinner is served already. And before you ask, I have made roasted eggplant curry today. I know both of you like it a lot." She smiled and walked away toward the dining table, followed by her husband and son.

Lying down on the comfortable bed, Vihaan tossed and turned relentlessly, replaying the words of Dr. Shah in his mind. "*But, on a side note, I do want you to consider the lobectomy. Of course, the surgery has its risks, but we can't let you slip away like that. Moreover, we all have tackled the biggest menace, which is to be born into this world.*

All the others are puny in front of it. Remember, life is the risk we must take." Frustrated, he picked up the pillow, and putting it over his head, shouted into the sheets. "I want to go to Jatin's party. I want to hang out by the pool, drinking cocktails. I want to live the life of a normal young man. But this stupid disease will never let me do that. I just want to live, God damn it!" Saying so, he threw the pillow at the table, which knocked down his office bag placed on it, spilling its contents.

Grumbling, he got up to collect the materials to put them back. Just as he was picking the last of papers, his hands caught hold of the book he had borrowed from the café, and an involuntary smile made its way to his lips, as memories of the time he had spent there rushed through his mind. 'Well,' he thought, 'let me read this book. At least, my mind would be diverted for some time.' And so, picking up the novel, he sank into his bed, and started skimming through the words. After about an hour, having read quite a bit, a yawn escaped Vihaan's lips. Putting the book down by the nightstand, he turned off the lamps and drifted off to dreamland.

The next day, while typing on his laptop, Vihaan felt two palms close around his eyes, blocking his vision. Feeling through the skin, he recognized the softness of it. He held his hands and murmured, "Jatin? Lord, please remove your hands." A chuckle escaped his friend's lips, as he settled down into the seat beside him. His bright, upturned eyes scanned him from head to toe, before he said, "Man,

I missed you terribly yesterday. The party was a bore without you. By the way, where were you? Went out somewhere? Did something fun?" Vihaan smiled at Jatin's affectionate words and replied, "Yeah, sorry about that. I went for a drive and spent some time at a bookstore café. It was quite a new experience. I even borrowed a book from the owner. She mentioned that it was quite intriguing, and I admit she was right. Last night, I spent about an hour reading it." His friend smiled, showing his pearly teeth, before asking, "So, how is your health? I know it is a sensitive topic, so if you want to leave it out of the picture, I understand." Vihaan's eyes dimmed a bit, but he decided to break the information to Jatin, because he knew he only wanted the best for him.

Therefore, he explained the situation his tumor was in right now, which to be precise was neither disheartening nor appealing to Jatin, just reassuring. Before starting off with the day's work, he smiled feebly and hugged Vihaan as he mumbled, "You are one of the strongest people that I know, Vihaan. God, I would have collapsed under desperation, if not under the disease, if I were you. I love you so goddamn much, and am honored to call you, my friend." Vihaan smiled widely, before turning to his desk.

Hours flew by quickly, and before anybody knew, it was already time to leave. Jatin packed up his belongings and gave one glance toward Vihaan, who was still immersed in a spreadsheet, and announced, "Hey, I will be back from the Human Resources representative's office In a few minutes. Until then, pack up, so that we can leave. It is raining, and I want to get home before the weather worsens." Without waiting for a response, he marched toward the door, and

Vihaan got up, heaving a huge sigh, and started collecting his things.

In a few minutes, they were in the parking lot, and after bidding their goodbyes, moved toward their respective vehicles. Vihaan got inside his car and started off, while listening to some music on the radio. The wiper removed the pouring droplets of rain which fell like transparent gems from the sky above, moistening the air and filling it with a gush of petrichor. The song playing on the radio was cut short, and a sweet, feminine voice spoke, "Yesterday, we had asked our listeners to describe how a person feels when they are truly in love. We had promised that the best response would be read out loud, which is as follows. Congratulations to Mr. Shekhar Jha for winning the contest. Here is how it goes:

'Falling in love feels like you are prepared to take any other fall head on, because you have the one special person beside you, who will never let you down. The one who will hold you, support you and nurture every good feeling inside. You will easily slide under each other's wings like two soulful puzzle pieces clicking together with the purpose of expanding one another's journey with support, loyalty, and understanding. There is no fear in love. It makes you connected, yet spiritually makes you elevated. You feel free, and at home at the same time. You can experience heartbreak again and again, and it is one of the most terrible feelings. But, when you truly, boundlessly, abundantly fall in love, that is only one time. Only with one person. And that person is the one who makes the fall feel like flying.'

Well, this was an amazing explanation. I am sur--" The voice was cut short, as Vihaan switched the radio off.

He smiled remembering the words. Soon he reached his house, and dashed toward the porch, where he swatted his coat a few times until the excess water was removed. After that, removing his shoes he walked inside, where his family greeted him joyfully, and they all made their way toward the dining table.

The next few days passed by in a blur, as work took on a languorous pace. Although, a new task had been added to Vihaan's timetable: reading the book he had borrowed from the café. Every time he opened it, he felt the smell of warm coffee surround him, and the small drawing etched on the front page made him reminisce about the meeting he had with Freya. This was why the book was completed within seven days, and Vihaan decided to return it to the café the next day.

Fortunately for him, the evening was calm and peaceful. The sky was lit up with stars, and as he made his way toward the café, Freya's face floated into his mind. Her round, soulful eyes that radiated warmth, the mocha brown hair that fell carelessly over her shoulders, the mellow voice which sounded like ripples produced in a lake, all came rushing in fervently.

Soon after, he stood right in front of the door. He entered, soundlessly, which was why when he spoke, Ritul was startled. "Vihaan sir, you almost scared me. Welcome. Have a seat." He pointed to one of the empty tables, as the others were occupied by a few other people, either reading or sipping on their coffee.

"What would you like to have, sir? You may choose from the menu. I will be back in a minute." Ritul offered while turning away, but was stopped when Vihaan said, "Oh no, I have already decided. Today, I would like to have a macchiato. I wanted to try out different flavors, as I usually take Americano wherever I go." With a nod, Ritul rushed inside, and within a few minutes, presented him with the coffee he desired.

Sipping on the brown liquid, Vihaan enquired, "Is Freya here today? I wanted to return the book." The young boy smiled toothily and informed him, "Oh yes, she is here, just talking to someone inside. She will be back in a few moments. Enjoy the coffee, sir." With that, he left. Vihaan nodded and started to look around for some interesting books to read. Soon, he heard the door to the room, which was near the front desk, leading to somewhere inside, open. He lifted his head up, only to see Freya talking politely with a woman who was well into her fifties, not paying attention to the conversation they had going on between them. His eyes were fixed on Freya's back, where her hair, brown as ever, were swaying without a care in the world. Her locks, for some reason, reminded him of wicker baskets, woven skillfully into one another, shining brilliantly.

Soon enough, she finished the conversation and took notice of Vihaan. She directed a smile toward him, which he returned with an equally enthusiastic one. Asking a few customers if they were doing well, she moved toward him. "Hello, Vihaan. I did not expect you to be here today. How are you doing?" "Very well. How are you?" He expected her to reply something along the lines of 'same here,' but he saw the shine in her eyes dim. Not wanting to sound too intrusive, he let the topic slide past, and softly said, "I-well- I read the book that I borrowed, and I must say, it has been quite an experience. It might as well be the start of my journey to become an avid reader."

Instantly, he noticed the sheen return in Freya's eyes, as she excitedly asked, "You did read it? I am elated that you found it interesting. Only a few people around here pick this book up; even less try to read it properly. Take a seat, I will be back in a few." Saying so, she left the spot, and Vihaan trudged back to the seat he had occupied earlier. Settling down, he scanned through the pages of 'New People' once more, purely out of boredom. Just as he was about to flip it closed, his eyes again caught the sight of the dartboard symbol drawn on the first page. Idly, he started tracing the lines and circles, landing right at the center.

Lost in his thoughts, he was startled when Freya's voice called out to him. "I see you found the dartboard symbol quite peculiar. Want to know about it?" she asked in an intriguing manner. Thoroughly confused by the fact that the engraving was not some idle art, rather had a meaning behind it, Vihaan nodded. Freya sat down beside him and placing the steaming cup of cappuccino on the table, commenced the tale of how the little drawing came into being.

"You see; the dartboard is not just a random doodle which I made out of pure boredom. It holds a meaning. Basically, the dartboard symbolizes my mind, soul, and heart. It is the representation of my thought process. And, as for the arrow, it is the manifestation of the mark, the imprint that the particular book has left on me. So, all in all, the dartboard and the arrow are a collective symbol of the fact that the book has left a significant impact on my mind."

Vihaan was quite astonished by the hidden meaning that the symbol possessed. "Very impressive of you, Freya. I could never have imagined it on my own." He praised her. She giggled and proceeded to take a sip from her cup.

After a few seconds of silence, he asked, "So, are there any other books here too that have this symbol on them? I am asking out of pure curiosity." "Of course, there are. In total, there are eight books, including this one, which have this special mark on them. All of them are very dear to my heart." She replied. Before Vihaan could say another word, Freya held her left shoulder tightly, and removed the cup from before her to settle her elbows on the table. Panicked, he asked, "Oh God, are you fine? Do you want me to call Ritul? I can take you to the hospital if you want." Freya shook her head and said, "Oh no, I am fine. It is just a minor muscle pain; it will subside soon." But she knew that it was not as simple as a throbbing joint, but something more than that.

When she felt Vihaan's hand on her shoulder, she lifted her head up to look at him. As soon as her eyes met his, she clearly noticed the concern floating in them. For a few seconds, neither of them said anything, just gazed at each other. The only difference was that Vihaan's eyes were brimming with concern, while Freya's were full of admiration. She realized that up close, his eyes were quite striking. They were so basalt, yet a part of them was agate, like the evening sun against a rainy sky. They were overflowing with concern, but she knew that they held a lot of other emotions inside them too.

"Are you sure? I mean, you don't look quite fine to me." Vihaan's voice tumbled into the empty space between them. She inched back a little, and plastering a small smile on her face, straightened her back, "I told you; I am fine. I am just tired today, maybe from the lack of sleep or due to overworking. I was anyways going to finish the coffee and head home, because I seriously think I need rest. You don't have to worry, Vihaan." She got up, and taking the cups in her hand, bid goodbye to him, and headed inside. Vihaan was thoroughly confused by her behavior, but shrugged it off, thinking that she indeed was tired. He picked up the book, and placed it back on the shelf, exited the café.

On his way home, he kept on thinking about Freya's health, and decided to visit a few days later to check up on her. Concluding so on the issue, he pushed it toward the back of his mind, and diverted his thoughts to the upcoming project discussion meeting which was due the next day.

"And this is my take on how we should move on with the highway construction near Ghaziabad." Vihaan concluded. He was working on a major highway construction project, and his core team, which consisted of Jatin, another coworker Karan and himself, was required to present their ideas and viewpoints regarding the impending work which laid in front of them.

"Very well done. I am highly impressed." Mr. Bakshi, CEO of Lumen Infrastructure commended the whole team, as he proceeded to say, "That is all for today. I request all of you to return to your workstations." Smiling widely, Vihaan hugged Karan and complimented him, "I know you are relatively new here, but you have genuinely amazed me with the amount of dedication you have shown toward the project. All the very best." Saying so, he took his leave, and returned to his seat where Jatin was already waiting for him.

"Well, I am glad that the project went well. I had visited the site a few days ago, and everything seemed to come along nicely. I wanted to take you along with me, but they decided against it, because traveling too much is not good for your health. Anyways, are you free this evening?" Jatin asked.

"Yes, I am. Where do you want to go?" Vihaan enquired.
"Nowhere in particular. Do you have a place in mind?"

"Why don't you come to my place today? My family would be pleased to meet you." He suggested.

A huge smile formed on Jatin's face. "Really? I surely will. I am also excited to meet your parents. So, the plan is fixed. You can't even imagine how much I miss home cooked food. Back in Meerut, my mother used to cook the most amazing food, especially cauliflower curry. I loved it. Finally, I would be able to taste some homemade meals. I am excited beyond words."

Vihaan hugged him and said, "We are not friends for nothing. Thanks for supporting me with everything, especially whenever I get tensed over the tumor. You are very precious to me, and I hope you know that."

"I am precious to everyone, dear. It is an absolute delight to have me around." Jatin smiled, and with that, they both went back to work.

Time flew by, and before they knew it, office hours came to an end. Vihaan and Jatin packed up their bags and headed outside. They both got inside their cars, and Vihaan started off, with Jatin following him close by. Within a few minutes, they were outside the ebony gates, and Vihaan opened the doors for Jatin to come in.

Once inside, Jatin greeted Vihaan's parents respectfully, and before anyone knew, it was almost as if he was a part of the family. He laughed with them and also shared Vihaan's clumsy moments in the office with them. And although the latter blatantly refused to accept that he had almost shredded away the current project's file after confusing it with the one related to the previous project, his parents chose to believe Jatin.

Before anyone knew, it was time for dinner, and when Vihaan opened the casserole, Jatin was genuinely surprised. "Cauliflower curry?"

Mrs. Sharma spoke from behind, "Jatin, Vihaan told me how much you missed the curry your mother prepared. I am not sure if it would be up to your taste but do have a bite. I hope it is nice." She smiled, and without a word, Jatin hugged Vihaan tightly. He thanked him again and again, and Vihaan just hugged him back, smiling softly.

After a few moments, everyone settled down, and enjoyed the meal. Jatin praised Mrs. Sharma numerous times for preparing the delicious curry, and all of them felt warmed up inside seeing him gobble down the food.

Half an hour later, both the friends were laying on the couch placed on the porch, talking casually, until a question popped up in Jatin's brain. "So, you had told me you went to a café the day you didn't attend the party. How was your experience? I can't believe it has been four months since I visited one."

A faint grin bloomed on Vihaan's lips, as he recalled the day when he first discovered Café Athena. He took a deep breath, and began explaining how he discovered the place, borrowed the book, met Freya, and had gone there again the last day. All the time, there was a smile etched on his soft features. He also added the fact that Freya was one of the very few people he was able to open up to, and that she made the already pleasant bookstore a hundred times more lovely.

After the short yet sufficiently detailed explanation, Vihaan closed his eyes and laid back on the couch. Jatin was silent for a few minutes, brooding over something. Eventually, he spoke, "So, what I derive from your description is that both the book café as well as Freya have had their impact on you, which, due to being with you for a very long time, I have realized is quite difficult. I mean, it is not every day that you talk to strangers so freely. You are a fairly reserved person.

Freya must have some out of the box quality in herself to grab your attention. I wish to meet her too. That is, if you don't have a problem with it." He waited for a response, and when it came out in the affirmative, he continued, "So, when can we go? It would also be a delightful experience for me at a bookstore café as peculiar as this one."

Vihaan listened attentively to him, and after a few seconds of silence, he finalized, "I think it would be awesome of you to meet her. In my opinion, visiting her after two days would be nice. You can come along with me." Jatin beamed enthusiastically and hugging his friend for the last time that day, got up from the couch. Before leaving, he said, "Do tell your mother that the curry was mouthwatering. It was exactly how my mother makes it. I will also tell my parents about it. Bye, meet you tomorrow."

Vihaan bid him good night and entered into the welcoming warmth of his house. As he already felt drowsy, and the night breeze had further played its role perfectly in adding to the slumber looming over him, he mumbled a 'goodnight' to his parents who were busy watching a web series and headed to his room. As soon as his head hit the pillow, all the thoughts he had flew out of the window, and sleep engulfed him in its endless arms.

Chapter 3
RESPLENDENCE

Two days passed by in a blur, with the impending project discussion taking up a lot of time. As Vihaan breathed the morning air on Friday, his tired thoughts delighted in two things: One, the upcoming two days were holidays, which meant that he could relax. Two, it was finally the day he could meet Freya. As soon as her prospect crossed his mind, his lips curved into a faint smile. He got ready for the day and headed to the office.

As soon as he settled himself on the chair, Jatin swiveled it toward his direction with a questioning glance, "So, how are you today? Thank goodness it is a Friday, I could finally spend some time at home, away from the bustle of the office. Anyways, we are going to Freya's café today, right?"

Vihaan replied in the affirmative, and was about to say something else, when suddenly, a thought popped up in his mind. Without saying another word, he turned his chair back, and started off with his work.

Hours passed by in a jiffy, and before long, it was half past five in the evening. Vihaan glanced up at the clock and turned to Jatin, informing him, "Hey, be ready in half an hour. I will be back in a few." And before Jatin could ask any other details, he was already inside the elevator. Pressing the button to reach the ground floor, he muttered, "Anthurium."

Plopping down on the driver's seat, he drove to a local nursery, which was known for housing a large host of both exotic as well as local plants. Being a nature enthusiast himself, Vihaan was a frequent visitor of the place, and consequently had made friends with Mr. Naqvi, the owner of the luscious and calm hideout. As soon as he reached the place, he hopped out of the car and entered the nursery, bubbling with joy.

He called out to the owner, who appeared from behind a tree, and as soon as his eyes landed on the person in front of him, his face lit up with the effect of a smile. "Hello, son. It has been quite a while since you have visited here. How have you been?" Vihaan politely answered his questions, as Mr. Naqvi was almost a part of his family, and enquired further, "Sir, I would like to ask if you have any anthurium plants in here?"

Mr. Naqvi thought for a while, and then, his eyes lit up as he guided him toward the back of the greenhouse. "Here, they came in a week ago, and you can choose whichever you like the most." Saying so, he left the place, in order to give him time to pick the best one. Vihaan skimmed through them, trying to pick the one that stood out and was effective enough to materialize his thoughts. After searching for about ten minutes, he settled on the one with two flowers, claret and glassy. He gently picked it up and carried it to the counter, where Mr. Naqvi was waiting for him. As soon as he placed the plant in front of him, a compliment flew out of his mouth, "Good choice, young man. Do you want me to put it in a pot or something?" Vihaan nodded his head and responded, "I would love it if you chose the pot for me." The elder man smiled widely, the edges of his eyes crinkling slightly, and then he disappeared inside, only to emerge a few moments later with a pot in his hands. Vihaan noticed that it was tinted beige, with little blue hearts emerging from a corner. He instantly likened it to Freya, whose personality was much like the appearance of the planter itself, simple yet captivating.

"Do you like it?" Mr. Naqvi's voice broke the train of his thoughts, as he nodded. The older man carefully placed the plant inside the pot and handed it over to him. Vihaan thanked him deeply and headed out of the place, back inside the car. He carefully placed the planter on the backseat and drove off to the office.

Within a few minutes, he was back inside the building, where both him and Jatin were packing the last of their belongings. As soon as they were done, the two of them exited the premises, and entered the parking lot. Vihaan asked Jatin to follow him while driving, and both of them entered their respective vehicles.

The drive was not quite long, and shortly, both the cars were parked in front of the lane which led to the café. Jatin and Vihaan entered the small road and trotted down the path. Upon seeing the exterior of the café, Jatin was awestruck. It seemed aesthetically pleasing to him too, and the sweet smell of the honeysuckles made him nostalgic, as his thoughts went back to his father who loved them.

He opened the door, only to be enveloped in the warmth of the place, which was magnified tenfold due to the burned and nutty smell of coffee. As usual, most of the seats were occupied by customers, some reading, some relaxing, and the only free spot was the table at the far-left corner. Ritul came into view with an empty tray in his hand, indicating that he had probably come back after a serving trip. As soon as he noticed Vihaan, he greeted him enthusiastically, but the cheer dimmed when his eyes fell upon Jatin, as he was an unknown face to him.

Seeing the look of confusion written on his face, Vihaan introduced the two of them to each other, and before long, Jatin and Ritul were chatting away as if they had known each other for ages, while the one who had introduced them sat in his seat quietly, scanning the place. "You would not believe it, Vihaan, but Ritul is from Meerut too. It has been such a long time since I had last met someone from my hometown. What a real pleasure it is!"

Vihaan laughed heartily at the news, as the two of them went back to discussing about their city.

Before long, a man called out to Ritul for a cup of black coffee, and off he went to serve the customer, but not before exchanging greetings with Jatin and promising to stay in touch with him.

"So, Vihaan, where is Freya? Is she not here today?" Jatin enquired. "I am sure she is around here, maybe working inside. She'd be out here soon." He ensured him. As soon as the words left his mouth, the door beside the counter opened, and out came Freya, balancing a pile of books on her hands. Vihaan got up to help her, but Ritul beat him to it. He jumped up like a spring from where he stood and grabbed half the books from her.

As soon as the weight blocking her face was removed from view, her expression, contorted from the pain of holding the weight, shifted back to its soft features. She heaved a sigh of relief and placing the rest of the books on the counter, turned back toward the customers. Skimming through the people, her eyes landed on the familiar face, who was already looking toward her. A small smile tugged the edges of her lips, and she mouthed a 'Hello' to Vihaan, also taking into account the fact that he was not alone today.

After breaking eye contact with him, Freya moved toward the table in the front and greeted the middle-aged woman, probably in her late fifties, who occupied the seat. Vihaan heard her say, "Hello, Mrs. Patel. How are you? You have visited this place after quite some time, I must say. Did you not miss me?" The older lady, who most definitely was Mrs. Patel, responded with a small smile, "Well, I would not give any excuses, dear. I was down with a severe cold for a week. After that, it just took some time to recover. Therefore, I could not come to visit you. But, as a sincere apology, I have prepared this box of sweets for you. I hope you accept it." Saying so, she proceeded to pull out a tiffin box from her purse and hand it to Freya.

The young woman was surprised that Mrs. Patel had actually put in efforts to give something to her. She smiled and hugged her tightly. After reminding her to keep on visiting regularly, she placed the box on the counter and walked toward the far-left corner, where Vihaan sat with someone whom she assumed was his friend.

As soon as she neared the table, both the men got up from their seats and Vihaan greeted her, “Hello, Freya. You seem much relaxed today.” She smiled a little and looked over to the man next to him.

“I would like you to meet Jatin, my colleague as well as best confidant. And Jatin, this is Freya, my new friend. I am so glad you both finally met.” He introduced them to each other as Jatin reached out to shake hands with Freya.

After the short introduction, the three of them chatted for a while, before Jatin’s eyes wandered toward the clock that hung from the wall. “Oh, I guess it is time for me to leave, else it would be quite dark before I reach my house. Vihaan, you coming?” he asked, as he got up to collect his things. “I guess I can stay for a few more minutes. You may leave if it seems late, I will meet you tomorrow.” Vihaan replied.

Jatin moved aside from his seat to head outside before Freya’s voice stopped him. “Hey, would you like to borrow a book too, Jatin?” She asked. After thinking for a few moments, he nodded in the affirmative, adding, “I love reading George Orwell. Do you by any chance have any of his books?” Freya smiled brightly and left the spot, saying that she would be right back.

Moments later, she returned with a book clasped in her hands, and giving it to Jatin, informed him, “This is ‘Coming up for air’ by George Orwell. I hope you like it.”

Jatin smiled, and hugged her frame, "I would definitely love to read it, don't you worry. This is one of his books that I have been wanting to read for quite some time. Thanks, dear." Releasing her, he hugged Vihaan. Before leaving, he asked him to inform him when he had reached home. With that, he took his leave.

Freya turned to Vihaan and spoke, "He is one amazing friend you have got. I am glad we met. Have a seat, I will be back." She pushed a few stray strands of hair and turned around, making her way through the tables. When she was out of view, Vihaan rushed outdoors, and opening the backdoor of his car, took out the flowerpot carefully. He walked back inside, and sighed in relief that Freya was not there yet.

He placed the pot on the opposite seat, which was previously occupied by his office mate. After making the arrangements, he sat back in his chair, waiting for his new friend to arrive. Within a few minutes, she turned back up at the counter, sorting the books placed on the counter into various boxes.

As soon as Vihaan saw her, he called out, not loud enough to disturb the others, just to grab her attention. She looked up and saw him motioning her to come to his table. Keeping the books in her hand in a box marked 'DONATE,' she marched over to him. As she neared, Vihaan gestured her to close her eyes, and although a bit hesitant at first, she did so eventually.

"Here you go, Freya. This is the first gift I am giving you, my new friend. I hope you like it." Listening to his voice, Freya opened her eyes, and Vihaan saw her dark brown, round eyes widen in wonder. The chocolate of her eyes shone in sparkles, as her heart shaped lips parted slightly.

"This is for me?" She pointed at the anthurium, the sheeny red of it being faintly reflected in her sepia irises. Vihaan did not respond. He only peered into her eyes, which could have seemed ordinarily brown to anyone else, but not to him. In there, he saw coffee mixed with red shimmer, reflecting a thousand colors, yet absorbing all the energy in the world. They were like the earth after it rained, fresh and comfortingly warm, with the urge to sprout new seedlings. He could have sworn he saw all the hues of the world mixed to perfection, peering into those two mocha eyes, and that made him smile unintentionally.

Finally tearing away from her gaze, he replied, "Of course it is. As you know, I have succeeded in making you, my friend. Now, as a habit, I love giving presents to my friends. And when I thought of you, I immediately settled on the idea of presenting an anthurium. Want to know why?" She nodded, still clearly surprised by the unexpected gift she received.

As soon as she affirmed, Vihaan jumped up and excitedly started, "You know, anthurium is a symbol of hospitality. It is usually given to hosts, as a way to convey our regards that their service was splendid. And although you are obviously more than just a host to me, I thought about the hard work you do to provide the best experience to your customers. Therefore, without a second thought, I bought this plant for you. Everyone may not praise you for this, but I sure do. I do hope you like it."

Freya was silent for a few seconds, then avidly exclaimed, while trying to keep her voice low, "Like it? I love it! This is one of the most thoughtful gifts that I have ever received. Thank you so much, Vihaan. You made my day a hundred times better."

Warmth bloomed in Vihaan's heart when he heard those words. He grinned softly, his thin lips parting slightly and two dents like that on the surface of the moon appeared on his cheeks. 'Dimples.' Freya thought.

Before he could utter a syllable, the woman in front of him said, "Oh, just wait here. I will be back. Don't move." And without hearing another word, she left. He was left confused, but before long, his dubiety was cleared as he saw Freya come toward him with a polaroid camera in her hands. She smiled cheerfully and informed him, "Vihaan, I love receiving gifts. And working in this café since coon's age, I have made quite a lot of friends with the longtime customers. All of them are very special for me in different ways. And today, I found a new friend in you. I have a small habit of taking pictures with the people who gift me these presents, as it truly makes my day. I hope you don't mind doing so. I would be glad to have this picture."

Vihaan was pleasantly surprised by this new information. He quickly agreed and added, "I think the pot should be in the frame too, so that it is also cherished." Freya nodded, and placed the pot on the table, both of them sat on opposite sides. She was trying to adjust the camera on the bookshelf to take the picture easily, but it would not stand stable. Irritated, she was about to turn, when a customer offered help.

He asked her to sit down, while he gladly snapped the picture. Freya thanked the man and placing the freshly processed polaroid and camera in her hands, he left.

Taking a good look at the picture, Vihaan smiled at the way Freya was holding the pot gently, as her eyes smiled along with her lips. Freya took the photo and placed it on a shelf, balancing it gently. Then, she took a good look around the space, and moving forward toward the entrance of the café, placed the planter on one side.

Vihaan had come up to the door too, holding his bag and folders, as he shook hands with Freya. She was comfortably surprised by the welcoming warmth of his hand as he enveloped hers in his. Her small palm fitted like a puzzle piece in another inside his own. He gently pressed her hand before letting go, and she felt herself longing for the mellowness. She looked outside on the street, where her eyes caught Vihaan's retreating figure moving toward his car.

She wanted to stay for a little longer but found herself peeling away from the view as a customer called her. She turned away and walked toward the table.

Vihaan revved the engine of his car and drove off to the comfort of his house. On the way, he received a call from Jatin which he chose to ignore, because he took pride in being a vigilant and responsible driver.

Once he reached his house, he completed the routine tasks and plopped down on the queen-sized bed of his room.

Sighing, he fished out his smartphone from the pocket of his trousers, and lazily unlocking it, dialed the number of his closest ally.

As expected, after a few rings, an excited Jatin picked up the call. Before Vihaan could say anything, he beat him to it, "Hello, best friend, how are you? First of all, I am so glad I got to meet Freya. She is one amazing person. I am pretty sure you feel the same too. I have always said that the dynamic between two people can never be the same with another person. With me, I have noticed that you are comfortable in a friendly manner. I feel you to be the person who solves my problems."

"Really?" was all Vihaan could blurt out. He never expected to hear such deep words from his frolicsome friend.

"Yes. I hope you feel some sort of special connection to me too. And as I noticed from today's interaction, Café Athena seems to be your comfort space. I saw the way your shoulders relaxed when you sat down on the chair. Also, the way you talked to Freya was different. Your words did not seem directed and modulated, rather felt free and flowing. She seems to bring out the inner Vihaan, the one that is somewhat hidden under the outer, professional façade. You opened up to her in a new way, and I absolutely adored you in that moment. I hope you know that she is one of the realest persons I have ever met, and although the interaction was brief, I can see it in the future that we would become great friends."

"I hope so too, Jatin. She seems to bring out the original me, and I really wish to become a comfort person to her, too."

Although Vihaan could not see, Jatin smiled gently at the words of his friend, who was more like a brother to him. Before long, the conversation diverted, and after talking about odds and ends, Vihaan hung up, as the soft and deep sleep called out to him, and he gladly held its hands, as he snuggled into the warmth of his duvet.

The next few days flew past quickly, with piled up work taking up a major chunk of both Vihaan's and Freya's time. With the project picking pace, Vihaan was left with even less time to relax, and the stress really took a toll on him. His appetite had reduced drastically, with regular skips of lunch. Jatin too was engrossed in work, regular site visits wearing him out constantly.

On the other hand, Freya too had a few people to meet in the span of a week, due to which she could not be present at the café for most of the days. Although she was quite sure that Ritul would be able to manage the place just fine, she could not shake off the worry lingering in the back of her mind.

Therefore, the newly found friendship seemed to be on pause for a while, with Vihaan cursing himself a couple of times for not taking Freya's contact number when he had met her, whenever she floated in his mind. Nevertheless, he looked forward to the weekend, which would be a breath of fresh air, and when he would finally have time to relax and meet his new mate at the café, so willingly described as his 'comfort place' by Jatin.

When Friday came to a close, Vihaan's face was marked by two contrasting expressions. His eyes seemed tired and dull, begging for a night of peaceful sleep, but his lips were tugged up by a blinding smile, because he knew that the next two days would be quite unwinding and snug. He packed his belongings in a lazy manner, and bidding a good night to Jatin, whose eyes were still glued to the file he held in his hands, he walked up to the elevator, which took him to the underground parking spot.

Once inside the car, he started the engine, and listening to some old melodies, which teleported him to his childhood days, he drove down the streets of Delhi, humming gently to himself.

Not quite later, he found himself parking the car outside his house, as he thought to himself, 'Music really does make time fly by faster.' And with random thoughts roving inside his head, he entered the drawing room, the warmth enveloping his tall frame, as he slid off the shoes and walked up to his mother, who was preparing the dinner in the kitchen.

Upon feeling Vihaan's presence behind her, she said aloud, "I know you are here, son. But before you say that you are hungry and want dinner, I must remind you to clean up." Her voice was soft yet firm, just like it had been whenever Vihaan decided to throw a tantrum to avoid going to school, and she giggled lightly as she felt a pair of arms snake up her waist, as Vihaan kept his chin on her head. She pinched his cheeks and nudged him a little, a signal for scurrying off and cleaning up before dinner was served. Vihaan laughed heartily, and backing off, he shouted from the hallway,

"You need to spill out the secret, mom! How do you recognize me?" His mother did not say anything, just smiled a little, before returning to the work at hand.

By the time Vihaan made his way downstairs, dinner had been served and both his parents were sitting on the couch, waiting for him. As soon as they saw him come, they stopped whatever discussion was going on, and stood up instantly, walking toward the table. If he noticed the behavior, Vihaan chose not to comment on it. He sat down along with his parents, and all three of them ate their dinner in silence.

Just as he got up to leave, his father stopped him, saying "Son, don't leave just yet. We have something to talk about."

Listening to his father's words, the young man sat down, unsure of the proceedings that were to follow. Soon enough, his father cleared his throat and began, "As you know well, Vihaan, the tumor in your lung has not been showing any growth, but neither has it shown any positive reaction to the medicines. You went in last week too, but Dr. Nitin had called me today, to inform you that you need to take the consideration of the lobectomy quite carefully. It might give your life a complete turn. Remember dear, none of us would ever want any harm to befall you, let alone put your life in any danger. We all are well aware of the suffering this disease causes you, the irritation you feel consuming innumerable tablets, but it is for your own good, son. This operation is like a ray of light in a dark, cold tunnel. We need to wisely move toward it, not run away, afraid of change."

Vihaan listened to his father carefully, and when he looked up to meet his eyes, he saw pain, care, warmth, and worry swirling inside. Moving on to his mother, he saw her face marred with an ache, a longing to see her son in a healthy state again, and that broke his heart. And when he listened to his own heart, he became conscious of the fact that it was beating irregularly, and that he was absolutely terrified of the idea of such a major operation to be done on him. Yet, he inhaled, and releasing a shaky breath, slowly said, "I am honestly terrified of the surgery, dad. But I do realize that it is as crucial for both of you, as it is for me. Therefore, I have decided to give it a go. But not instantly. I need to prepare myself both mentally and physically, and therefore, I request to continue with the chemotherapy sessions for a few more months, and by that time, I am sure I would be in the right state of mind. I hope you understand." He completed in a single go, before anybody could interrupt his train of thoughts.

His eyes were closed, and fists clenched, but he relaxed a little when he felt his mother's hand hold his face. He opened his eyes, and she said in an almost hushed tone, "Son, I am so proud of you. I never thought you would agree. Do you even realize how brave this is of you? I love you from the bottom of my heart, we both do, and I am elated just by the idea of my dear son being all hearty and robust again."

Before he could say anything, Vihaan felt a warm hand on his shoulder, and he looked up to see his father holding his shoulder tightly, and a faint smile was plastered on his lips.

He did not say anything, just hugged him tightly. Tears stung the corners of Vihaan's eyes, but he pushed them back. Indeed, he knew that he was fearful of the surgery, but inside the rational part of his brain, he knew that this was for his own good.

When his father released the hug, he felt the warmth leave his body, as the cool air brushed his sides. An involuntary shiver ran down his spine, and when he looked up, he saw both his parents looking toward him with a concoct of love, adoration, pride, and concern painting their faces.

Vihaan looked toward his mother, whose warm brown eyes were always dripping with the purest care to ever exist, and which looked like hot cocoa filled in mugs.

He then looked toward his father, the pillar of the family, whose steely gray eyes he had inherited. Those eyes seemed cold at first glance, but when one took the effort to look past the steel, soft cotton was all they could find.

He smiled, the curve of his lips hurting every cell. Yet, he got up, hugged both his parents, and retired to his bedroom, where sleep waited eagerly to engulf him in its depths, which was the refuge from all the problems in the world.

Chapter 4
LACUNA

December had always been one of the most peaceful months for Vihaan, who was currently strolling on the office balcony, a cup of latte macchiato in his hands. It had been two days since the deep and downcast conversation regarding the impending surgery with his parents, and it had been imperative for him to tell Jatin since he wouldn't stop pestering him with innumerable questions.

Slowly, Vihaan had been trying to build the courage within him, piece by piece, but it would all crumble down at the thought of one fact: Only about 40% of people diagnosed with a benign lung tumor are able to have surgery because most of the times, they are found after the disease has already progressed.

Dr. Nitin had shared this information with him, so that he could make an informed decision, after weighing all the pros and cons whatsoever. His heart told him to go for it, after all, as he had been lucky enough to be diagnosed this early, it was fairly possible for him to make it out successfully as well. But, the logical part of his being, his brain, advocated the fact that the number of casualties in the procedure were far too more than successes. He should continue with the medicines, and not put such a hazardous risk in front of his life.

While these thoughts were dueling inside his being, one sentence by Dr. Shah stood out, above all the turmoil and chaos. '*Life is the risk we all must take.*' This is what constantly kept him going, not letting him crumble in front of the herculean troubles.

Sighing, he turned around to walk back inside the office, when Jatin walked out, licking a small cone of ice cream. When their eyes met, he smiled widely, like the cheerful person he was. Vihaan smiled too, but it did not reach his eyes. When his best friend noticed this, his expression turned somber. He slowly trudges toward him, and without saying a word, hugged the other tightly. Vihaan was slightly shocked for a second, but the next moment, he wrapped his arms around Jatin just as securely.

After a few seconds, the two parted, and Vihaan smiled. It was a tired expression, but the sincerity reflected from it was truly amazing. He had always been a person who valued relationships, and he thought that putting his heart and soul to nurture a bond would always reap results, no matter how long it takes.

"So, when are you visiting Freya? You know, she is a good friend. You shouldn't abandon her like this when you are in a crisis. I think she would help you make a clear decision regarding the issue. Did you ever give her a hint about your condition, though?" Jatin asked.

"No, of course not. I would never like to burden her with this sort of depressing information. She is a very important person for me, and I don't think I want my medical condition to come in between the special bond that we have." Vihaan stated clearly.

Jatin nodded, his eyes glinting with sorrow, yet Vihaan could spot a ray of hope shining at the edges. Both of them walked back toward their desks and resumed the work at hand.

Two days went by in a blur, and it was December 4, when Vihaan decided to visit Freya. He had taken a round of the medicines prescribed to him a few hours ago, and as he had come to notice, they always made him feel a bit nauseous and dizzy. However, they were potent medications which had the capacity to produce such side effects, as told by Dr. Nitin, which was why he wasn't too concerned.

It had been a while, and now that he thought about it, he realized that he missed the café and the people there a lot. He did not want to say that the café was a distraction from his mundane and difficult life, because it would degrade its position to a mere entertainer. For him, in fact, it was a homely abode, where he found his heart and soul at peace instantly, and where the sweet aroma of coffee- and a specific person- floated incessantly.

So, in the evening, he drove leisurely toward the local nursery once again, where he was met with Mr. Naqvi, who was bent over a collection of roses, inspecting the lot. Vihaan walked up to him, and casually patted the older man's shoulder, whispered, "You need to rest too, you know?"

Mr. Naqvi did not turn, just chuckled, as he recognized the familiar voice. Dusting his trousers as he got up, he said, "Son, I have rested well. And after all, my heart resides within these plants. I need to be with them. They fill me with serendipity. Anyways, enough about me. What brings you here?"

On being enquired, Vihaan expressed the desire to purchase a plant of hydrangea. When he did not receive a response, he decided to stay quiet. After a few seconds, Mr. Naqvi thoughtfully said, "I am in awe of how lucky you are. Believe me when I say, a whole batch of beautiful hydrangeas arrived just yesterday. They are inside, as I haven't had the time to organize them yet. I will show them to you, come with me."

With this, he led Vihaan to the room, where the plants were placed. In all honesty, each one beat the next. Delicate hues of red, maroon, orange, blue and pink mashed together to present the most soothing fusion of colors to the eyes. Each petal curved delicately together, enfolding into itself. The stark contrast from the darkness of the room added to the magnificence they exuded.

Vihaan stared at them for a few minutes, having visible difficulty in choosing one of them. Assessing his turmoil, Mr. Naqvi stepped forward. He proposed, "I can plant more than one of them in a bigger pot, you know? Do not worry about picking one. Choose as many as you want and leave the rest to me." A smile graced Vihaan pained expressions, as he turned around to hug the older man tightly.

After freeing himself from an eager Vihaan, Mr. Naqvi picked up the best flowers from the lot and proceeded to place them intricately inside a large planter. The blue mixed with the maroon, which whispered delicately into the pink, which gave way to the orange. When he was done, Vihaan was left speechless, as he eyed the deep blue pot in awe. Finally, taking it from the expert flower arranger's hands, he said, "I never knew you were so talented. I hope I am able to see much more of this in the future." Mr. Naqvi laughed heartily, and patting on the young man's back, bid him goodbye, before leaving for the backyard.

Vihaan too, walked up to his car, where he placed the pot on the backseat carefully, so as to not break it. Then, with clammy hands, he drove to the café, his peace and refuge.

He never understood why going to the place brought out the nervous side of him, as if he was going to an interview. But the feeling was not of dread. Rather, it was always of bubbling excitement, which pushed his emotions into a pumped state.

With these thoughts playing in his brain repeatedly, he didn't recognize when he reached the café. He parked the car on the sidewalk and walked toward the place.

When the gates opened, a swoosh of dark mocha brown hair greeted him, smelling of vanilla and cinnamon.

Freya turned around, pleasantly surprised to see Vihaan at the doorstep after a long time. A bright smile graced her lips, as she put out a hand for him to shake. He shook it firmly, his own palm lingering there for a few more seconds than intended. When he let go of her and let his eyes wander in the café, every cell in his body seemed to relax at the feeling of being inside the comforting space. It was as if the room had a pace of its own, different from the world, and where people were always welcome to relax and unwind from the grueling reality of life.

Finally, his eyes came to rest on the beige pot placed by the door, in which the anthurium was still planted. The plant glistened softly, indicating that it had received a shower recently. His eyes curved into little crescents as he smiled softly at the memory of Freya being elated on receiving the present.

As he walked further inside, he decided to sit on his usual seat, the one at the back. Walking forward, his eyes caught the sight of a beautiful photo frame, blue and green, with seashells decorating the borders. His pupils widened when he realized that the picture it housed was the same polaroid which Freya had taken the other day, along with the plant.

As he stood there, admiring the frame and the photograph, a mellow voice broke his train of thoughts. "Like it? It was special to me, and therefore I decided to frame it." He turned around to see Freya standing there, with a cup of latte in her hands. Not receiving a response, she continued, you really hope you. I came to ask what you would like to order today. Any preferences?"

After pondering for a few seconds and realizing that his indecision would not let him come up with any name, Vihaan said, "Actually, if I may ask, what is the one in your hands called?" Freya laughed lightly, and Vihaan could have sworn that the ringing voice alone set his heart at an erratic pace. She said, "You really are clueless about coffee, aren't you? Well, it is a latte. And of course, you can have it. Would you like some toppings, like cardamom, coconut milk or chocolate?"

"Chocolate sounds pleasant." He said, without thinking much. "One latte with chocolate topping coming right up, sir." Freya said, and turning around, walked toward the door that led to the kitchen. Vihaan sighed, not sadly but contentedly, as he reclined back in his seat. Closing his eyes, he rested his head between his arms, and massaged the eyelids. Not much later, he felt a plate being placed on the table, and as he lazily lifted his head up, he eyed Freya, and for the first time, took in the clothes she was wearing. It was a pine green bohemian blouse, paired with charcoal pants. The choice of the hues radiated the perfect aura for the word: comfort. He smiled, and taking the cup in his hands, muttered a small "Thank you." Freya smiled, and walked away, saying that she had to attend a call.

When she came back, she noticed Vihaan looking outside the window, with his face resting lightly on his palm. His skin was clear, like solidified caramel, and his smile was soft and gentle. But it was his eyes, which she probably noticed in a different light for the first time, that made her breath hitch in her throat. His eyes really were gray, gray enough to be able to seem muted, yet there was something in them that brewed and churned life. The shade, if she was being sure, was nothing short of striking, and it reminded her of the glisten of the hair of an old woman, grinding spices in the sun, definitive and experienced, yet brilliant and reflective.

One of his hands held the cup firmly, while the other acted as a support for his visage, which looked ever so soft and gentle, as if it were made of glass, and life was breathed at the last moment in it.

After a few seconds of standing still, she strolled toward him and sat down on the opposite seat. As soon as he saw her, a smile crept its way onto his lips as he welcomed her to sit. They talked about odds and ends for about half an hour at a stretch, with topics ranging from the illogical work pressure in corporate offices to the most emotionally moving stories ever written.

In the middle of the conversation, Vihaan's mobile phone buzzed, and when he picked it up, he saw that his father was calling him. Looking at the time, which was half past eight, he realized that he had been conveniently late in reaching home, thanks to the mesmerizingly sweet and interesting words of a certain young woman.

When he looked up, he saw Freya already standing, holding the used cup in her hands. She said, "I know, it has been quite late. Your parents must be worried sick. You should go home. Although, I must say, your visit here has been the highlight of my extremely monotonous week."

Vihaan got up too, the thought of what he was about to do tingling his insides. He smiled, "Thanks a lot, Freya. And in all honesty, I too feel a sense of relaxation and serenity here, at this café. See you soon."

When Freya smiled softly, he directed his feet toward the door, passing the anthurium once more. Internally, he whispered, 'You were my first gift. The second is soon to follow.' With this, he walked briskly to his car, and taking out the planter, gave it one last look of adoration, as he silently thanked Mr. Naqvi for his skills.

Without wasting much time or thought, he trotted back to the café, where an unsuspecting Freya was leaning by a shelf.

As soon as he entered, without making any sound, she turned back, leaving him slightly surprised. "Back again? How may I help you?" she asked, a slight tinge of astonishment in her own voice. Toward the end of the sentence, her vision drifted toward the pot, and that is when her eyes widened, while a small smile made its way onto her lips.

Her brown pupils faintly reflected the soft hues, and Vihaan almost saw the muddy matrix giving way to the starry dimension ahead. "Another beauty? If this is how you pamper your friends, then I am sure that it is one of the best ones I have ever experienced." She spoke. "Hydrangeas." he said.

"What do they signify, if I may ask?"

'*How do you know what I am about to say?*' Vihaan thought. "Hydrangeas are a symbol of heartfelt emotions and gratitude. They are extensively used to express the feeling of deep-set sentiments and acknowledgment. And being the amazing friend that you are, I felt the need to shower you with reasons to celebrate your feelings, because you may not know, but they float beautifully in your eyes, lighting them up with a delicate sheen."

Freya's smile grew by inches, as she said to herself, "It is a first for me. It is a new sort of appreciation." She went on to hold the plant in her own hands, and when she inspected it closely, a flush of memories invaded her as she remembered that those were the plants here mother used to grow back in their old house, when they lived in Agra. She delicately ran her fingers over them, and when she reached the tip of the last orange flower, one of her hands held the pot in place, while the other instantly wrapped around Vihaan's wrist, as she dragged him toward their table. "We surely have to take a photograph with this one too, because I want to treasure this small yet colorful moment forever." She explained, taking out the polaroid camera.

Before Vihaan could say anything, she called out to Ritul, who appeared with his usual pearly smile. "Yes, mam? How may I help you?" he asked, wiping his palms with a hand towel. Freya explained the procedure of using the camera to him, and after she was assured, he could use it without any difficulties, she moved forward to place the planter on the table, while sitting across from Vihaan. When both of them smiled, Ritul snapped the picture, giving the camera back to Freya. She took the film out, and after shaking it gently for a few seconds, the clear photograph emerged on the shiny surface on the sheet. She placed it on a shelf, away from the tables, so that it could dry easily.

It was at this moment that she heard Vihaan's voice from behind, speaking ever so softly, like the gentle rustle of wind from between the viridescent leaves in a calm tropical forest. "I think I should be taking my leave now. It was lovely meeting you, and I hope you like this present even better than the last one." He finished with a tired but jovial smile on his lips.

Freya walked up to hug him softly, and he gladly returned the gesture. As he waved at her while walking down to his car, she couldn't help but notice his outfit this time round. He wore a white shirt, with a pine green argyle pattern decorating the pocket and cuffs. His coat hung loosely on one of his arms, while his formal pants were a deep charcoal black. She smiled as she turned around, walking back to the counter, when her eyes landed on a mirror, which reflected her form. In less than a second, she noticed the mix of shades in front of her. Pine green and charcoal black. She noticed this recently, didn't she?

And then, her lips parted a little, as realization dawned upon her, and before long, a genuine yet amused smile made its way smoothly on her lips as she said, "Maybe our frequencies meet more than I tend to recognize. Thanks for lifting my mood today, Vihaan." With this she walked off, smiling at her customers, all of whom greeted her with the same beam.

(FOUR HOURS AGO)

Freya had been breaking her back over arranging a few books inside, when she heard the door open. She also heard Ritul greet the person as he requested them to take a seat.

She walked out smiling, ready to take the order, but her feet halted, and cold sweat broke on her forehead when she took in the frame of the person. He wore a long black trench coat, underneath which were a pair of stone washed jeans and a white shirt.

"Hello, Freya. Nice to meet you after such a long time." The man said, with a look of compassion and kindness in his eyes. "Nice to see you, too." Freya breathed out. The man ordered a cappuccino and asked her to take a seat. Although she was hesitant, she complied to his request and sat down.

"I hope you are doing better now. What happened can't be changed, but what would happen in the future can be.

I truly wish you a better life ahead, dear." The man softly said, while looking out of the windows.

Just then, Ritul came back with the coffee. Both of them thanked him, and he silently left.

"How is he, Ishan?" Freya asked, clearly shook by a memory stirring in her brain. The man, who was Ishan, breathed out heavily and spoke in a low tone, "I can't say too much too specifically. But I can surely inform this much to you, that he is in a better place now, than a few years ago. I think it is good progress."

"I hope so too. It was nice meeting you. Take care." Freya got up and trying to shake away the trembling of her palms, made her way back inside.

Ishan looked at her retreating figure, and when she finally went out of sight, got up, paid for the coffee, and left quietly.

Chilly winds were blowing on the evening of December 9, when Vihaan decided to step out of the office and visit Freya, as it had been five good days. He drove leisurely to the nursery, where he bought a small plant, and placing it on the backseat, drove straight toward the café. He entered without much thought, bringing the plant along with him this time. After greeting Ritul who was absolutely devouring a pack of chips, he sat down on the usual spot, which used to be miraculously empty every time he came to the place.

He was scanning through the bookshelves, and soon enough, a novel caught his eyes. "To the lighthouse by

Virginia Woolf." He read out loud as he settled into the soft cushioning of the chair. It had barely been a few seconds when he heard a low, mellow voice from behind. "I see I am about to receive another present today."

When he turned around, he saw Freya, holding a cup of macchiato in her hands. A knee length mulberry dress adorned her, while her hair was done up in a loose bun. He walked up to her, and picking up the planter from the table, stopped an inch short of their shoes touching, "Seems like you sure are about to."

With this, he took the cup from her hands and pushed the flowerpot into them. Holding it, she whispered, "Carnations." The yellow flowers swayed gently, in stark contrast with the dark soil underneath them. Their citrine was soft and calming, just like the presence of the woman holding it.

He smiled fondly over her figure and whispered, "I am glad you liked it." Freya looked up from the amber beauty in her hands and asked, "What do they symbolize, Vihaan?" He went silent for a second, peering closely into her coffee eyes, and then cleared his throat, "Carnations symbolize admiration. I bought them for you because your personality deserves all the appreciation. Hope you like them."

Freya giggled, and placing the pot on the table, went ahead to take the polaroid camera out and said, "I like it well enough to take a memorable photograph with the gift and the one who gave it." With this, she kindly asked a customer nearby to click a photograph, and when it came out, she gladly placed it on a distant shelf to let it dry off.

"You did not know that my favorite color is yellow, right?" she asked. "No, it was by pure instinct. I am elated, though, because the color must mean a lot to you." He replied, clearly pleasantly surprised from the revelation.

Freya smiled, and as her eyes traveled to the book placed on the table, she excitedly asked, "You picked this book up?" He nodded, not able to comprehend the enthusiasm. Understanding his visible confusion, she requested him to pick the book up and open it.

As soon as Vihaan opened the first page, the engraving of the bullseye caught him off guard. He never expected to stumble upon another one of Freya's favorite books. In awe, he said, "I never knew this would also be one of your preferences. Do you mind if I keep it for a few days? I promise I will return it to you soon."

Freya shook her head. "Not at all a problem. You may return this on your next visit when you drop by with another present. I would be more than glad to lend it to you." With that, she waved him goodbye, and walked off in another direction.

On December 9, Vihaan learned that Freya's favorite hue was yellow. He was sure to remember that.

On December 14, the sky was slightly pewter, but a particular person's spirits were quite high. As Vihaan drove to the café, another flowerpot was placed on the back seat of his car. The red and mauve flowers stood tall, and as he pulled up in front of the café, he looked at his reflection for one last time in the rear-view mirror. An amber-colored sweatshirt adorned him, and when Jatin had asked him about the choice of color, because he rarely ever wore yellow, he had brushed it off by saying that he was up for a few changes in his life.

Little did Jatin know that a swap of shades was not the only difference in his personality.

When Vihaan walked up to the glass doors, with the planter in his hands, he caught a glimpse of the woman he had grown to be fond of, holding a pile of books in her hands, as she struggled to find a place to keep them. Smiling silently to himself, he coolly went forward, and placing the pot on a side table, grabbed half the stack, and when Freya's eyes met his, she smiled widely as a greeting spilled from her lips.

She casually asked, "So, what is my present this time? I expect a new, lesser-known species, you know?" she flipped her hair, as both of them burst into fits of laughter. Then, Vihaan turned her around gently by the shoulders and pointed toward the table. Her eyes lit up, and so did his, the gray in them glowing like freshly solidified iron.

"Hyacinths. They symbolize playfulness, and I sincerely do wish that your ebullient nature may remain the same, forever. There're only a handful of people I've met with the same enthusiasm for life as you, and I adore that." His veiny hands went forward, gently touching the flower tips, while Freya stood with her back in front of him. He breathed in, and what enter his lungs was not only oxygen, but what smelled like life, like purity. A soft smell of vanilla and cinnamon wafted from her, and he wished he could stand there for eternity, and his life would be complete.

Just as she turned, he remembered to return the book he borrowed to her, and went outside to his car, where he rummaged through his bag to find the novel. When he found it, he strolled back into the building. Nearing the usual spot, he noticed a cup of flat white placed on the table, with a small post-it note attached to it. The note read, 'Hope you enjoy the coffee as much as I enjoy the presents.'

He sighed contentedly as he plopped into the seat and drank the coffee. Halfway through it, Freya came back, and without any delay, Vihaan returned the book to her, saying that it was one-of-a-kind experience to read it.

She chucked, and sitting down on the opposite chair, started a conversation about the novel. Before long, the dialogue somehow diverted toward cuisine preferences, and Vihaan excitedly said that he preferred one dish above all, and that particular one was vegetarian baked spaghetti.

When he asked her about her favorite cuisine, she replied, "I love bruschetta. It just feels warm and comforting."

She had been going on about the eclectic burst of tastes that the dish leaves her with when she abruptly stopped mid-sentence. Vihaan was looking directly toward her, his gray eyes as if boring into her soul. He looked so engaged that he even forgot to acknowledge the fact that Freya was no more rambling. For a second, her heartbeat picked up, his gaze making her slightly nervous, before she waved a hand in front of his face.

Instantly, Vihaan's trance broke as he shook off the shock, a lazy smile making its way on his face.

"Did you hear anything?" Freya asked, hoping to receive a 'no.' But she was beyond surprised when she heard his deep voice, "I did. I learned that you like the comforting warmth of the bruschetta as soon as it arrives. I also heard that you don't like basil on it. As well as that you like cheddar over parmesan as a topping. I was paying attention, Freya."

He finally smiled, his eyes closing into crescents. If she was to be honest, Freya felt shocked, yet a blooming sense of warmth suffused inside her as she beamed back.

Before anyone could register, she noticed that it was well past eight into the night, and that is when she politely asked him if he wanted to stay longer, to which he rationally replied in the negative, before picking his suitcase and heading toward the door, blissfully unaware of the soft stare that followed his way.

Slight rain pattered on that glass windshield of Vihaan's car on the evening of December 22, as he once again parked at the same spot, not far from the damask building, as he took out a dark green planter from the seat next to him. With fast steps, he neared the café, the drops soaking into the cotton of his shirt. Hurriedly, he opened to glass doors, and almost tripped over the anthurium planter placed gracefully on the side, a new flower sprouting from its bud.

Vihaan turned around to greet Ritul, but from behind the counter emerged Freya, with a few books in her hands and sweat beads decorating her forehead, half of which was hidden by a mop of her brunette locks. She placed the books before taking notice of the surroundings, and at the same time, she saw a planter being slid toward her.

Half surprised and half elated, she smiled gleefully on seeing Vihaan's face, with those ashen eyes curving into small crescents.

"I see my present has not been concealed well, but I must say, I like it anyways. So, which one is this beauty?" She asked, before lightly skimming her fingers over the garnet petals. "Well, they are rhododendrons. My mother loves them too because they symbolize femininity, strength, and beauty. Also, the unique shade is personally very soothing to me."

After a few moments of silence, Freya lifted her head up, and asked, "You think I am beautiful?" Silence engulfed Vihaan's insides and features, as he pondered over the question put forth him.

He wanted to say that that the copper barricades of her eyes invited him in incessantly, and how drawn he was to fall into them. That he thought of pointless topics to talk about, just to listen to her mellow voice speak to him, take his name. That she made him want to be close not only to her, but also to himself, love himself in ways he never had before. That he knew that even though she would never consider his words to be true if he said that she was the most beautiful being, inside out that he had seen, he wanted her to realize that her hair were cascades of the soil that nurtures life, her skin was the honey that the world considered the most valued fluid, and that her heart was what all the gems and priceless metals of the world would never equal to, it was precious and of immeasurable value, much like herself.

But he resorted to just saying, "Yes. Very beautiful."

Cheeks burning with the dust of mars, she accepted his compliment, never ceasing to emphasize on the fact that he was equally charming, if not more.

Soon enough, the sky changed colors, as it silently transitioned from a dusty orange to a matte shade of indigo, a gentle reminder that night had approached, and that people should return to their homes, where a loved one might be awaiting them.

It was December 25, and as expected, people were shivering through their bones, and although all offices and businesses were closed for the day, the streets were bustling with people either buying presents, or enjoying themselves in the cold, chilly weather.

It was on this day that Vihaan drove down to the café again, clad in a large trench coat, with a scarlet scarf adorning his features. He stepped out of the vehicle, but this time not only one, but both of his hands were occupied. In one, he held a viridescent spider plant, while in the other was occupied by a small green box, wrapped up in a red ribbon.

Walking inside the café, he crashed into the glass doors, hurting his shoulder in the process. Sighing at his clumsiness, he gently placed the planter on the counter, which was currently empty, although the café was quite full, even though it was only five in the evening.

Before he could put much thought to the matter, he heard the voice he adored from a corner, "Merry Christmas, Vihaan!" An involuntary grin grazing his lips, he turned around, only to be greeted by the sight of a very cozily dressed Freya, clad in a red maxi dress, along with a dark green cardigan to protect her from the chills.

Vihaan sauntered up to her, and engulfing her in a one-sided hug, since the plant was still in one of the hands, wished her too. When they parted, Freya said, "I see you have brought me a lush spider plant, and I sure do want to know about it. But what is in that box over there?" she asked, the heightened curiosity in her eyes making them go round. He chuckled silently, picked the box up and handed it to her. He eyed her in an amused manner as she opened the small carton in anticipation.

Once it was undone, her lips stretched in a small, genuine smile, as she took hold of the rum cake inside, which said, 'Thank you, for existing.' As she lifted it up, something rustled inside the box. On picking it, she noticed that it was a pendant. She eyed it appreciatively, but confusion flashed on her face. Vihaan smiled internally, and from the back, whispered near her ear, "This is a pendant representing the molecule of serotonin. It is also called the happy hormone, as it is a mood elevator. I want you to be happy forever, Freya, and therefore, I have gotten this gift for you. Merry Christmas."

The words were spoken so genuinely, that Freya couldn't help but smile involuntarily. As she turned around, Vihaan immediately pushed the plant in her hands, as he said, "The spider plant is a beautiful symbol of mindfulness and health, and I always wish that you may be mentally healthy, because it is extremely crucial."

The woman's brown eyes warmed up, and without saying anything, she brought out the polaroid camera, and indicated Vihaan to pose for the photograph. She stood next to him, and with one hand holding the pot and the other intertwined with his, she smiled beautifully, and in that moment, Vihaan could have sworn on his life that it was the most genuine, pure, and mesmerizing smile he had seen, and for second, his breath hitched in his throat. The words were at the edge of his lips, but he pushed them back with a gulp.

Turning toward the camera, he smiled widely, and as soon as the click sounded, Freya rushed toward it, and after shaking it for a bit, the photograph appeared on the film. She eyed it appreciatively as a loose lock of hair swiveled down the side of her face. Vihaan noticed it, and it took him every ounce of willpower in his body to not tuck it back.

Freya gently placed the photograph on the counter and said, "Wait for a second here, Vihaan. I will be right back." Without waiting for a reply, she turned toward one of the bookshelves, and before long, brought a book back with her. Handing it to him, she looked on, as he read the title. "The affair of the Flacons by Melissa Rivero." Vihaan read it out loud. "What is it about?" "Well, I wouldn't disclose much, but it is basically about immigration and the troubles that come as a baggage with it, quite literally. I am sure you will enjoy your time reading it." Freya informed.

"I would definitely read it and make it sure to share my opinions with you." Vihaan affirmed, placing the book in his bag.

They sat for a few moments, talking about miscellaneous topics. Just then, a question popped up in Vihaan's brain, "You told me you had a degree in sociology and one in market research, right? What happened after that, after leaving college? Was the café already in the plan or was there something else?"

Freya visibly stiffened, her pupils slightly shaking, as if she was trying to come up with a possible explanation. Vihaan sensed her discomfort and gently said, "You don't have to tell me if you don't want to, Freya. I was just curious. Sorry if I bothered you." Freya felt guilt rush inside her, as she spoke in a low voice, "It is nothing. I just remembered something from long ago, and I didn't mean to spoil the atmosphere. You don't have to apologize." She tried to muster up a smile but failed miserably. Seeing her state, Vihaan decided to give her some space and got up, thanking her for the coffee and the book.

Freya smiled, and hugged him gently, her hair brushing the sides of his arms. A soft tingling sensation crept up his throat and separating himself from her felt herculean to him.

Eventually, he walked back to his car, after bidding bye to Freya for the night, his heart constantly telling him to spill what it held. On the other hand, Freya, while placing the polaroid on the bookshelf, murmured to herself, "I am so sorry, Vihaan. I don't want to lose an important person from my life after trying immensely hard to regain control and composure. I don't want my bygone years to have any impact on my upcoming ones." She sighed, looking back at the picture. Suddenly, warmth and security invaded her insides. "I think gray might be my new favorite color." And with this, her eyes smiled along with her lips.

Frozen winds caressed Freya's cheeks on the evening of December 30, as she sipped on a cup of latte, looking over on the road. A small smile graced her lips, as she spotted a jacket clad Vihaan, a muffler wrapped around his neck, walking toward the café, his steps fast, as he balanced a planter of lucky bamboo, wrapped up delicately in a yellow satin ribbon, lush and bright.

Even before he could knock on the door, Freya promptly moved forward and opened it, a welcoming warmth instantly draped around him, as he sighed in pleasure. His eyes were closed when he heard honey being poured into his ears, "So, I see you brought me bamboos?" Smiling in contentment, Vihaan opened his eyelids and affirmed, "Well, yes. They are lucky bamboos, which symbolize good fortune and longevity. As New Year is approaching fast, I wanted to give you something which would mark the beginning a beautiful one, so here you go, my present to you, for New Year." He sighed, as he placed the planter on the table.

As usual, Freya took a memorable polaroid photograph, and shared a cup of hot macchiato with Vihaan. Just as he was leaving, a book fell from the shelf, and Freya bent down to pick it. It was at this moment that the shiny serotonin pendant dangled out from the neckline of her sweater.

Vihaan's eyes softened at the sight, and although no words were spoken, his smile widened. Before long, he was inside his car, and as he drove off into the night, he realized that love is not a feeling, it is an existential question. It is the mark of an inquiry imposed upon everything you have known to fundamentally exist in your world, a challenge to your perception of the world as you know it.

But he chucked and shook his head as another thought registered in his brain: he finally found an answer to the long impending question.

It was finally New Year, and as expected, everyone was still in the spirit of the enthusiasm of the phenomenon. It was on such an evening of Thursday, that Vihaan drove to the café once again, this time carrying a pot of yellow chrysanthemums, their petals spread our vividly, and the green of the leaves contrasting with the tone of the flowers.

As he stepped into the café, ashen eyes searching for a particular face, he saw a woman walking up to the door from the opposite side. He could have sworn he had seen her somewhere, but he couldn't pinpoint the exact location.

Letting the thought settle in the back of his mind, he resumed his search for a particular figure, until his pupils rested on a curled-up Freya, clad in a long indigo trench coat, sitting with her hands folded against her knees. She looked so unhappy, that for a second, Vihaan's heart dropped in his shoes. However, he walked up to her, and placed the planter on the table, in her field of vision.

As she lifted her eyes up to meet his, he smiled gently at her, eyes forming the softest crescents ever. She returned the gesture, but Vihaan didn't miss on the slight quiver of her lips.

Sitting across from her, he simply said, "Chrysanthemums symbolize love and joy."

A sigh rustled through his lips. "Now, I need to know what happened to upset you so much, Freya. I would feel restless without getting to know about it."

Freya's eyes widened, and unadulterated terror flashed in her warm pupils for a second. "Nothing, just feeling a bit down. I would be fine if I rest." She was about to say more, when Vihaan interrupted her, "I know it is not the truth." Then, holding her hands gently, he continued, "I really do hope you trust me, Freya. I want to know about you, and I am absolutely unafraid of whatever comes along with it."

When she didn't respond, he crouched in front of her, holding her face in his hands. "I know you are not telling me something, Freya. I know so, because involuntarily, your fingers interlace, and you keep on brushing your thumbs against each other. You start biting your lips, and your eyes start shying away from making direct contact." He brushed a thumb over her cheekbone. "So, tell me."

A lone tear escaped the muddy depths of Freya's eyes as she brokenly whispered, "It is about my health. Well, you see, I have been unwell for quite a while now." At this sentence, Vihaan could physically feel his whole body drop, not by the force of gravity, rather by the undulating tension in the atmosphere. "What happened to you?"

Taking in a deep breath, Freya whispered, "I, well, I-" a shudder ran through her arms, as Vihaan waited for an answer. "I suffer from coronary artery disease." Although he did not completely understand the subject, Vihaan was convinced that it was concerned with the heart, and if so, it was incredibly serious.

The world started closing in on him, as the full force of the truth that he himself was a patient, an ill person, dawned on him. The truth that he has to still bite the bullet suffused dizziness in his body.

Sure, he was well aware of the fact, but these past few weeks, he had been feeling rather healthy and open spirited. And even though he knew that the lobectomy was due in a matter of months, he chose to see the brighter side.

Now, however, he started feeling asphyxiated once again, but still holding the small hands of Freya, he managed to ask, "For how long?" With tears streaming down her soft features, she replied, "It has been a little over a year since the diagnosis."

Finally slumping back in his seat, Vihaan held his forehead in his palms, and drawing a deep breath, rose from the place.

Freya stood up too, and before she could even move a muscle, Vihaan took two long strides and engulfed her in a bone crushing, but heart-warming hug. She gasped, not able to process the actions, but melted, nevertheless. She felt teardrops dampen her scalp, and when Vihaan backed away, she saw moisture surrounding his unbelievably beautiful eyes.

He murmured, his words barely above a whisper, "I know, Freya, that words are poor comforters. And therefore, I am not going to say anything right now. I just want you to know that come what may, you will always remain special to me, and that diseases are not hindrances in between two people. They can never fathom the depth of the connection between them." After completely backing off, and instantly feeling cold and washed over, he said, "I hope you know that this revelation would never change anything between us, ever." A palm stroked Freya's cold, damp cheek, and for a second, both of them wanted the world to cease to proceed forward, but it was a futile desire. Therefore, work immense difficulty, he walked over to the glass doors, and without a single twitch of nervousness, was out of the café.

Freya, eyes now dry but incredibly tired, looked over to the planter, a photograph missing this time. 'Next time. There will be a next time.' Her heart said, and she placed a palm gently over it.

From the corner of her eyes, she looked over to Ritul, standing beside the counter, and nodded gently, a feeble smile tracing her lips. He sighed, and came over to where she had been standing, and engulfed her in an extremely lovable hug. She hugged him back, as he softly said, "It was difficult, but good, wasn't it? Now, go home and sleep, mam. I will take care of the café and close it timely. And remember, I am and will always be your younger brother." At this, Freya smiled widely, replying, "The best brother I could ever ask for."

On the other hand, arrantly uninterrupted tears streamed down like torrents from Vihaan's eyes. Everything seemed lost in the moment, as he drove, not to his home, rather to someplace else. A thousand thoughts whirled in his brain, robbing him of the normal rhythm of breathing, as his arms and legs quivered slightly.

After a few more minutes of driving, he stopped at his destination. He got out of his car and walked toward the familiar teal green house, with caramel pillars adorning the corners. Primrose and gardenia lined the small cobblestone pathway, and two dimly lit lamps flushed the dark atmosphere with a soft yellow glow.

With one trembling hand, Vihaan knocked the door, and a voice replied almost instantly, "Coming!"

Within a few moments, the wooden door opened up to reveal a man, clad in faded sweatpants and a light purple sweatshirt. Seeing Vihaan's disheveled state, he exclaimed, "Dear God, what happened?"

Vihaan's voice, feeble and weak, came out in the most desperate plead, which alone was enough to bring tears pooling around the other's eyes, as he asked, his voice a mere quiver, "Jatin, do you think I am cursed?"

Chapter 5
REDAMANCY

To say the least, Jatin was extremely perplexed to see a terribly distressed Vihaan at his doorstep, eyes reflecting the immeasurable hopelessness that moved in leaps and bounds in his heart. He immediately brought him inside the house, which was decorated in a minimalist fashion, with beige and burnt orange accentuating each corner.

Almost instantly, Vihaan collapsed on the sofa, mental tiredness and an overdrive of emotions turning themselves into salty tears that ran down his pristine face. Jatin brought a glass of water along with some fruits, and placing them on the coffee table, sat down silently on the opposite end of the russet tinged sofa. He kept silent, letting the other man collect his thoughts.

After a few seconds of straining, ear-splitting silence, Vihaan finally spoke, his voice barely above a whisper, "Am I not allowed to possess even a single ray of hope, Jatin? What crime have I committed that whenever I get close to anyone, it leads to some sort of despair?" Jatin cleared his throat, and said in a soft voice, "To help you Vihaan, I need to know who or what has hurt you?" And just like that, the room was again plunged into silence.

After a few strenuous moments, Vihaan finally murmured, "Freya."

Jatin was beyond shocked. The woman that possessed a saccharine charm, the one that made his best friend divulge his mind from all the problems in his life, could not have hurt him. There was no way it would ever occur. "How did she do that?" He asked.

"She thought that keeping her problems to herself, and not revealing it to the me was a nicer option, than letting me get hurt. I completely and fully understand, being in the same state as her, and I am in no way in the position to point out anything about her. I would have done the same." He breathed in, "She hid the fact from me that, well.... she suffers from, coronary artery disease." The last words came out as a tensed whisper, the one that is made when you don't want to speak the thoughts you have in your brain.

Jatin was left immobile. He could never have imagined that Freya could have ever been suffering from such a major health issue. Her cheerful, sunshine personality had well-hidden the fact that under the layers of her skin and muscles, her small, fragile heart was struggling. It did not take long for him to understand the fact that although her disposition was naturally quite bubbly and lively, with a deep sense of emotional intelligence embedded in it, a part of it was a sure coping mechanism, developed by her to overcome the fact that she was a terminal patient. It was as if she forced her brain into believing that if she maintained the cheerful persona as a cover-up, the disease would eventually subside. And this realization hurt and shook Jatin to the core, beyond belief.

One involuntary hand went up to Vihaan's shoulder, while the other stayed on his thighs, while he tried to digest the information. After a few seconds of shattering silence, he began, "Well, diseases are no small topics, and I know that quite clearly. But I strongly do believe that what you both share extends beyond any physical impairment. And trust me when I say that Freya is definitely one of the strongest persons that I have come across, in the sense that she dealt with such a grave topic by herself. I am sure she might have cried herself to sleep on many nights, with her pillows soaked to the core. But, now that she has told you, her heart might be feeling light as a feather. I do realize the extent of shock you might be under right now, but trust me, it gets better with time. When you told me about your condition, I felt my world shake from the force of it, too. Moreover, I do urge you to keep on meeting her. She would be totally devastated if you stop seeing her. I expect you to understand the emotional trauma and stress, Vihaan, because you yourself are suffering from something massive. We all are different, but in the end, we are connected by the fact that we all long for love and a person to confide in, at the end. If she opened up to you, you need to consider the fact that you must be very important to her, and how challenging and burdensome it might have been for her to go through the process."

Vihaan stiffened, his heart visibly thumping faster than before. The words that Jatin spoke rang in his mind. *Love*. The existential question that had been answered. And love is not bound. It is free, and it sets everything free.

All inhibitions, all insecurities, and all the hopelessness vanish when you peer into the special pair of eyes.

Was he ready for it though? Was he prepared to take all the obstacles head on?

He breathed in, deeply and slowly, releasing the air gently. Opening his eyelids, the gunmetal of his eyes met the carob of Jatin's, and a small involuntary smile crawled up on his tear-stained lips.

With a sigh, he got up from the sofa, and gathering his belongings, turned around and hugged his best friend tightly. Without wasting a second, Jatin returned the gesture, his heart going out to the man in front of him.

After a few seconds, they separated from each other, and Jatin whispered, his voice not allowing him to increase the loudness, "Remember my words, Vihaan. She would be shattered if you stop communicating with her out of the blue. I request you to not do so. Will you oblige to my words?" Not able to form any sentences, Vihaan nodded his head slightly, and began walking up to the door.

Once he was out on the porch, he cleared his throat and mumbled, "I will never want to see her in as devastated a state as she was in today. I will do everything I can to make her content in her decision of opening up to me." And although he had said that to himself, Jatin heard him discreetly, and his upturned eyes closed into two curves as he smiled, raven hair falling on his forehead, shielding his closed pupils.

"You truly fall in love once in a lifetime. Truly, abundantly, boundlessly. And with that one person, who makes the fall feel like flying." Jatin said to himself, chuckling. "Well, I guess the thing about love is that even if you have never felt it wholly, you are never untouched from the essence it holds. I really should be thanking Mr. Shekhar for coming to me for help on writing an answer for some question asked on the radio. I think I am a really nice neighbor."

With that, he strolled to his bedroom to sleep, the events of the day running through his brain.

Winds caressed the back of Vihaan's neck and cheeks as he drove back to his home, dried tears staining his face. He still needed to come to terms with the situation at hand completely, but with the assistance of his best friend, he was able to realize a few things.

He was falling in love with Freya, fast and hard, yet slowly and gracefully, and he himself had no idea how it began. He just was here, at this point of time, craving her warmth next to him, wanting to hug her and feel her heart beat next to his. Now that he thought about it, he saw how dangerously close he was to stepping over a line and reach out to her in a different way. He knew pain, because he was aware of what happens when you are gone, separated, and can never reunite. But he shuddered at the thought of never seeing her again. He breathed in and recalling all the small moments he had shared with her, said out loud into the night, "I love you, Freya. And I would rather let you consume me than let my doubts do so."

As he said so, silent tears streamed down from his tired eyes once again, and he shut them, preventing the brine from running his emotions haywire. He sighed, and affirmed to himself, "This is going to be one amazing and worthy life, now that I have you." With this, he parked the car in front of his house, which he realized for the first time was welcoming yet somewhat incomplete. He patted the walls as he walked along, making sure not to wake his parents up.

As soon as he reached his room, he shut the doors, and after washing up and having a light dinner, he walked up to his desk. He retrieved a paper and a pen from the drawer, and without giving it a second thought, began writing something. His hands trembled, but his words flowed out seamlessly, as if his pent-up emotions had finally found a warm release.

After about twenty minutes, he was done, and without giving the inked sheet a second glance, he folded it nicely and placed it inside an envelope. Next, he walked into his balcony, and after a thorough search, found the planter housing a bush of orange roses. He carefully picked one up, and placing it in an empty pot, whispered to it, "You are rare, just like her. Everything about you in intriguing. Therefore, I am giving you to her, to make her realize something important."

With this, he placed the planter by the envelope, and switched the lights off, drifting into a heavy slumber.

Next morning, the sun shone mildly in the sky, as slightly gray clouds covered it, shielding the city beneath from the harsh heat. The soft gushes of wind caressed the tips of leaves. A mottle of baby blue and slate blended to fashion the serene morning sky. The awakening magic touched each corner of the city, and Vihaan woke up rather late that day, the emotional stress having worn him out the last night.

But the sun promised the world with hope and positivity, with a belief that things always take a turn, no matter how bleak.

As he got ready for the day, a certain languor took over Vihaan, and he almost skipped office, but the orange rose sitting on his table reminded him otherwise. He got ready, slipping a walnut cream trench coat over his all-black wear, his slight bangs almost hiding his gray pupils.

Breakfast was served at the table when he arrived downstairs, his parents getting ready to start with it. He wished his parents a good morning, getting a plate to help himself to the meal, a spread of roast pumpkin and lentil salad.

Within a few seconds, he finished the delightful nosh and walked back up to his room, and carefully picking up the pot and the letter, rushed downstairs. He placed the contents in his hands in his car before walking back up to his parents inside, and hugged both of them at the same time, tightly. He whispered, "I love you both, mom, and dad, and I hope you know that at every second of the day. Have a great day." When he separated from them, his mother kissed him on the cheeks, and his father patted his back.

Getting inside the car, he took a deep breath and revved the engine. "Today is going to be one of the most memorable days of my life." He affirmed to himself, and as a small twinkle shone in his eyes, he drove off to his office.

Once he was seated in his chair, he immediately felt two hands on his shoulders, and he wasn't surprised in the least. Softly, Jatin's voice spoke from behind him, and Vihaan could feel his upturned eyes staring at his back from behind his raven hair. "Not much, just here to say that I hope you are in a better state than last night, though I know how discombobulated you may feel. Always know that I am here for you, Vihaan."

Vihaan rubbed his palms over the arms and try as hard as he might to suppress it, a smile of pure happiness adorned his face. Turning around, he hugged his best friend, who was a bit surprised, but returned the gesture immediately.

Separating from the hug, Jatin said, "Let's get some work done, shall we? The best employees of this office don't look good idling around." He pointed toward the numerous glass cut, gold lined awards lining the walls with titles like 'Employee of the Month' or 'Outstanding Performer' engraved on them, awarded to two of the best members of the office.

Vihaan chucked, and settling around again, opened an unfinished file on his laptop. Jatin, on the other hand, walked out to attend a meeting.

Hours flew by, and before any of them knew, lunch hour had arrived. Both the friends ate their meals, and before resuming their work, Vihaan called Jatin to the rooftop, asking him to come as soon as possible. Within a few minutes, the said man was leaning on the parapet of the office building. Settling himself on the corner, he enquired about the reason for asking to meet him.

Vihaan took a deep breath and explained everything slowly. He informed Jatin about his turmoil the last night, and how he put all his feeling in the letter, which he wanted Freya to receive. But after the intensely emotional episode they had the last day, he felt that he should not be the one to directly present it to her, because he was a ball of nerves to say anything properly to her. Therefore, he wished Jatin, the one he trusted with his eyes closed, to be the one to deliver his small present to her.

Jatin looked up at him, and he saw a nervous boy, hands fiddling with each other and feet tapping the floor consistently, peering back at him. A throaty laugh escaped him as he declared, "I will surely do it, only if you treat me to a plate of red sauce pasta."

Vihaan relaxed a bit, his shoulders evidently dropping down from the tense state. "Of course, I will. You are the best friend I have ever had, Jatin. I don't think I thank you enough for that. But I want you to know that you are one of the most crucial people in my life. My parents love you more than me, and that says something."

"As I said, I am an absolute pleasure to have around. Consider yourself blessed. Now, let's get downstairs." Jatin patted Vihaan's back, as both of them turned on their heels to go back to their cabins.

Getting out of his car, Jatin smiled, looking at the neatly stuck envelope and the planter in his hands. It was quite late, and the night had settled in deeply. He glanced at his wristwatch and noticed that it was almost nine. He took a deep breath, and walked up to the café, which was almost empty now, save for the last man paying his bill. As he entered, the man turned to walk out too, and the two shared a smile. Before he could say anything though, Freya's gentle tone brushed his ears, "Jatin, is that you?" He turned around and smiled warmly on seeing her standing in front of him. She was wearing a burgundy wrap coat over a porcelain top and obsidian denims, her hair falling down her shoulders onto her back. Her eyes shone slightly on seeing Jatin after a really long time.

Breaking the silence, she asked, "What brings you here?" Although she almost knew the answer, she was still eager to hear it from him. Pointing toward the planter and the envelope, he said, voice barely above a whisper, "I just had to give this to you. I am not going to say much, knowing what is going on inside your mind. I urge you to read it." With this, he stepped back, not leaving, just giving her the distance.

With a trembling hand, Freya touched the deep tangerine rose, while with the other, she took hold of the envelope. Opening it slowly, she slid out the letter. She felt the need to sit down because the anticipation was making her dizzy. After pulling out a chair and settling on it, she opened up the folded paper, and began reading. The very first words, arranged neatly into beautiful alphabets, made tears sting the back of her eyes. However, she pushed them back, knowing full well it was a futile attempt, that they would flow down eventually.

My beloved Freya,

I am writing a letter to you, which in no way is necessary, when I can voice my emotions to you. This isn't a love letter, just a way to express what my heart can't comprehend.

Whenever I think about you, all I can feel is a surprising warmth invading my senses, with all essence of everything wrong in the world being dissolved into nothingness. You hex me beyond imagination, and you may never believe it, but I do notice you. I notice every small detail, from the gentle curls of your luscious hair to the calm yet confident gait.

The way my name rolls off your lips so effortlessly, has me thinking at times about the beauty that your name holds, and I may reveal it to you, I have pronounced it quite a few times when alone.

Your mere touch unleashes bouts of collywobbles throughout the entirety of my body, and I am willing to confess that it is the most rapturing feeling ever.

When I peer into your eyes, I feel all my smallest emotions come alive. If someone would look into them, they would see plain, bland tea. If you swirl a spoon in it, you'd see waves of cinnamon decorating the edges, pecan embedded in the middle, and ever so slightly molten copper flowing out of the darkened, musing pupils. Yet, to others, it is tame, mundane tea. When I look at you, I feel breathless, and yet it seems I have never felt more alive. Does it make sense?

The way you smile lights up my being, not in the way the sun does, rather in the pattern of the moon, soft and calming, a sheen I want to bask in.

Whenever I hear your voice, I don't want you to ever stop speaking, because it feels like pure, unadulterated honey to my ears.

You remind me of rain, of crystals, of filtered sunbeams, of unsolved metaphysics and above all, of blissful euphoria.

You defrost me of the feeling of fear, emptiness, and trouble, and I can never thank you or your simple presence enough for that.

Last night, I was fearful, trying to run away from this unprecedented, blooming sensation. But, when your singular entity erupted in my mind, I realized that we always run away from the one who stays inside us, and over these weeks, you have become home to me, and I hope I am something to you, too.

So, I guess I would have to contradict what I had said earlier. Yes, I am abundantly, incessantly, deeply in love with you, and I would have it no way other than that.

With sunshine, warmth, and crystal love,

Yours in every way possible,

Vihaan.

Tears blurred Freya's vision as she ran her fingers over the sheet, her eyes glossing all over again.

"Did you like it?"

A mellow voice asked, and Freya could have sworn she felt her heart stop for a second, before it began pulsating erratically. She turned around, wiping the salty stains from her cheeks.

There he stood, the man that was willing to accept her in the bare reality. Still carrying the same charm and yet giving off a playfully refined aura. Within his slaty eyes danced a thousand emotions, yet all of them coalesced to melt into an expression of true affection.

He walked forward, diminishing the distance between them. In four strides, he was directly in front of Freya, where she could feel the gentle warmth radiating off of his body.

"You are a snowflake, you know?" Vihaan started. "Soft, flawless, precious, and fleeting. God forbid had I not entered this café on that particular day, I would have never met you, Freya. And you know, I was afraid, not for myself but for you. Even if loving you wholeheartedly and helplessly would have been a mistake I had committed, I would do it all again in a heartbeat. But the truth is, loving you is not a flaw, it is the remedy. It is the cure to all things wrong with me. I feel content and complete when I am with you. So, will you let me love you?"

He saw a tear escape Freya's eyes and slide down her cheek. Before it could drop below, he gently wiped it off with his index finger. Then, he smiled at her.

In that moment, Freya physically felt her mind go hazy. That smile carried genuine sincerity, and all she could do was whisper, "Would you let me love you too, Vihaan?" It was as if deliverance washed over him when he heard his name escape her lips. Tears brimmed in his eyes as he nodded slightly, and instantly wrapped his arms around her, enveloping her into a warm, homely hug.

Freya felt herself melt into a pool of satisfaction as she hugged him back, encapsulating him. Her tears soaked through his shirt, but both of them were past caring now, as home was more important to them, and home was right here, in each other's arms.

Outside the café, Jatin smiled softly to himself, wrapping the scarf tightly around his neck, walking away to his car, which Vihaan had parked safely at the end of the street while he was inside the café.

Chapter 6

NOVALUNOSIS

Vihaan was sitting by the balcony of his room, listening to a few songs. The evening sun was glowing with a red hue, casting its glow over every available surface. Then there was him, lost in thoughts crashing upon the brinks of his mind like the waves that break on the shore.

Exhilaration rode over him due to the fact that he had been able to admit his feelings toward Freya in front of her, satisfaction flowed in his vessels when he remembered the look of pure admiration on her face, and a strong feeling of wanting to do something to make her believe that she was indeed significant and important to him bloomed in his body.

Being with her was so singularly visceral and binding that he never wanted to look away. He wanted something just like that, something to make her feel as connected to him as he felt to her.

He went over a million ideas, from a simple coffee date to a museum visit, but discarded all of them, because they felt too conventional and straight forward. It was as if no thought felt put in them, and he went for them mechanically.

Sighing, he was about to give up, but just as he got up to go back inside, his arm brushed against the leaves of a fern plant standing proudly in a corner. The leaves were showy and verdant, and it was as if the touch lit up an idea in his brain.

Immediately, he called someone up to help him take care of the arrangements, a permanent smile having plastered itself on his face.

After placing the call down, he decided to take a quick shower to relax his body, when a notification went off on his phone. He picked it up and a message from Jatin greeted him, which went, '*When am I getting the red sauce pasta?*' Vihaan burst out laughing, remembering he had promised to treat his best friend to it. He quickly replied that both of them could go to restaurant tomorrow to have some of it. Then, placing down his phone, he strode off toward the bathroom to douse off the tension between his muscles.

The next day was quite fast paced, with both the friends working their heads off in the first half of the day, so much so that their necks had started to ache. When lunch time finally arrived, it was as if the heavens had smiled upon them, and Vihaan dragged Jatin over to his car, in which they both traveled down to a chic restaurant in the heart of the city.

The insides were absolutely breathtaking, designed in azure and lined with black frames. One whole wall was entirely made out of glass throughout the height of the building, which gave a striking view of the expanse of the city.

Both the friends sat down on a table, and as soon as the waiter came along to take the order, Vihaan said, "One plate of red sauce pasta, and do add some extra oregano on top." Jatin smiled, reveling in the fact that he remembered how he liked his dish.

After that, they started talking about various topics, ranging from the project they were working on to Jatin's parents visiting him soon. Within ten minutes, the pasta was in front of them, and without wasting much time, they dug in.

After a few minutes, Vihaan decided to break his thoughts to Jatin. He informed him that he had been thinking of taking Freya to a place as distinctly alluring as her, and then proceeded to reveal his plans for the same. Jatin sure seemed impressed and patted his back for putting in so much thought to it.

Then, Vihaan proceeded to ask, "This doesn't seem enough, though. I want to do just something else, not going overboard, but enough to make her realize her worth and charisma. Do you have any ideas?"

Jatin went silent, and it appeared as if he was going over various prospects in his brain. About ten minutes later, his eyes lit up as he revealed, "I have the most amazing idea for the two of you. The only condition is that you have to agree to it." Vihaan nodded, curious as to what it was. Jatin dusted his hands as he proceeded to explain the plan he had in mind. Once he finished, Vihaan was left speechless. "You should be a dating expert or something. I knew you were creative, but this is brilliant! Thanks a lot, dear." He said, hugging him. Jatin returned the gesture, and both of them made their way out.

Three days later, Freya received a message from Vihaan in the morning, stating that it would be nice if she could close a bit early today, because he wanted to take her somewhere. Anticipation and confusion tugged at her heart as she replied in the affirmative, going back to placing cups of coffee on the tables.

The day was fast paced, and soon enough, it was half past four. Freya was just closing when she heard the familiar honk of Vihaan's car. She smiled and locked the door, walking out over the cobblestone to reach the vehicle. Vihaan got out and opened the door for her, taking in her frame. She was wearing a tangerine dress, ribbed in the middle, ending right above her knees.

Once they had set in motion, Freya asked where they were headed. Vihaan, though, was tight lipped. "A place as unique as you, snowflake." This gave no answers to Freya, just confused her further.

About fifteen minutes later, they were parked outside a nursery, which spread over a large piece of land. In the front, the ground was littered with hundreds of plants arranged in small batches, while a building in the middle separated the area from the backside. After crossing the front yard, both of them entered the grounds behind it, and the whole place left Freya shocked.

It was a large greenhouse, with a dome shaped ceiling, and an octagonal interior. The entire structure was made of glass. The flooring was made of brick, which conferred it a rather countryside touch. Creepers slithered down from hanging planters above, and the sunlight reflected off of every available surface, creating a transparent cascade of colors. A small pond sat in the center, gray stones lining it on the inside. The water was calm, with slight ripples forming occasionally.

Plants and flowers were arranged in an alternating manner, leaving ample space for the glass to be uncovered, to let the light in. One whole surface was covered in blue and orange flowers, which consisted of the Himalayan poppy, delphinium, canna, and begonia among others. Another one was a cascade of blues and green, ornated with hydrangeas, passion flowers, and Boston ivy. Yet another was a show of lilac and white wisteria at the top and balloon flowers at the bottom. The last one was the most diverse, each inch covered by a medley of rusty nasturtium, rouge zinnias, sangria foxgloves, amber pansies, and alabaster candytufts, bound on the borders by a thick growth of devil's ivy.

The whole place smelled heavenly and sublime, and Freya was lost in the beauty of it, when Vihaan tapped her lightly on the shoulder and directed her toward the center, whereby the pond, two elegant chairs were placed along with a table, food served out on it.

The floor was littered with monstera and other creepers, which made the place feel like it was a part of a forest.

Once they had made themselves comfortable on the seats, Vihaan removed the lids from the dishes, and Freya saw that the meal consisted of black hummus served with pita bread, some Mexican fiesta rice, and a plate of lemon cheesecakes.

"How do you like it?" Vihaan asked.

"It is beyond anything I could have imagined, Vihaan. I don't know how to describe the feeling of contentment yet excitement inside me. It is as if I am at home, surrounded by love, and the fact that you are here only adds to my pleasure. I never could have thought of it myself, and I am overwhelmed by the gesture. Thanks a lot."

A smile bloomed on Vihaan's face, as he urged her to begin with the meal. It was delectable, and the servings were finished in a jiffy. After a few moments, he held Freya's hands, which sent a wave of tingles rippling through her, and asked her to look up.

When she did so, the most spellbinding sight greeted her. The evening was closing, and the sky, clearly visible through the dome, was painted in indigo, crimson, and tangerine, with the occasional shimmer of stars glimmering on the sheet like engravings of love on the heart of eternal time.

Freya smiled, and held his hands tighter, almost forgetting to breathe for a second.

After a few moments, both of them got up, and Freya once again profusely thanked him for allowing her to become a part of something so carnally magical.

Vihaan, though, closed in on her from behind, and the moment his body made contact with hers, it was as if the bubbles of exhilaration inside her burst, and all that was left was the soap water of breathlessness. "This was half the date, snowflake. The other half still remains." He whispered in her ears.

"This was half?" Freya managed to ask through her bewilderment. "Of course, it was. We should get going now, I can't wait to show you what else is in store for you today." "Someplace more beautiful than here?" "I hope so, because for someone as salubrious as you, this is a speck of dust, incomparable to the rejuvenation you provide me with." Vihaan excitedly said and dragged her outside, where they got in the car and drove away.

During the entire ride, Vihaan did not let any information slip past his lips, although enthusiasm and alight nervousness rippled beneath his calm exterior, eager to tell everything to her.

When the car finally reached the destination, Freya saw a beautiful ivory colored gate covered in mandevillas, an entrance to what seemed like a fairytale garden. Both of them stepped out, and Vihaan brought out a piece of black clothing from him pocket. Before Freya could do much, the fabric was secured around her eyes, shutting off the light and plunging her in darkness. She panicked a little, but calmed down as soon as a soft voice reached her ears, "I am right here. Just hold my hand." It was all she needed to ease out, and without any hesitation, she followed Vihaan inside.

After what felt like a few minutes of walking, both of them stopped, and Vihaan announced, "Now, I am going to remove the cloth, and you will honestly tell me how you like my actual surprise." The rasp in his voice led to goosebumps forming on her skin, and she felt a hand slowly release the cloth from her vision.

Within a few seconds, her eyes adjusted to the dark, and what she saw left her speechless.

Astounded.

Amazed.

Stunned.

Dazed.

An expanse of berry blue and indigo enveloped the whole room, the light reaching every corner beautifully. White luminary dots were scattered around the dark cover, giving the impressions of the most exquisite blanket of universal pattern to ever exist. An undertone of sangria added to the natural warmth of the ambience, and the whole place teemed with an otherworldly pristine yet welcomingly mysterious aura. A whole cosmic performance had unraveled right in front of her eyes, and Freya did not know what to think, much less say anything.

"I might never be able to bring the actual stars for you, as they are unreachable, but I can always do my best for the one who brings the best out of me. So, real constellations might be difficult, but I thought you would appreciate the idea of a rendition of the same covering the expanse of this room." Vihaan said. After a slight pause, he continued, "Do you know why I specifically chose the universe to cover every nook and corner of this room, and not flowers or something like that? Well, the reason lies within you. You are the embodiment of the universe, Freya. My universe. Your eyes are the beautifully deep abysses that we call black holes, as nothing ever comes back from them, just like I did not.

Your hair is the perfect form of the milky way, dropping down your shoulders and onto your waist, just like the incessant flow of the most astonishingly dazzling galaxy ever. Your whole presence and being is like that of the cosmos, mind boggling and larger than life. And simply put, that is why I fell in love with you. You speak to me in stars and constellations, and I can hear you for hours. I love you in light years, and I want to love you till infinity, because you are the only end in sight, and with you, there is no end. So, do you like the surprise, snowflake?"

Freya was shell shocked, to say the least. No one had ever done anything remotely like that for her. Never in her wildest dreams had she imagined that something so precious would come to life in front of her. Words were not able to present themselves in her brain, and all she could do was walk forward, her eyes brimming with brine, which dropped onto the floor below when she hugged Vihaan as if her life depended on it. His gray eyes shone with an unmatched sheen, as he wrapped his arms securely around her, in an unspoken promise of never letting her fall, of making the fall feel like flying.

Half an hour later, both of them were still reveling in the cobalt shades, when Freya felt Vihaan's palm on top of hers. She looked at him softly and was instantly able to recognize the little wave of discomfort and sadness that had floated in those eyes. She said, "You know that if there is anything bothering you, I am always here to listen, without judging you." Her words were like a shower of solace for him, as he cleared his throat. "I know you will never judge me, snowflake. It is myself I am scared of. But I wouldn't hide it anymore. I-" Words were in his throat, but hesitance was pushing them down. So, he closed his eyes, breathed in, and said, "I am not as perfect or content as everyone makes me out to be. In fact, I am so imperfect that I cry into my pillow sometimes, just so that nobody might ever make out that tears had flown down my eyes. But I am so scared, so afraid, that it numbs my bones. Freya, I am ill too. I have a benign tumor in the lower lobe of my right lung. It was not so bad until a few months ago, but in the recent past, it has not shown many signs of any improvement, and that is forcing me to make the most difficult decision I have ever had to make. All my doctors have asked me to consider a lung lobectomy, a surgery to remove the damaged lobe. I really want to get well, but going under the knife is a very difficult task, and I am honesty stuck. I know that eventually I would agree, but it is your support that I require to be assured that I would make through it."

Tears were flowing down Vihaan's eyes by the time he had finished, but Freya stood still, her eyes focused on the far distance, on nothingness. Eventually, she said, "Don't you think we are perfect for each other? Just the way we are, broken, twisted, sick and vulnerable. Even if our health eludes us, we have our souls, Vihaan. And all I know is that souls are made of something irrevocably pristine, unharmed by anything. Also, I know that there could be no other Vihaan Sharma for me, or for anyone for the matter, who would book an entire greenhouse for someone, much less project the most precious stars for their beloved. So, in sickness, in health, in hope, in bleak despair, in brightness, in stormy pain, in melting pleasure, in every form and every emotion, you have me forever, sunshine."

Silence persisted in the room for two minutes, not heavy and unsaid, but rather calm and fluffy. Then, in two long strides, Vihaan had enveloped Freya in his secure arms, and the girl had responded instantly, by hugging him back. He kissed her on the forehead, and whispered, "I need you, Freya. I need you more in every next breath of mine." A content smile crept up on Freya's face as she replied, "Me too, sunshine."

Under the stars, bathing in the soft sheen of calmness and bonding, the two entangled people smiled softly at each other, peering at the universe enveloped by the irises of the other's eyes. At this precise moment, Freya said, "I love you." And although it was a simple sentence, it stirred a thousand emotions inside Vihaan's heart, and the most prominent one was elation.

Chapter 7

SELCOUTH

It was five days after the beautiful night had unraveled, that Freya was arranging the books on a distant shelf in the corner of the café. The place was not buzzing with people, but not empty either. She was feeling particularly lightheaded since the past two hours, and as she sat down on one of the chairs, she noticed a woman, probably in her late forties enter the place along with someone very important to her. Knowing both of them, she smiled and walked up to the door.

The woman, looking serious yet calm, brought a particularly powerful vibe with herself, which was soothing at the same time. The man, dressed more casually in a long-sleeved T-shirt, was older, probably in his fifties. Freya hugged both of them and asked them to wait while she prepared coffee.

Within a few minutes she came back, holding two cups. One was an affogato, which she presented to the woman dressed in a more formal attire. The other cup which was filled with macchiato was served to the man.

Finally, being seated, Freya asked the older man, "What brings you here, dad, and that too along with Dr. Kriti?"

Her father took a sip of his favorite drink, prepared by his favorite person, and replied, "Dear, Dr. Kriti had called me up yesterday to talk about something important. She knows how easily you panic, and therefore she chose to inform me first." Then, he looked at the woman. "Dr. Kriti, you may proceed."

"Well, Freya we all only want what is the best for you. And although you are comparatively healthy right now, we all know that with your condition, you would have to get a bypass graft sooner or later. And your latest reports have shown that the occlusion has increased to about fifty-five percent, and that your vessels have narrowed further. So, I request you to please consider the surgery in the near future." Dr. Kriti said.

For a few seconds, Freya was completely silent, as she stared at her father's troubled expression. Then, she asked the doctor, "I have known for a long time now that I have coronary artery disease. It is almost as if it has become a part of who I am. But would you please explain me in detail this once about the disease and the surgery?"

Dr. Kriti smiled and nodded. Then, she began explaining, her tone laced with comfort and knowledge, "Your heart is supplied by two coronary arteries. A right one and a left one, which divides into two main branches. Usually, the lumen of arteries is the space from where blood flows. But sometimes, substances and factors like alcohol use, high lipid diet, genetic predisposition and high blood pressure can trigger the deposition of cholesterol in the lumen, which narrows it and prevents normal flow. If not cured, the heart muscles would not get proper oxygen, and this can cause heart attack. Luckily for you, the type of this condition is stable and ischemic. But still, we would have to perform a surgery.

Basically, a bypass surgery follows the same rule as a flyover, that if the main road is too busy, another path is followed by the traffic. In this procedure we take a part of some other vessel of your body which is healthy, and graft if from the point of start of occlusion to its end. In this way, we ensure that the blood is shunted to this new vessel and flow is maintained. Also, it is not as dangerous as it sounds, so you don't have to get too stressed over it."

After receiving such a clear explanation, Freya was comparatively calm, and turned to her father. She smiled softly, and holding his hands, asked what he thought about the matter. With a slim line of tears in his eyes, he responded, "I know it is terrifying to think of undergoing such a major surgery. And to be honest, both me and your mother are scared to the bones. But we realize that it will only do long term benefit. I know very well that there are a million thoughts in your mind right now, but the most prominent feeling would be to be healthy again. So, although I would never force you, I suggest you should undergo the surgery before it is too late."

No words escaped Freya's throat, as she silently got up and hugged her father. Her little heart thumping wildly inside her chest was scared too, but she hoped for the best.

Then, turning to Dr. Kriti, she said, "I think I need some time to think about it, although I am pretty sure I want it soon. But can I inform you in two days?"

The doctor nodded in the affirmative, saying that it was indeed a very big decision to make. Then she got up, hugged Freya, and left. Her father chatted with her for some time, during which the entire focus shifted from the bleak thoughts of the surgery to more merrier ones of odds and ends, including one particular memory when Freya had almost been separated forever from her family because, once, while they were all aboard a train, she thought that they had to get off at the next station and had remained seated inside while her parents were dragging the luggage outside. Her father had to hop on the train, which was beginning to move, to rescue a seven-year-old, teary-eyed Freya. To this day, the memory left them in splits.

A minute of silence passed, after which, with slight hesitation, Freya finally told everything about Vihaan, right from how she met him up until their last meeting under the stars, and when her father listened to his daughter's genuine words, especially when she said that Vihaan had the most beautiful ashen eyes in the world, that seemed so full of life and never dull, he smiled to himself. Finally, when Freya showed a picture of Vihaan to him, which she had taken when he had gifted her a plant, her father patted her head and said, "You have one great man here, Freya. From the way you describe him, I feel he genuinely cares for you and loves you deeply. Also, his features convey his inner persona accurately. I hope you stay together forever."

A small smile crept over Freya's lips, as she held her father's hands and said what she was the most afraid of. "Dad, I know you would always want the best for me. And I strongly believe Vihaan is better than the best out there.

But there is one thing you ought to know about him." And she told him about the lung tumor Vihaan had. She did so very gently, not wanting to shock him. But her father listened calmly, not at all flinching at the mention of such a life altering information. Finally, when she was done, he looked up at her, a smile on his face as he said, "You both love each other, and that is all that matters. Diseases are surely big road blockers in any journey, but life is all about crossing hurdles together, right? Moreover, love isn't a roadway. It is a vertical travel, which only leads to newer levels of serendipity. And if you have fallen in love with him truly, he will make you feel content and warm." After a pause, he continued, "All I wish for is that the past may never repeat itself."

Freya's smile dimmed a bit, and as soon as her father took note of it, he patted her back and encouraged her to think positively, that his concern was only as a parent. Freya looked back up, "I know, dad. Another thing I know is that Vihaan is who he is, both inside and outside. He has a very caring and gentle heart, and the shadow of the thought of hurting me would never cross his mind." Her father smiled warmly, "From your words, it sure does seem so."

With that, he got up and gently reminded her to ponder over getting the surgery done, as it was for her own benefit. Kissing her on the forehead, he left, but not before picking up a small novel from the bookshelf, placing it discreetly in his suitcase. Freya laughed seeing his actions and returned to work, muddled thoughts about the future prospects of her health switching tides in her mind.

The next day, as the sun was starting to radiate its saffron sheen and the temperature had dropped down, Vihaan entered to café, his hands as usual carrying a planter, this time blooming with an anemone. Along with that he also had a packet in his hands. As soon as he placed the items on a table, he saw Ritul walk up to him. He pulled out something from the bag, and handed it to him, saying that Freya had informed him about his birthday two days ago, but official engagements had prevented him from coming.

Now there, he was elated to see the young boy's surprised face, as he evaluated the two crisp shirts from a high-end brand, never having laid his hands on such expensive material. After coming out of his trance he leaped toward Vihaan and wrapped him in a tight hug. Patting his back, Vihaan wished him again.

It was at this exact moment that he heard a sigh. Turning around, he was met with the sight of Freya bent over her knees, turning the soil over one of the planters he had given her earlier. Smiling, he soundlessly walked up to her, and picked her up by the waist, spinning her around once, before putting her on the ground. A small squeal escaped Freya's lips. His hands around her waist knocked the air out of her system. She felt her skin heat up, as his warm breath stroked the back of her neck. His strong arms around her body gave rise to goosebumps on the entirety of her skin, and although she laughed, her insides burned as his touch seeped inside her senses.

Still a bit surprised, she turned around to hug him. Excusing herself to wash her hands, she returned a few minutes later, only to find Vihaan going over the bookshelves. Silently, she waited for him to pick up a book.

After much thought, Vihaan's hands traveled down to pick up a book in the far-right corner, and he chose 'The Duke and I' by Julia Quinn. A wide smile spread over Freya's face, as she placed the cups of latte she held, on the table nearby.

When both of them had settled on the table, Vihaan opened the first page of the book, and the sight that greeted him was beyond beautiful. A dartboard drawn right in the middle of the page. When he looked up at Freya, he saw her eyes sparkle, and he leaned forward to hold her hands, pressing them between his own to create warmth.

"I see you like this book a lot. I hope you liked my present too." he said, pointing over to the cream-colored planter settled on the counter. Freya nodded, her hair bouncing slightly.

He picked it up, and the lavender flower swayed lightly. "This is an anemone. I especially like the story associated with it. It is said that the anemone sprang from the tears of Aphrodite as she mourned the death of Adonis, which is why, it has become a symbol of protection against any harm and represents overcoming anxiety and adversity."

Freya took the planter in her hands, and as usual, both of them took a polaroid with it. Although none of them had spoken about the topic much, but inside their hearts, this small ritual seemed magnanimously important. After that, she took a step back and asked, "Would you like to have something?"

Vihaan thought for a moment, and then, a mischievous smile bloomed on his face. "A cup of Americano, please."

"Sure, anything else to go along with it?" she asked, out of habit.

"You."

Slight surprise registered on Freya's face, which turned into a smile upon seeing Vihaan's face. She cleared her throat and said, "A cup of Americano along with a side of Freya coming right up, sir." Both of them burst into laughter, after which Freya went inside to prepare the order. Once back at the table, she put the coffee- and herself- in place.

Clearing her throat, she spoke, a hint of doubt floating in her eyes, "Vihaan, I have to tell you something. My father had visited me yesterday." With that, she told him everything, from the surgery to the fact that her father now knew about him. Vihaan was mildly surprised to know that her father actually approved of their relationship. But the major news for him was that Freya, his small, delicate, and amazing Freya would be under the knife sooner or later. Hesitantly, he asked her if she had agreed, and she said that she had finally decided to undergo the procedure, and that she would inform her father in the next day.

That was when Vihaan said, "Well, snowflake, I have to tell you something too. In fact, it is more or less the same. The other day, my parents and I had a long discussion with Dr. Nitin, and he has convinced me to undergo lung lobectomy soon, after much persuasion. I think I should finally give my body a chance to live and breathe. And although it is terrifying enough to think about my lungs being opened, I think it would get easy by the presence of my parents, Jatin, and you by my side."

Freya got up and hugged Vihaan, obviously aware of the panic his heart was in. She whispered, "I know that you are afraid, and rightfully so. But everything you want is on the other side of fear. So, sunshine, you needn't be afraid. Believe me, everything will fit just fine."

Separating from him, she sat back down in her seat and grabbed her cup of coffee. Taking a sip, she asked him, "So, which hospital are you being taken to for the surgery?"

"Broadmeadows Multispecialty Hospital. How about you?"

Freya visibly dropped her cup, regaining her composure a few seconds later. Vihaan was confused, but before he could speak, she enquired, "The one in Golf Links?" When he nodded, she smiled broadly and said, "Me too, I am also being admitted there. It had one of the best cardiothoracic departments in Delhi."

Vihaan laughed out loud, and running a hand through his dark locks, confessed "I sometimes feel you are a part of my bones, soul, and everything around. Really, as we said the other day, we will be together in sickness and in health. And as it is evident, we are."

Freya laughed too, and after a few moments, Vihaan got up, saying that he had to reach home. Both of them hugged each other tightly, and he mumbled in a husky voice, "I am aware that anything can happen, and that I might not be able to see you again, but it makes me the most joyful man in the universe to be able to share these moments with you." Freya lightly hit him on the head, scolding him for thinking such pessimistic ideas. Then, she waved him bye, and returned to work, a very happy Ritul smiling behind the counter, elated that one of the best persons in his life found something so precious: love.

Chapter 8

HELIOPHILIA

It was three days later when Freya received a message from Vihaan saying that he wanted her to meet someone, and for that, he had requested her to wear something yellow, her favorite color. This confused Freya a bit, but eventually, she decided to go with the flow, being aware that with him, even bleak despair could turn into calm moonlight.

In her closet, she dug through the piles of clothes for a very long time, until she found the perfect attire for the evening. It was an amber hued ankle length dress, with long, elegant, puffed sleeves. It had a slightly deep back, which conferred it a perfectly shaped look.

The entire day, anticipation washed over her in waves, and when it was finally dusk, she heard the familiar honk of Vihaan's car outside the café. Her body bubbled with exhilaration and anxiety as she stepped out of the doors.

To say Vihaan was dumbfounded would be an understatement. His shadowy eyes grew wide as he took in her frame, walking toward him. Smiling, she opened the door on the other side, but as she was about to step inside,

Vihaan's deep voice reverberated in the space, "Stop right there." Her feet halted, as she looked up at him. "That look, that smile on your face, it is priceless. Keep it on forever, snowflake." He smiled widely.

Laughter bubbled up in Freya's chest, as she stepped inside, closing the door. Vanilla and cinnamon invaded Vihaan's senses, as his eyes remained fixed on her. Finally, she signaled him to start the car, and they set in motion.

It didn't take long before they were outside large ebony doors, the vehicle coming to a smooth halt. Confusion bloomed on Freya's face, as she asked him about the place. A mischievous grin appeared on Vihaan's face as he announced, "Welcome to my home."

Fear rose from Freya's spine and spread all over her body as she sat dumbfounded before a wave of panic washed over her. She immediately started begging Vihaan to let her go back, but he calmed her down, and promised to be with her all throughout the time.

After ten minutes of heavy persuasion, Freya finally stepped out of the car and through the doors. Rows of plants and trees greeted her, arranged wisely to provide stunning hues to the place. Sangria fused with cobalt that spoke to emerald and mustard, which gave way to bronze shading a patch of scarlet, all blending together to create a passionate harmony of hues. Walking along the small entrance path, Freya touched the petals of dianthus, as a smile spread over her face. Vihaan, standing beside her, silently prayed for his parents to see the light he saw in her. He had already had a conversation with them about all that had happened in the past few months, and he had not forgotten to mention the details ensuing her health.

Soon, Vihaan opened the door to the house, and the interior took Freya's breath away. Beige tones covered the tall walls, and dark chestnut pillars accentuated the warmth. Family portraits adored the corners, and the calm luster of false ceiling lights bounced off the walls.

"Welcome, dear." A voice startled both of them. Vihaan turned around to see his father holding a tray with bowls of tomato soup along with croutons, while his mother was smiling beside him, her mitten covered hands indicating she had been baking something.

Walking forward, he hugged his parents, then introduced Freya to them. Not much had to be said, before his mother cast the mittens aside and hugged her, as she gladly exclaimed, "It is so nice to finally meet you in person! Vihaan has been going on about you nonstop for quite some time now. And I must say, you look an absolute dream in that dress."

Freya chucked, as she greeted his father too, who hugged her lightly, patting her head. Vihaan's mother asked them to sit, while she went inside the kitchen to resume whatever she was baking.

Once comfortable, Vihaan's father asked Freya a few questions here and there, and before long, his mother had joined the conversation.

Time flew by, and after about thirty minutes, they proceeded toward the dining table. The magnanimous size baffled Freya, while Vihaan chuckled and asked her to sit beside him. One by one, his father uncovered the dishes, and stuffed zucchini, butternut squash curry, falafel and bread baskets greeted them, the enticing aroma wrapping them in comfort. At the right moment, Vihaan's mother walked in with a platter of double chocolate cookies, and settling them down, asked everyone to begin the meal.

The first bite felt like home and earthly aromas mixed in a delightful concoction to Freya. She looked up to see the three people beside her enjoying it just as much as her. In a short duration, the dinner was over, and Freya helped Vihaan's mother in doing the dishes, even though she refused multiple times.

Finally, settling down on the couches, Freya thanked Vihaan's parents for accepting her warmly and making her feel a part of their family. After a few moments of silence, Vihaan's mother said, "You know, both of us were extremely excited to meet you, as this is the first time Vihaan has brought a girl home. You must be very different, and I hope you know that we love you for who you are, regardless of any issues or health problems. A person like you deserves all the care and love in the world."

A hint of shock appeared on Freya's angelic face, as she turned toward Vihaan, who explained, "I had told my parents about you and the condition, and if you are angry or upset by it, I totally understand. I just didn't have the heart to keep anything from them, especially about someone so important to me."

Tears of elation and adoration pooled in the brown warmth of Freya's eyes, as she smiled brightly, nodding her head. Soon though, the tears were replaced by resounding laughter, as the four people started discussing lighter, more vibrant topics.

A few minutes later, Freya got up, saying that she had to be home soon, and all the three other people got up along with her. Vihaan offered to drive her home and walked her out before doing so himself.

Once in the car, Vihaan asked how she felt about his family. With constellations in her eyes, Freya replied, "Like home. Your family is literally the epitome of togetherness. I loved this evening, and this shall remain one of the finest days of my life."

Vihaan smiled, his smoke hued eyes curving into those adorable crescents, as he asked her for directions toward her home.

Within ten minutes, they were in front of a two floored alabaster toned house with cobalt borders, cedar wood doors gating the entrance. Plants neatly lined the balcony, and the house looked extremely aesthetic. Opening the door for Freya, Vihaan hugged her tightly, and she let his embrace bloom warmth inside her.

Finally letting go, Vihaan said, "I know this isn't the time to break such news, but my surgery would be performed in about twenty days from now, but I would have to be admitted for the same three days in advance, as they would like to keep a check on my airway passages and such." A sigh escaped Freya's lips, as she placed a palm over his own and informed him, "My surgery is probably in three weeks, as my father told me. Aren't the coincidences getting too peculiar, Sunshine?" Suppressing the urge to spin her around, as the nickname sounded heavenly on her lips, Vihaan said, "Well, is it weird? Because as far as I know, soulmates are together in everything, even the toughest of times."

"I love how you turn everything gloomy into the most hopeful thing ever." Freya chuckled and bent over to pluck a small dark mauve flower from one of the planters outside her home, and handing it to Vihaan, informed him, "This is a zinnia. This is one of the most beautiful flowers in my entire home. And my father told me that it is particularly remarkable as it symbolizes lasting affection, just like the one you shower me with. I really want you to keep it." Taking the blooming stalk in his hands, Vihaan studied it for a few moments, before his eyes closed into the same mesmerizing crescents that Freya had fallen for, and the purest laugh escaped his lips.

"You amaze me, woman." He said, before kissing the top of her forehead.

"You will forever remain the melody of my heart, the imprint on the sanguine surface of my organs, the last thought on my mind when all haze surrounds it, and the first drop of elixir that brings back the life and consciousness within me." He spoke directly next to her ear, and with a final hug, got into his car and drove off.

Freya stood there, roses blooming on her cheeks, much more resplendent than the ones beside her on the ground.

Two days had passed since their last encounter, when Vihaan's message popped up on Freya's phone. He asked her if she was up for a small detour, and she had gladly agreed, Wednesdays being less busy than others.

Twenty minutes later, both of them were turning a lane, when Vihaan asked Freya to stop. Gently, he asked her to close her eyes, promising that the place would cheer her up. Animation tugging at her veins, Freya turned the corner with her eyes shut, and after a few steps, she felt Vihaan tap her shoulder. She opened her eyes, to find herself standing in front of a brightly colored building, splashes of vibrant hues filling her peripheral vision. Vihaan whispered in her ears, the sensation causing the hair on the back of her neck to stand, "This is a place to let yourself loose, Snowflake. Are you ready to let all your inhibitions pour out on the canvas?" She nodded, her eyes taking in the color scheme once more.

Once inside, both of them picked up a canvas, and setting it up on opposite ends of the room, began working on their pieces. After about an hour or so, Vihaan sighed loudly, grabbing Freya's attention. She walked over, wiping her hands with a rag, and he turned the canvas around to let her see his work. Her feet stopped, and the shimmer in her eyes brightened as she took the content on the canvas in.

A perfectly symmetrical snowflake was painted on the blank sheet, but what drew her in was the center of the work. A girl with brown hair swirling like the wisps of smoke was drawn, facing back, so her expressions were not visible. The chestnut shade of her locks was brushed with streaks of golden at some places, giving it the desired depth.

"It's you." Vihaan said from behind the canvas, and Freya's hands moved on their own accord as they ruffled up his tousled umber hair. Comfort washed over him in waves as his eyes involuntarily closed, while his soul relished in the soothing graze of her fingers against his scalp. A smile warmed up his features, and he opened his eyes after a few seconds of sheer bliss. Then, he insisted on seeing what she had made in the past hour.

Though he sensed a bit of hesitance from her, he encouraged her, and she finally gave in. Walking across the room and turning her board around, she gauged Vihaan's expression. He stopped and admired the strokes, as his hands came to rest on his hips. "You are one heck of a talented person, Freya." Hearing him praise her relaxed the tensed muscles on her forearms, but listening to him say her actual name in that particularly deep voice was what sent her heart in a frenzy.

Then, his face shifted from being serious to excited once again, as he walked up to her and held the frame in his hands. Against charcoal darkness of the painted sheet, stood out a million stars made from shades of alabaster. Still, the most priceless part was the silhouette of a couple standing near the corner, hand in hand, admiring the expanse of inky midnight beauty in front of them. It was captivating to say the least.

Vihaan tugged on Freya's sleeves, and she looked up at him. He leaned down and planted a soft kiss on her cheeks, and that is when Freya realized that she was down bad for this man. She had already known that he was the one for her, but the brush of his lips against her cheeks had set her insides aflame and had provided her the most calming response together. She knew that this was what falling in love feels like, for the kiss made her soul soar up, and yet she felt the depths of his simple presence engulf her completely, until no other thoughts invaded her mind.

Four days later, Vihaan showed up outside Freya's house for the first time since dropping her off, and ringing the doorbell, he waited for someone to open the door. As it was past nine in the evening, he expected her to not show up. But, in a matter of seconds, Freya was in front of him, though both of them were unable to see each other due to the cedar wood partitions. As soon as the door opened, Freya was surprised, as she smiled and asked him to come inside. But Vihaan was unable to speak for a minute because this was his first time seeing her in such a cozy state, and not in some formal or work wear attire. An oversized olive hoodie was placed over her like a blanket, while she wore gray sweatpants, which were so long they were pooling around her ankles. She looked like she was about to go to bed, and Vihaan felt a little bad for interrupting her. He asked her about it, and she responded with a smile on her face, "I might have been getting ready for bed, but I hope you don't mind me being seen with you in a state like this?" "Like what?" Vihaan asked, a little frown on his face. "Like I desperately need a fashion therapy and spa treatment. I am in sweatpants for crying out loud."

"No. You are going out like this, and you are going to look the absolute best, because that shines from within you."

"Can I get to know where we are headed?"

"Nowhere." He smiled, and although that didn't answer her question, she preferred to let the events unfold at their own pace.

With that, Vihaan left his car by her door, and both of them walked hand in hand, roaming about in the night, talking about childhood memories, like when Vihaan had dropped a bottle of honey all over the kitchen counter, and how even after cleaning it many times, ants had flocked around it. He skipped the part where he had gotten a good scolding from his mother, but Freya understood without him saying it. Similarly, Freya shared with him the time she had messed-up the dance to be performed at their annual fest in school, and even though she was in the front row, performing the opposite steps, her parents had cheered the loudest for her.

Talking had never really come easy for Vihaan, who felt way more secure and safe in his own bubble, beat his own trusted people, whom he opened up to. Never in his wildest dreams did he think of sharing such intimate and personal details with a woman he had met mere weeks ago.

But then, this was also his first time falling hard and fast for a woman who nurtured an ocean of sunlight within herself, and when you dive into sunlight, you leave behind the promises of fear and hesitation, for all you see after that is clarity and a soft, warm glow enveloping you, and you never want to get out.

So, blabbering about the most random topics Vihaan had never found himself comfortable opening up about to others, they reached back to Freya's home, where he hugged her tightly, and waving bye for a final time, went off toward his home.

Three days later, Freya was standing outside the café, clad in an indigo ribbed top and a pair of wide legged, stone washed jeans. Her whole being exuded a vibe full of enthusiasm, as she paced lightly over the cobblestone. She had called Vihaan about an hour ago, asking him to pick her up. He had tried to ask where she was headed to, but she had refrained him form asking too many questions and had hung up. Now that she saw his car turn the corner, her heartbeat picked up, and she adjusted her clothes one last time.

As soon as he parked, she walked up to the car and opened the door, making herself comfortable. When Vihaan asked her about the destination, she asked him to follow her directions, and the way her carob eyes shone, forced him to obey her.

Meticulously giving directions, both of them were now in a quieter part of the city, which was a surprise for Vihaan, as Delhi was always bustling with noises. After a few more minutes, Freya asked him to stop in front of a road, shrubs lining either side of it, as she got out. Vihaan followed, and Freya held his hand, "I hope you enjoy this duration of time you spend with me." Vihaan's heart swelled, as he nodded softly.

In a few steps, both of them stood in front of a mulberry shaded building, adorned by fairy lights and ivy vines. A few people were inside, wearing aprons, working away. The board above their heads read 'La Risa,' which Freya told Vihaan meant laughter in Spanish.

She opened the door, and the soothing warmth and smell of freshly baked goods invaded their senses. She informed, "This is a self-baking café. Here, you can make your own baked goods, and also add your own twists to the flavors. I hope we have an amazing time here. This is such a quaint place; I couldn't resist bringing you here."

"This is perfect. I don't know how you do it, but somehow you always manage to surprise me in the most unexpected ways possible." Vihaan expressed, still taking in the aesthetics of the place. Freya chuckled, then proceeded to ask, "So, what would you like to make?" After a few moments of pondering, he responded, "Stuffed caramel brownies."

Freya was a bit amazed, as she thought he would pick up a material like sweetbread. Nevertheless, she held his hands, and after talking a bit with the head chef, they were assigned a counter with all the materials required, and shortly they began with the procedure.

Soon, both of them were immersed in the work, kneading the dough and such. At one point, Freya slightly hummed, as Vihaan came up behind her to pick up a bowl of sugar resting on the tabletop.

Oblivious to it, she backed up a little bit to dust off the thick layer of flour that adorned her apron, as well as parts of her face. It was then that she felt his arm next to his cheek.

Her feet froze, as he leaned down to pick the bowl up. She felt his chest, warm and strong, against her back as he smiled down at her.

He moved back, and just like that, the warmth was gone. But her body still stirred a bit as she remembered her back pressed against him. Her heartbeat was blatantly refusing to slow down, but she somehow brought it under control and continued with the work, the recent memory giggling playfully in the back of her mind.

In the next hour, the counter was covered in a layer of butter, sugar, flour, and cocoa powder, as were Vihaan and Freya. But they had been successful in completing the task at hand, along with clicking a few very memorable pictures. Sitting down while waiting for the oven to ping indicating the sound of completion, Freya put her head between her arms. In a few seconds, the brownies were done, and Vihaan got up to open the door. Instantly, a sensual, creamy, nutty smell surrounded them, and Freya helped him get the batch out on the table.

"Well hard work pays off for sure." Vihaan said, while taking a bite into the chocolaty goodness. Freya followed, and soon, both of them had finished half the batch, while packing away the other half to take home.

While heading out, Vihaan kissed Freya lightly on her cheek, and while her insides did a complete somersault out of sheer bliss, she managed to smile. "This was the calmest, most relaxing place I have ever been to, and being with you simply enhanced the experience. Thanks for bringing me here, snowflake."

Then, holding hands, both of them walked back up to the car and drove off.

Vihaan had become silent, but Freya didn't mind. She basked in the unspoken beauty of the moment.

When she got out of the car, Vihaan followed suit, and without thinking much, gripped her by the arm and dragged her down to the end of the street, which was rather quiet and opened into an alley.

Once there, Freya felt a tad bit confused. But, before she could gather her emotions, he gently but firmly grabbed her shoulders and backed her up into the wall. Her heart raced up, as he bent down to her ears and asked, "Do you know why I was so silent during the drive?" She shook her head in the negative. He continued, "I was thinking about you."

A smile formed on his face when he saw her hands close into fists. He moved his face closer to her cheek so that they were skin to skin and whispered:

"I don't think you are a dazzling, luminous ray of sunshine." He stopped and felt her gulp down.

"You are the dark right before the first ray of sunshine grazes the earth. You aren't the brightness craved by everyone. But then again, I never wanted or had a bright, sunny life. You are the calm darkness that puts one to sleep, even if it masks the imminent arrival of a blinding shard of light to disturb it all. You are fleeting and momentary, yet the conclusive state of the universe, eternal night.

And believe me when I say that in brightness, there may be hope, but you are visible. Each mistake is clearly seen. But, in darkness, there is room for expansion. There is space to create mistakes and learn, to revel and all illicit deeds and never speak of them. The dark depths hold them for us." He breathed out, and physically felt Freya shiver from the impact of it on her skin.

"You are those depths. You are the cave where I open up my deepest, rawest form in, without the fear of being judged. And however fast the speed of light may be, the brink of darkness always comes first. You are the brink, Freya. You are the depth of my secrets and the wholeness to my hollowness."

He kissed her lightly on the junction of her neck and shoulder, and she practically melted in the alleyway.

He backed up, a smile etched on his perfect face. "Go on now. Your customers would be waiting." He prompted.

"Yes." She replied after three seconds, seeming dazed. As she walked away, Vihaan chuckled to himself. 'It's fun to make her breathless.' He thought, before making sure she was inside the café, and once he was assured, he drove away.

Chapter 9
QUIDDITY

About four days had passed without Freya and Vihaan seeing each other, both of them busy in their professions. Vihaan was adamant on explaining all the details of their ongoing project to Jatin before he took the medical leave, while Freya was occupied with clearing out the accounts and other documents of the café. She wanted to do as much work as possible, so that Ritul wouldn't be unnecessarily burdened.

On the evening of the fifth day, Freya sat down on one of the chairs of the café, feeling lightheaded. Her palms were sweaty, and although her breathing appeared to be normal, she felt the need to inhale deeply in order to feel conscious.

Ritul, who had been by the counter, had noticed her health wobble throughout the day, and therefore, was by her side with a glass of cool water in an instant. With the customer flow reduced, it was easier for him to do so.

Gulping down the refreshing liquid, Freya asked him for something to eat, saying anything would be fine at the moment to keep her energy up. Quick on his feet, Ritul went inside the pantry and brought out two sandwiches, made by him a few minutes ago for any incoming customers. A weak hand went out toward the plate, as Freya grabbed one of the sandwiches, biting into the warm potato and cabbage filling. The first bite felt like the revival of her soul. She sighed deeply, chewing slowly on the goodness of the buttery bread.

Just as the situation was starting to seem slightly less bleak, Freya felt her vision go a bit blur at first, and before she could give more thought to it, onyx expanses covered her vision. The last thing she saw was Vihaan's form entering the café, with a planter as usual in his hands, before collapsing on the floor.

Vihaan had been wanting to gift Freya a gladiolus for quite some time now, as it was a symbol of strength, which was highly required by both of them when the situations were as dire as the one, they faced. That was the reason he had stopped by at the nursery to buy a mauve flower and had driven straight toward the café.

But the scene before him had his breath stuck in his throat, as his knees buckled under him. He almost lost his balance completely, but the counter at the doorway helped him stabilize himself. Before his own unbelieving eyes, he saw Freya go limp, before hitting the cold, hard floor. Ritul tried his best to hold her up, but his panicked state didn't help much.

Vihaan rushed toward her with every ounce of power in his already tired body, as everything in his being screamed her name. In mere three strides, he was beside her, kneeling down. Gently picking her head up, he shook her to get any response, any sounds. But he was met with only ragged breaths. His eyes brimmed with tears which were threatening to spill over the edge, as he rubbed them back.

Quick to his feet, he tucked one arm below her knees and one below her head, asking Ritul to open the door. Placing her inside his car, he asked him to close the café and get in. In less than fifteen minutes, they were inside the hospital, evidently due to breaking a lot of traffic signals.

Haggard and restless, Vihaan shouted for doctors again and again, until a couple of young female doctors rushed over to him and helped him get Freya out. Immediately, one of them brought a stretcher out and helped the other get Freya onto it, and Vihaan rushed inside the hospital along with Ritul, not wanting to leave her side.

It was physically fracturing for him to see the love he wanted to protect from any harm lying on a hospital stretcher, trying to breathe, which came out in shallow, broken intakes of air.

Once they had reached inside, the doctors knocked on a door, and soon, Vihaan was greeted by the sight of a woman in her mid-forties, wearing an apron with Dr. Kriti Desai written on it. She took one look at the stretcher behind the young doctors, and walked over to it, placing away the documents in her hand onto a side table.

Recognizing the person as her long time patient, she immediately asked Vihaan about the time when she collapsed and instructed her juniors to start an intravenous dose of disodium EDTA. Saying so, she herself made space for her in the critical care ward, and then left after repeating the instructions and patting Vihaan's back, a signal for him to not lose courage.

Dread washed over Vihaan in hyphens, as his palms trembled every time his eyes fell on Freya's lifeless form. He knew that this was the time to believe everything would turn out for the better, but deep down, fear gnawed at his insides, and a molten feeling of despair pooled in his gut. Not wanting to think any more about the bleak situation at hand, he got up and walked out of the room, only to be met with the sight of Ritul pacing down the hallway.

"Why are you here? You should go inside, Ritul. Or better, come with me to the cafeteria and have something to eat." Vihaan gently said, holding his hands and walking toward the food booth. Once there, he ordered a small plate of pasta for Ritul, and settled on a large cup of Americano for himself. After taking the first sip he sighed aloud, putting his head between his palms, and closing his tired eyes. Ritul asked in a small voice, "Will mam be alright? What has happened to her?" Vihaan patted his back and assured him, "Well, as far as I know, Freya is a tough person. I am sure she would be fine."

Ritul still seemed a bit shaken up, but the elder's words brought an ounce of relief to him. Soon, after finishing the meal, Vihaan called for a cab to send him back home, promising to keep on updating him. Then, he returned to the room Freya was kept in for observation.

Sitting down back into the chair near her bed, he held her palm and stared at her for a few moments. Unknown guilt pooled inside his chest. In a raspy voice, he began, "Snowflake, I know you can't listen to me right now, but I hope my voice reaches your heart. You know how scared out of my mind I was when I saw your body go limp in front of me? Terrified is more like it. In that moment, I felt like the most powerless, weak, and lonely person in the world. I know how hard it must be for you to endure all the pain your body has to go through every day, but the way you manage it is enchanting. You are not only a snowflake, but the embodiment of the entire winter season. You are the crystalline, frozen joy of each step in the crispy snow on a chilly morning. You are that singular flower on a dewy hilltop, standing out against all the stony backdrop, filling the surroundings with an abundance of exhilaration. Your presence is exactly like that singular bloom in my life. You are the spectrum of my emotions because you might not know this, but with you, thinking about you, I have felt almost all the possible feelings stir up inside me: fear, enjoyment, happiness, gloom, anxiety, satisfaction, affection, envy, and above all admiration. It really baffles me to no end, when I think about the impact you have on the little things in my life. Earlier, I wasn't really a fan of donuts with coffee, but over time, sitting with you by the large glass windows, I felt myself grow a liking for these sugary delights so much that now, I have found a local bakery near my home to bring some back whenever I want to. Similarly, I was not much interested in reading biographies either, but the week you gave me 'Radioactive' by Lauren Redniss, I felt myself get attached to it dearly. You might be unaware of this, but the walnut sensations of your eyes always put my head in a frenzy and my make my palms a bit sweaty.

And I swear to God, there is nothing in this world I would trade for feeling this. I have fallen and will continue to fall in the depths of your being, your essence, till forever falls apart. So, you might not be in the prime of health right now, but as I promised, we would be together in health and in sickness, and I am here. Always, till the end of time."

"I hope everyone finds love like you, Vihaan." A voice broke from behind him, and Vihaan turned to see Dr. Kriti along with another doctor looking over him fondly. He was tall, with peculiar hazel eyes, his tousled hair making him look a tad bit playful. He was considerably younger than the woman beside him. "This is Dr. Dev Shah. He is one of the finest young minds around here. Vihaan, you should feel free to ask any questions from him." Saying so, the elder woman left.

Dr. Dev walked in with an air of cheerfulness yet knowledge, and the atmosphere lightened up instantly. He sat down on one of the chairs, and after looking for a moment toward Vihaan, he asked, "Did you inform her parents?" The latter nodded, remembering the trembling voices of Freya's parents as he told them who he was, how he got their contact number from Ritul and what had happened. They were in Noida at that time, so it was natural they weren't present at the moment.

"Nice. Patients are always more comfortable around the ones they love, rather than nurses and doctors. Mind telling me who you are?" The doctor asked, a playful smile ghosting his lips as he picked up a toffee from a bowl on the table. Vihaan hesitated for a moment, as he had never said the words out loud. "I- I am her best friend."

"Hmm, best friends don't make each other's palms sweaty now, do they?"

A wave of surprise passed over Vihaan's face, as the doctor continued, "I get it, she is your girlfriend. Just say it out loud. It is clearly evident that you care deeply about her. In all honesty, it is a rare sight nowadays."

Vihaan smiled, his pigeon hued eyes closing into the two crescents everyone adored. But soon, he felt the atmosphere simmer down to gloom once again as his eyes fell on Freya. Noticing his confusion and fear, Dr. Dev gently began, "I know you are scared. And I would say rightfully so. Freya was in a really serious state when you brought her here. Any more delay and the golden hour would have passed. Now, I am glad to inform that all her vitals are stable. Her heart muscles are just weak, because of the blockage in her coronary arteries. This could have increased because of any reason, most prominent being stress. That is why she had been feeling restless. Now, you must know that the blockage is still present, though instant doses have reduced the tension a bit. Still, as her surgery is near, I feel everything would be fine." After a pause, he continued, "I take it that you are also soon to be admitted here, and if I remember correctly, isn't it because of a benign lung tumor?"

Vihaan looked up in surprise, and before he could say anything more, Dr. Dev cut him in, "I know this because this is a teaching hospital. We have rotational postings in various departments here. It was the day we were being handed out a few files which were to be studied and reported. It so happened that I got your file. That is where I remember you from. I must say you have a charming face." As he finished, a small grin appeared on his features. Vihaan smiled widely too, as he commented, "I am compelled to say the same about you." Dr. Dev laughed out loud, and getting up, he hugged Vihaan tight, and said softly, "I am sure both you and Freya would be all fine in no time. And believe me when I say that I predict the outcomes of surgeries quite well. Take care." With this, he excused himself.

Vihaan sat back down on the chair, and gulping down a glass of water, closed his eyes for a few moments. Soon, he was fast asleep, his head by Freya's hands, some raven hair brushing the skin on her forearm.

His slumber was interrupted about twenty minutes later, when he heard some commotion outside. Getting up to check what it was all about, he noticed a couple, roughly in their late fifties, who were evidently troubled. It didn't take him much time to recognize them as Freya's parents.

He walked up to them and asked them to sit down, telling them his name. Freya's mother was in a terribly panicked state, and for a moment, Vihaan felt his defenses fall again. But he collected himself and held her hand firmly, repeating again and again that Freya was fine now. It took a few minutes, but it worked, and Dr. Dev, who had entered the area a few seconds ago, explained them the situation calmly. Meanwhile, Vihaan brought two glasses of cool water and handed one to each of them.

As was evident from the washed expressions on their faces and trembling hands, they were highly shaken up by the incident. The flint in Vihaan's eyes shone with freshly settled dew drops as he tried his best to fight back the developing tears. However, Freya's mother strode over to him and held his hands in hers, as her voice came out scratched and heavy, "Son, I am aware that we both don't personally know each other, but as far as I have managed to gather from what Freya has told me, you are a gem of a person. I really hope I could have met you in more joyful circumstances, but-" her voice cut off as she choked back on a sob. Instantly, Vihaan wrapped his arms around her, and soothingly rubbed her back. After a few seconds, she regained her composure and turned toward Freya's father. "We should go see her now." She spoke. He nodded and getting up feebly, walked over to the room. Vihaan followed them but stopped at the gates in order to let them have some time alone.

Once inside, Freya's father's tears rolled down his cheeks once more, as he hugged her tightly in his embrace. Her body was warm to the touch, and although her features seemed weak, there was still a slight rosy hue to her otherwise pale skin.

Her mother pressed her cheeks together, as she whispered, "Freya, my golden child, I am so sorry because I was not there when you felt dizzy. I should have probably called you home a week ago. Look at you. Don't you eat properly?" She but back a pained sob. "Anyways, when you get well, I am taking you back home and I will make it sure that you eat malai kofta, shahi paneer and dum aloo with naan and tamarind chutney, just the way you have always liked."

Fresh tears brimmed on her waterline.

"I know you can subconsciously hear me; I can feel it. So, get well soon dear. God is supremely gracious, and I know for a fact that no matter how many cold showers of troubles He may pour over us, once they are all over, the most astonishing rainbow of contentment and relief spreads over the sky of our life. Look at you father. He is so scared. After all, you are his best friend and television companion. Get all healthy soon, my child."

Her father kissed her forehead, and a few teardrops fell on her smooth skin. He wiped them off and sat back on the chair. After a few moments, Vihaan entered the room too, and politely stood near the entrance, until Freya's father asked him to sit as well. Tiredness was well evident on his slightly wrinkled face, which was devoid of all colors, because of the piling tension and stress. Vihaan said, "Sir, I am well aware of the tremendous emotional and mental pressure you are under. After all, your only daughter is in the question. I want you to know that she is one of the best things that has happened in my life, marking her presence right from the first day I met her. Freya is one-of-a-kind, and although I have seen plenty of people battle with chronic, life threatening diseases with a smile, I know for a solid fact that her way is the most unique. Beneath the soft, shiny layers of her magnetic persona, she is still a vulnerable, innocent person who finds amusement in the smallest things. She is not afraid to accept the fact that she indeed is physically weak, and she embraces it. This is what makes her special. Medical conditions have not dulled her spark and enthusiasm for life at all. I was shell shocked when I saw her fainting right before my eyes, and to be honest, I felt like crying a river of tears in the café. But, fortunately, with Ritul's help, she was here in record time. I don't want to think about what could have happened if I was stuck in a traffic jam or something."

Freya's mother wiped her face with the back of her palm, as she softly said, her voice still hoarse from all the tears, "I know how much you care for our daughter and love her, son. I can feel it coming from you. Also, Freya has been talking about you in bits and pieces over the phone whenever I called her. It was fairly evident in her voice that she was always delighted when the conversation involved you. Now, all I wish for, is to hear her voice again. To call me, her father, you, everyone just like she used to. What happened to the ball of soft happiness that jumped about in our house, like the wind that loves frolic?" Her voice broke toward the end, and she stopped.

Freya's father continued, his eyes fixed on her palm, "As a kid, she always used to fear sleeping alone in her room. At times, she was so petrified that she woke up in the middle of the night, sweat coursing through her back, to knock on our door. Even though we persuaded her to be brave and not fear, deep down, I knew that her imagination would run rampant the moment she found herself alone under the blankets. And more than anything, I hated seeing tears in her eyes. So, I went with her to bed, where we used to talk about the most random topics, from her friends to her dreams, and she amazed me at times. She always had a penchant for studies involving social settings, which is why she chose sociology. Then, she went on to pursue a degree in market research, and we were elated. Everything seemed rosy, but all I wish for is that she never met Pranay." He paused, rubbing his thumb over her wrist.

'Pranay? She never told me about him.' Vihaan thought but didn't question the man. "That was the time she stared having small bouts of chest pain. Earlier, it was too inconspicuous to be taken note of, and we thought it would go away. But then, one day, she fainted from the impact of it." His hands shuddered. Vihaan's palms itched to hold them, but a slight burn of unfamiliarity stopped him. He was at the awkward junction of knowing him and yet not knowing who he was, and that only furthered the uneasiness.

"My mother had started showing the same symptoms around the age of seventy, and when I connected the dots, I was terrified for Freya. I had seen my mother go weak in front of my very own eyes, and to think that the same could happen to my daughter, the young, effervescent girl that ran up to hug me the moment I stepped foot inside home shuddered me to my bones." A tear dropped down his cheekbone.

He continued, "Anyways, that was the day we took her to the hospital, where the doctors diagnosed her with coronary artery disease." A shudder involuntarily ran through his body. "To say we were shocked is an understatement. I had prayed to every God and deity imaginable to avert this very possibility, but the world has a distorted way of functioning, and I was mortified by the realization. Still, we couldn't even come a hair close to realizing how she would have felt. But, over time, she became braver about the situation. This was when she expressed her desire to open up the café, because she wanted to be able to be the source of a space where people could come to relax and unwind. She learned to smile again; the same pure joy that had been lost for a few months. Luckily, her condition was stable, and the medications were helpful. The doctors had suggested us to consider a surgery soon, but being parents, we were too scared. All the wrong possibilities popped up in our brains, and now we are here. Although, on top of that, I must say that Freya is one of the strongest people I have ever seen. Had it been me, I would have probably succumbed to the building pressure far sooner. I love her, and I make sure to tell that often to her." He bent forward to hold her hand and rubbed circles on it.

"Freya is blessed to have parents like you. I can imagine how beautiful her childhood must have been." Vihaan smiled, although it was an empty feeling that clouded his chest.

Just then, Dr. Kriti entered the room, holding a few papers in her hands. When her eyes fell on Freya's father, she walked up to him, and greeted him softly, doing the same to her mother. Then, she proceeded to sit down on an empty chair. "So, as we all know, Freya's bypass surgery is scheduled in the next four days. And as far as I know, your lobectomy is also on the same day, right Vihaan?"

He nodded, the back of his neck heating up from the evident stares of the two other people in the room. "Right. Just so you all know, Freya is going to be absolutely fine, and this is a promise. In no time after the surgery, she would be able to do all the chores normally, without having bouts of chest pain or experiencing fatigue." She paused, and everyone nodded. Continuing, she said, "As for you, Vihaan, let me accompany you to Dr. Nitin, to have a conversation with him."

Vihaan obliged and got up. Before leaving, he had a look at the faces of Freya's parents, and though her father seemed relatively calm, hazy confusion still adorned her mother's features. He nodded toward the older man knowingly and left.

Upon reaching the room of Dr. Nitin, Dr. Kriti left, patting Vihaan's back. Hesitantly, he knocked on the door. Within seconds, a voice asked him to come in. Judging by the look on Dr. Nitin's face, he was not expecting his most adored patient to walk in. Nevertheless, he was delighted, and hugged him tightly. Settling down on the seats, Dr. Nitin asked him about his arrival. Briefly, Vihaan told him all about Freya's episode, and her impending surgery.

Dr. Nitin said, "Well, I am absolutely sure that Dr. Kriti is an amazing surgeon, definitely one of the best in cardiothoracic department in Delhi, and I can assure you that Freya would be completely healed." Then, after having a swig of water, he continued, "As far as you are concerned, I was thinking of calling you up today, for the tests to be done prior to the surgery. It is a coincidence you came along."

Suddenly, Vihaan felt his palms turn a bit moist, and his heart rate increased. Dr. Nitin noticed it and asked him to calm down. "Vihaan, you have absolutely no need to worry. You know very well that Freya's surgery is far more complex. I can assure you that I will never let anything happen to you. You too, are in the hands of a good surgeon just like Freya, if you don't know." At this, Vihaan chuckled. Dr. Nitin had always been like family to him. Therefore, he had grown up to be frank with him. He got up and shook the doctor's hand. "When would I be admitted?" he asked. "If you have no issues, we could admit you tomorrow, as I think your family would want to be there. And the nice thing is that even after admission, you can get up and walk around. No need to be tied down to the bed."

Vihaan smiled and turned around to leave.

Once outside, he leaned back against the wall, exhaustion evident on his face. He ran a hand through his hair, tugging on them slightly. This helped ease a few knots and released a part of the pent-up tension inside him. He dragged himself up to a seat and plopped down. His hands roamed near the pocket of his pants, and he felt for his phone. Once he pulled it out, notifications of missed calls and messages bombarded his sight. His graphite eyes widened when he realized that his phone was on the silent mode, which was why no calls of his parents along with Jatin had been received. Panicked, Vihaan called up his mother. He was well aware about all the thoughts that might have stirred up in her brain in the meantime.

Two rings later, the line was picked up and he heard a hastened "Hello?" As soon as he replied, his mother almost yelped. "Where were you, Vihaan? Me and your father have been trying to reach out to you for the past two hours almost. We were more worried when Jatin told us that you left office as usual. Where are you? Are you hurt?" Vihaan breathed in, and replied in a calm yet drained tone, "Sorry mom, I am well aware of how much undue tension I might have put you all in. I would have picked up the calls, had my cell not been on silent mode." His mother breathed in, then said, "You don't know how relieved I am feeling right now, hearing your stable voice. Now, tell me where you are at the moment." Vihaan hesitated, as he did not want to pile her anxiety. But, once he heard his father's voice too, saying how worried he was, and had almost called the police, he broke down.

For the first time since the events had taken place, he let all his fears and inhibitions turn into molten form and flow out of his eyes. His breathing became slightly heavy, and he finally let it all out. He told his parents he was at the hospital, then briefly narrated all that had happened up until then, along with his meeting with Dr. Nitin.

His parents listened shell shocked on the other line, unable to form a single word. Now that they had met Freya, they knew the cheerful demeanor she carried with her. Imagining her lying on the hospital bed, not able to move, her heart beating weakly, had their knees buckling. Finally, his father offered to come up to the hospital. A beat of silence passed.

But Vihaan was tired. He was exhausted from the day's events, and although a part of him wanted to stay up all night near Freya, the more rational one suggested him to go home, as his body ached for some rest. Moreover, he himself had to be admitted tomorrow, so he wanted to spend some time at home.

His heart told him to visit Freya's room once more, but he knew that if he strayed toward that side, his being wouldn't allow him to leave. So, he got up with a sigh, and made his way toward the exit. Once he sat down inside his car, he silently prayed to God, the same words on his lips again and again, until it became a chant. He prayed for Freya, for himself, their parents, and their wellbeing. Finally, he started the vehicle, and drove off into the night.

Twenty minutes later, he was sitting on the sofa of his living room, his eyes closed due to exhaustion, his head resting on his mother's lap. Meanwhile, his father prepared a simple meal for him. He almost fell asleep there, but his mother shook him gently to ask him to consume some food. Groggily, he walked up to the dining table, where he sat opposite to them, and ate with small bites. Once his meal was finished, his father moved around the table to sit next to him. He hugged his son tightly and ran a hand over his back. Vihaan sighed at the sensation, and his eyes felt heavy again.

"You know, we were planning on asking you to bring Freya home again." His father started. "It is very rare nowadays to meet such a pure, kind-hearted person. It amazed me how well she fit in the first time. It was as if we had known her for quite some time." He paused and cleared his throat. "But, when you told us about her today, we felt the ground from beneath us shift, and not only because it was her that was admitted. It was also because I had almost imagined you there, and it knocked the wind out of my lungs. I cannot even begin to imagine the kind of trauma and stress her parents might be under. We are going there tomorrow, and before meeting up with Dr. Nitin, I think we should see Freya."

His mother also approved of the idea, and added, "I am so proud of you today, son. You have essentially played a part in saving someone's life. I adore you a lot. Now, go up to your room, take some rest. Also, before you sleep, please do call Jatin. The boy was scared to death when he couldn't reach you."

Vihaan nodded and got up to climb the flight of stairs that took him to his room.

After showering under cascading warm water, he slumped into his bed. Taking out his cell phone, he called Jatin. Once he picked up, Vihaan immediately started speaking, not letting his friend utter a word. Once he apologized for not picking up the calls and explained the reason, Jatin responded, "No worries, dear. I was just concerned for you. Knowing you, there aren't many places you visit other than the café, the office and the nursery. I just wanted to know you were safe. Also, I think I should go see Freya tomorrow. Whenever you leave, do tell me. Now, I suggest you to not worry and take some rest. As the doctor said, Freya is stable, and you don't want a sleepless night, which might lead to you being tired tomorrow. Goodnight." Vihaan smiled internally, then wishing the same to his friend, turned off the lights.

As he crawled under the warm covers, his mind wandered to the events of the day. Although, it got stuck at one point. He remembered Freya's father telling something about a certain Pranay, and his curiosity didn't let him rest. He wanted to know everyone who was important to Freya. He wanted to know how she made friends, and what she expected from them. Compassion? Sympathy? Support? His mind whirled on, and before long, a yawn escaped his lips. Soon, his eyes turned heavy, and he drowned into the comforting sea of sleep.

Chapter 10

MOED

Next morning, Vihaan's mother woke him up, and although he still wanted to sleep, he got up to the thought of Freya, and of the hospital.

He had a quick shower and got down to breakfast. He was met with a decadent meal of spinach soup, breads, and paneer kofta on the table, along with some grape juice. As soon as his parents came down, all of them dug in. The meal was uncharacteristically silent, and only the sounds of slurps and clatter of spoons broke the blanket of quiet spread out. In the middle of his bite, Vihaan's father saw his eyes go moist. Abruptly, he stopped, and asked him what the matter was. "Will I come back to eat all of this again, dad?"

The spoon in his mother's hand almost dropped, as she held back tears as well, collecting her courage. She said in a mellow yet determined tone, "Yes. You will come back, son. I believe in you as well as fate. You are worthy of every nice thing in your life, and this one gray area can't overshadow the fact that you are going to be free of it in no time."

Vihaan nodded, and his father fed him a spoon of soup. Soon, all of them were ready. His parents asked him to check if he had left anything accidently, and once they were sure everything was with them, they left for the hospital. Vihaan texted Jatin about their departure and closed his eyes for a moment.

Soon, they had reached the hospital, and once the formalities were completed, they patiently waited for Dr. Nitin to come. It was a matter of a few minutes before he came, Dr. Dev behind him. He smiled brightly toward Vihaan, and he returned the gesture.

Greeting his parents, Dr. Nitin instructed them to follow him. Once they were inside his cabin, he instructed Dr. Dev to briefly explain the procedure the surgery would follow to them. Quick to his feet, the young doctor stood up in front of the family and proceeded to provide all the necessary information about the procedure. Once he was done, the senior doctor commended him, then proceeded to talk to them about the bills. "The surgery, well, it approximately costs two lakh twenty thousand rupees." He informed, and Vihaan's father nodded.

They had decided beforehand that he would pay for the bills, but Vihaan didn't want to depend on his father for all the expenses. He knew well that as he was a flourishing businessman, the amount was nothing much to him. But he didn't want to feel like a total burden. This was the reason he had decided to pay for half of the bills from his salary, while the other half would be footed by his father. His parents promised to deposit the check in the evening, and with that, all of them got up.

Dr. Nitin walked forward, held Vihaan's hands, and commended him for being able to take such a decision. Then, he asked all of them to follow him. Soon, they were at the same floor as Freya, and Dr. Nitin showed them the room where he would be admitted. It was quite close to the room where she was in, and that brought some relief into Vihaan's tensed posture. The doctor proceeded to say, "I don't think you need to be put on the bed right away. In fact, I think we can wait for another three hours. I anyways have a meeting to attend. By the time I come, why don't you go and meet Freya?" Vihaan's entire being lit up with the sheen of the moon as he nodded. With that, both the doctors left, and Vihaan proceeded to step out of the room. Just then, he received a call from Jatin, asking where he was. He told him the floor number and room number. After that, with a determined nod, he walked toward Freya's room.

As soon as he entered inside, he was met with her parents, both of whom were sipping coffee, fatigue, and debility pooling inside their tired eyes. It was evident they hadn't slept a wink yesterday. Upon seeing him, they smiled lightly, and Vihaan greeted them. Then he introduced his parents to the tired couple. As soon as they met, though, a spark of warmth and happiness crossed their features. Freya's mother smiled warmly, "I had heard about both of you from Freya. She was all praises. Now I know why." With this, they sat back down. Vihaan urged them to take a nap, registering their worn-out expression. However, they asked him if he could watch over their daughter for an hour or two, until they went to her home and came back, with some food and fresh clothes. "Gladly." He said, and they exited the premises.

Vihaan's parents came up to Freya's bedside, and his mother stroked her head lovingly. His father also patted her shoulders, as he spoke in a thick voice, "She is a strong woman." Vihaan felt a sense of pride bloom inside him, and he sat back down on the seat.

Just then, Jatin walked in through the doors carrying a bag, and practically ran to hug his friend. Vihaan did not expect such a huge reaction out of him, but he chuckled heartily. Then, he plopped into a seat as well. Both of them stirred up a conversation, and a sigh escaped Vihaan's lips as he placed his head over his forearms. Silence hung over the room, and no one dared to break it. It was one of those rare moments when the quiet didn't lay over them like a cold, stone dry feeling, and even though a lot of words were left unspoken, it still felt warm and complete.

After a few minutes, Freya woke up, mumbling something under her breath. When she saw the other occupants of the room, her face turned into a confused one, and Vihaan immediately got up. He sat by her side on the bed, and explained everything to her, slowly and carefully, so as to not freak her out. Once he was done, Freya slung her arms around his neck and put her head down on his chest.

"Why am I so weak?" she mumbled. Vihaan was taken aback. Of all the things he had expected to hear, this was not one of them.

"Snowflake, it is absolutely not your fault that your heart decided to act up and show a somersault out of nowhere. How were you supposed to know? No one plans beforehand for these things. You were perfectly fine one minute, and the next, you were on the floor. I can't even explain how petrified Ritul and I were. But you are here now. That's all that matters."

Freya loosened her grip on him and turned to his parents. She smiled, "Thanks a lot for coming here. I honestly am so honored to see both of you." Then, she turned to Jatin, "And as of you, I don't know how to explain but I am feeling like a brother has come to see me." Jatin chuckled, then walked up to her and handed her the bag. "It has a few cups of hot chocolate, some ramen and one of the books I like." Eagerly, she opened the knot, and taking out the edible items, picked up the book. "One Hundred Years of Solitude by Gabriel Garcia Marquez." she read. "I think I will really like it." Smiling, she kept the book down on a table nearby along with the other items and leaned back.

Vihaan's parents got up, and his mother informed that she would go about the premises to get her joints moving, and his father accompanied her. Jatin stood up too, saying that he would have to go to the office, as he had only taken a half day leave. Just like that, within a few minutes, the room was empty.

Vihaan pulled out an empty chair and settled down comfortably on it. Then, he held her hands. He brought them up to his cheeks and pressed against it. She soothingly rubbed her thumb over his cheekbone, feeling the sharpness of it. Finally, he opened his eyes, and smiled lightly. "Although I don't want either of us to relive the memories, I think you should let out all that you feel." Freya closed her eyes and inhaled deeply. "I felt restricted." After a pause, she continued. “I felt covered by a deep blanket of oblivion. The whole day, I had a worrisome, sickening feeling inside my chest. By late afternoon, it had turned into a sinking one. I thought it might be because of the medicines. As I had not eaten much that day, I asked for a sandwich. But as soon as I took a few bites, my chest started to clench again. I felt as the air had been pumped out, and try hard as I might, nothing was being inhaled. I felt a vacuum develop from the inside. And before I could process anything, it was all dark.”

Vihaan nodded, then asked, “And what did you feel when you were unconscious, lying here?” Freya sighed again, “I felt you. I felt you holding my hands. I couldn’t listen to you, but I felt your skin against mine. Then I felt my parents. The comforting warmth. I felt your parents too, subconsciously. But above all, I felt the air come back to my lungs when you were near. It was as if I was being cured.” She smiled, and Vihaan felt his elation heighten. He kissed her lightly on the crown of her forehead. She smiled, feeling a secure warmth locking inside her.

Chapter 11
TACENDA

Vihaan gulped down a glass of water, before proceeding to rest his hands over his legs. “Freya, I am going to ask you something. I hope you can truthfully tell me about it. That is, if you feel comfortable. If not so, I wouldn’t push you. I just want to know you better.” Freya nodded, confusion pooling in her eyes.

“Who is Pranay?”

Time and airflow as if stopped for a second. Freya’s earthy eyes widened, so much so that Vihaan could see his reflection in them.

“H-how do you know about h-him?” Freya stuttered, her palms beginning to shake. Her fingers interlaced, as her thumbs stroked the skin, a sign that she was hiding something. Vihaan held them, then said truthfully that he had heard the name from her father. He also assured that he didn’t presume anything about her.

She retracted her hands, and as if a switch had flipped on, her defensive mode took over. “Pranay Sehgal is a part of my life that I have buried long ago.”

Brows crashing together, Vihaan softly asked, "Why Snowflake? What has you so troubled suddenly? I don't mean to pry, but to get to know you, I need to know what happened." A sharp intake of breath reverberated in the room, while Freya closed her eyes.

Exhaling deeply, she responded, "I don't think you would understand, Sunshine. This is my own cross to bear." At this point, Vihaan was getting befuddled beyond measure. "Nothing is your cross to bear alone if it converts into an anchor that impedes your progress. I don't mean to sound overbearing either, but I thought we were at a point where you could tell me things without the fear of being judged." Hurt flashed briefly in his eyes as he fiddled with the collar of his shirt.

Freya felt a sharp stab of pain in her chest when she saw despondency and distance floating in those gray eyes. Still, she couldn't make up her mind completely. A part of her was begging to finally let the truth out in the light, while the other, more indignant part wanted to remain in the comfortable dark oblivion, the demented area it had created in the back of her brain.

It was not the fact the she felt Vihaan to be incompetent of understanding her in any way. If anything, she was sure he could see right through the layers she had. It was her who had created sky high walls around this aspect of her life. She had no right to be angry or mad at Vihaan. He had always been emotionally available and sensitive toward her. If she asked his to stop enquiring her, he would step back immediately. But now that she thought about it, she felt the need to let the beans spill, to let him get familiarized with the darker aspect of the woman he thought was made of rainbows. It was time to let him realize that she was also hiding the rain and thunder underneath.

Turning around to face him, she asked one final time if he would see her in a different light after getting to know about Pranay. When he firmly stated the negative, she took in a deep breath and began.

THREE YEARS AGO

An ivory top and midnight blue skirt were placed out on the bed, while a very unsure looking Freya held a teal gown in her hands, waving it in front of her mother.

"I think teal suits my skin tone more." She pondered aloud. "Then go with it." Her mother commented.

"But the ivory top has never been worn, and I like it a lot." Freya's complaining voice resounded.

"You would look great in it too, dear." Her mother responded.

"You aren't helping, mom! I called you here to choose one of them." Freya exclaimed, as she sat back down on the bed.

"Will you agree with my choice?" her mother asked. "Seeing that I am highly indecisive at the moment, I am ought to." She responded.

"Then, go with the top. I think the combination brings out your eyes and you would look gorgeous in it." Her mother declared, taking away the dress from her hands.

College had just ended, and Freya had been invited to a gathering. It was about two weeks after the graduation ceremony. At first, she had been moody and hesitant, but when she got to know that her friend from college, Navya, had personally come by the house to drop the invitation, while she was out shopping, she decided to attend the gathering.

The card mentioned the fact that it was a celebration of Navya's father's business had completed twenty years, and Freya knew that it would be massive.

Evening gathered up in the sky, and she reached the venue. Upon arriving there, she realized that she was super awkward and alone, mainly because there were only a handful of people she knew, which included Navya, her family, and another college mate, Vikas. Naturally, she couldn't tag along with Navya all the time, because she was the host and had a lot of people to cater to. Therefore, she sat down in a corner, and Vikas was long lost among the sea of people bustling around.

Just as she was about to go for another glass of a soft drink, because boredom does that to you, a man came out from the dark shadows around the hubbub and sat on the chair beside her. At first, she was startled because she had a tendency to grow awkward with strangers easily, but he himself opened up the conversation, "I really hope I am not making you uncomfortable in any manner. It is just that it was too loud in the middle, so I came to sit here for a few moments."

Freya smiled gently and asked him to feel free to relax. Slowly but steadily, both of them started talking, beginning with small topics like profession and interests, then moving forth. Honestly, Freya had never found herself to be the person who was able to initiate conversations or engage in them with strangers out of the blue. She felt too exposed, and that factor made her cower from the prospect of meeting someone new.

But she was experiencing a new dimension with the man in front of her.

"I am Pranay. Pranay Sehgal. Nice to see someone other than me who is not into extremely loud parties bursting with people. This is not my cup of tea." He said, a small smile forming on his lips, to which Freya responded, "I just came here because the daughter of the person hosting this event is my friend. She really wanted me to come, and I couldn't refuse." "Navya? This girl is really persuasive, I must say." Pranay commented.

Naturally, Freya asked him how he knew Navya, to which he responded by saying that since her father was a regular visitor of the hotel for which he was the procurement specialist, both of them were nice acquaintances. Therefore, he was invited at the party.

Nodding at him, Freya was amused when he proceeded with the conversation. "So, what do you do?" "Oh well, I have just graduated a month ago from college, with a degree in sociology. I plan to become a market researcher, but that is a plan reserved for the future. Other than that, I think the only hobby I have is reading."

"Market researcher is honestly such a diverse and opportunity-based job. I hope you achieve your dream." At this, Freya thanked him for the wishes.

Before long, both of them were talking as if they knew each other for years, and Freya was silently thankful for finding someone who made her relax at such a bustling place. Just as the night was coming close to an end, Freya's father called her, asking her to come home soon, expressing his concern for her. Getting up, she thanked Pranay for lending his company to her, and making her time at the party memorable.

"Well, we can spend more time together, outside of the party. That is if you want to." Pranay answered, a cheeky smile plastered on his attractive face. A hearty chuckle escaped Freya. "Mr. Sehgal, is this your way of asking me out?"

"Well, what if it is?" he asked.

"Then I am surely impressed, as your personality is very charming. I see no harm in getting to know you more. Where do we spend time, though?"

Pulling out his visiting card, Pranay said, "I think this place is nice. It has a lot of positive reviews. I have also heard from my friends that it serves excellent lasagna." A laugh bubbled up inside her throat as Freya took the card and promised him to visit soon.

After that, both of them parted ways, and soon, she was inside a cab that drove off to her home.

As she fiddled with the visiting card in her hands, she read, 'Tastel Restaurant, Hauz Khas, South Delhi.'

"Well, lasagna isn't that bad, is it?" She said to herself. Sighing due to the tiredness taking over her, she placed the card in her bag and closed her eyes for a few moments.

Soon, she was at her home, sliding under the warm sheets of her bed. She did not put much thought to anything, as sleep engulfed her in itself.

Next morning, she came down for breakfast after a long shower, and greeted her parents. Smiling at her, her mother asked about the party last night. Gladly, she told her about everything, including Pranay in her explanation, as he had surely rescued her from the extreme boredom she could have suffered from.

"Well, procurement specialist seems a really diverse job. I mean, I haven't heard many people follow this profession. Anyways, let's have breakfast." Her father commented. Welcomed by a spread of malai kofta and breads, Freya dug straight in.

Life seemed to drag on, and a week had passed since the party. One day, while clearing her cupboard, Freya found the visiting card Pranay had given her, and an idea struck her. She decided to visit the hotel the next day and kept the card on her bedside table. Then, she continued with the work at hand.

The next day, at around twelve in the noon, she dressed in a flamingo pink knitted turtleneck sweater along with a pair of jeans. Before leaving, she placed the card in her purse.

Upon reaching the restaurant, she was absolutely blown away by its aesthetics. The whole place was bathed in the soft glow of yellow lamps, which provided it a dark yet cozy vibe, unlike most of the hotels that went with extremely blinding bright lights. A huge, tapered drum lamp was placed in the middle, made out of frosted glass.

Around it, large cabriole sofas were placed, covered in light cream shades, matching the hue of the walls. After the main dining area, which was extremely large, was a bar, where bar stools were placed, and a few people sat on them. Posh drinks like masseto, pilsner and Glenmorangie signet were placed on the shelves.

But what made the place stand out more was that long parlor palm trees were placed in beautiful planters, and they lined the entire length of the room.

A mosaic of small chandeliers hung from the roof, exuding the same Tuscan glow. An earthy, balsamic smell lingered in the air, which unmistakably belonged to vetiver. It was a fresh change of senses from the usual flowery tones that other places used.

Just as Freya was assessing the place, a voice emerged from behind her, "Mam, how may I help you?" She turned around to see a woman, probably in her late thirties, smiling at her.

"Well, you see, someone who works here invited me to this place. Do you know a certain Mr. Pranay Shukla?" she asked. "Of course, I know! He is our procurement specialist. The best one we have had until now. Shall I call him?"

Freya nodded, and the woman asked her name. As she informed her with the same, the woman showed her a seat and took her leave.

A few minutes later, Freya heard the fall of footsteps and turned around. She saw Pranay, but he looked quite different from how he had appeared at the gathering. He was wearing black pants and a formal shirt in the same hue, along with a pine green coat. He also wore dark oxfords, which tied up his formal attire seamlessly. His hair was bouncy, though, which was a pleasant contrast from his rather sharp cut look.

She got up and greeted him, shaking his hand. Soon, both of them were sitting on one of the sofas, talking about odds and ends.

"I never really thought you'd come." Pranay said, sipping on a glass of champagne. "Well, I had to, after you told me that this place serves excellent lasagna." Freya responded. A hearty laugh left his throat when he remembered the conversation, they'd had a few days ago.

As she looked closely at him, she realized he was actually quite striking. His olive skin was smooth, with a natural glow to it. Tousled hair fell over his eyes slightly, while his forehead remained exposed. He had a high nose bridge, and sculpted cheekbones that gave his face a chiseled contour. Warmth floated in his tawny eyes, along with a hint of charisma. He had a long neck, and the veins on his arms were the proof that he worked toward keeping himself in shape.

"We sure do have some amazing varieties of the dish. Would you like to try some?" he asked. She nodded, to which he took out his cell phone and dialed a number, asking them to bring a sample each of all the lasagna varieties they had. After that, they resumed their conversation.

Within a few minutes, a host of plates were in front of them, with a portion of the varieties of lasagna on them. Pranay asked the chef to introduce them to her one by one. "This is the Italian lasagna, with a dressing of tomato sauce and ricotta. Our most popular variety." After that he allowed her to take a bite, and she was overwhelmed with the warmth and creaminess of it. The flavors burst deliciously on her tongue. Next up, he introduced to them the Mexican green variety, which had salsa verde dressing. This one tasted more earthy and had a hint of smoked spices to it.

He went on to name more varieties like whole wheat spinach, butternut squash, Bolognese, scamorza, eggplant, pesto, and mushroom.

Soon, Freya's stomach was almost bursting with the amount of food she had eaten. When they had finished, Pranay asked her which flavor appealed to her the most, and after thinking for a while, she responded, "I think the butternut squash one, because it had a distinct creaminess to it." Listening to this, Pranay ordered a plate of the same, but she stopped him instantly, saying that she was already full and just needed some champagne to cool off. Chuckling to himself, Pranay nodded, and they continued their conversation.

Soon, it was time for her to leave for home, and Pranay gave her a pack of the butternut squash lasagna as a takeaway. Thanking him once again, they parted ways.

After about twenty minutes, she was at her home, where her parents were tasting the dish, and her father seemed to be impressed by it. Her mother liked the dish too, but since she wasn't a fan of butternut squash, she only took a small helping.

Once inside the warmth of her bed, she opened her mobile phone and went to her chat box, where she found Pranay's name. She messaged him, thanking him for the takeaway and informing him that her parents liked it a lot. Then, tired from the events of the day, she covered herself in warm sheets and soon drifted off to sleep.

The next day, she woke up to her mother calling her downstairs for breakfast. Lazily, she got up and began prepping for a long warm shower, to set her in mood for the day.

She was pretty sleepy, so she dragged herself up to the bathroom, where she turned on the shower to warm and stepped in, relishing in the relaxing feeling it provided to her muscles.

After about twenty minutes she was done and came out, her hair dripping wet while she searched for something to wear. Finally, her eyes landed on cozy looking T-shirt and sweatpants, and she decided to go with the flow and wear them.

Soon she was downstairs, talking to her parents. At first, the conversation was smooth and easy going, but after a few minutes, she felt as if her parents wanted to say something to her but were uncomfortable in doing so.

Taking the lead, she asked them herself, "Mom, dad, is something wrong?" Her father looked up at her and she could sense the guilt in his eyes. He cleared his throat and said lowly, "Well, as you know, I have a transferable job, dear." Freya immediately cowered at the statement. She knew what was coming next. Anxiety suffused in her vessels. "No dad, we aren't moving this time. I don't want to shift cities again. Adjusting to the new environment, meeting new people, all of this has been repeated over and over again many times in the past few years, and finally for the first time, I have liked one of the cities. I don't want to leave it all behind to start a new life."

Her mother kept her hand on hers as she tried to reason with her, "But, what if you like the new city better, dear? Maybe it is more pleasant living there than here in Delhi." Obstinately, Freya shook her head. "No, mom. I know that I feel like being at home in this city. We have lived here before too when I was about three years old. I don't remember much from that time, but as far as this time is concerned, I feel as if this is where I belong. I don't want to stress out over something which could be avoided."

Taking a deep breath, she continued, "Moreover, as far as my plans after college regarding market researching are concerned, I don't think there is any place better than Delhi, the capital city to begin with. Living here would provide me with opportunities that I wouldn't have in any other place. Another aspect of it is also that I have grown to make a few nice friends for once. I don't want to lose all of that."

After keeping her point of view in front of her parents, she got up and left for her room.

Both her parents sighed together, as deep in their hearts, they know that it would be difficult for them to persuade her this time.

Soon, the morning gave way to afternoon, and Freya sat by the balcony in her room, looking out at the leaves falling from the azadirachta tree near her house. They were green and pale, falling out one at a time and settling on the neighbor's car below.

A knock on her door startled her. Getting up to open the door, she stumbled a bit on her way, and finally reached to turn the knob.

Her parents stood there, holding a tray of three cups of hot chocolate in their hands. She asked them to come in and closed the door. Her mother placed the tray on the bedside table, while her father sat on one of the stools by the mirror.

After everyone was settled in, her father began, "So, as we have come to realize that you don't want to move cities this time, we have also come to notice one more thing. I think all this moving around had affected you both socially and mentally, right?" he asked.

Freya nodded, her eyes stinging with tears. Her mother continued, "So, we have decided one thing. You should continue living here, as we don't want to strip you off of your social relations. Also, you are old enough to be able to live here on your own."

Her father continued, "But, this house would not be the one you live in, as this isn't our permanent residence. You would have to live in either a paying guest fashion or find a friend to share an apartment with. Now, it is up to you to decide what you want to do."

"Really?" was all Freya was able to say as tears rolled down her cheeks.

"Of course, dear. Your satisfaction is where our ultimate happiness resides. If you feel comfortable and seem to have more growth opportunities here, then so be it. We love you, and you will always come first for us." Her parents hugged her and left the room. Turning on her heels, Freya took out a canvas and her paints from the closet and sat down at her table to relax her brain.

A stroke of gray. This signified her confusion. Another one of green. This was a symbol of the peace of mind she was searching for. Another dash of blue. This was a representation of the sky, of the freedom she wanted. More splashes followed and soon, the whole canvas was covered in random straight strokes of paint running vertically. On finally being finished, Freya got up carefully, so as to not smother her bedroom walls with paint and placed the canvas to dry.

Washing her hands, she took a look at the mirror in front of her and was reminded of her younger self. The child who used to play in the mud and was always found running around with two pigtails swirling behind her. Smiling weakly at the memories, she walked up to her bed and as soon as her body hit the soft mattress, her eyes fluttered shut on their own accord and she went down the depth of endless sleep, where troublesome situations couldn't find a shelter.

The next few days were quite hectic, being spent with her applications being sent out to various institutions that mastered in market analysis and helping her parents with the packing up of the necessary items that would have to be shifted to the new place. Along with all this, Freya also had another situation lurking at the back of her mind. She had to search for a place to live, and time was running out fast.

Initially, she had thought of asking Navya regarding renting a room at her place, but later decided against it. Navya was a nice friend, but Freya was unsure in the aspect of being comfortable enough to live in a house with a whole another family. She wanted someplace where another person lived alone, so that she could fit in better. Living as an outsider with a family was mildly unnerving for her.

Her parents were due to move in a month, and with no friends available to rent a room with, the solution to the problem still seemed a farfetched dream.

Although, during this time, she had met up with Pranay a few times. For once, they had crossed paths quite near her house, and the issue of housing had inadvertently popped out of her mouth. Pranay had asked her to consider living with him as his apartment was quite large, but knowing how her parents would get about it, she couldn't quite confirm anything to him.

But now that a week had passed and desperation was gnawing at her insides, her last resort seemed to be Pranay, as renting a full apartment for herself wasn't something she was capable of, especially when she had no job of her own.

This was the reason she had asked her parents to sit down for once and listen to her. Once they were at the table, she began "As you know, I don't have a job at the moment, and paying rent for an apartment is a very big deal. I don't think you'd agree on this immediately, but I want you to give time to ponder over it." Inhaling deeply, she said, "Pranay, the friend whose hotel I had gone to earlier, had met me a few days ago, and had offered me a place in his house. Of course, I had avoided and turned him down earlier. But now that I think of it, I don't have a proper place to live, and his house is quite spacious as he had mentioned. So, if you are willing to meet him and also if you agree to go visit the place to see it for yourselves, I think I can make it work."

As soon as she finished, she closed her eyes and waited for her mother to start worrying and shouting. And it happened. Within a few seconds, both her parents started asking her a million questions. They had their doubts about the kind of person Pranay was, his job, his personality, work ethic, rent she'd have to pay, among many others.

When they had finally calmed down, Freya got up and brought two glasses of water from the kitchen. She placed them on the table and then expressed herself, "I knew you would have thousands of doubts regarding this topic, and this is why I have decided to call Pranay and ask him to come over, preferably tomorrow I know this is an extremely tough decision for both of you, letting your only child live with someone entirely unknown, but I think if you meet him once, you would be able to change your mind, or at least give it a try." With that, she hugged her parents and whispered, "I know warmth lies here with you, but I hope I find wind, to find room to expand alone, somewhere else." She kissed her mother on the cheek and walked away, her fathers' eyes trained on her disappearing figure.

Shutting the door behind her, Freya pushed her back against it, sighing loudly as she felt the imminent pressure approaching. Realizing she couldn't do much other than rest, she changed into pajamas and sprawled down on her bed, smothering the sheets with her natural scent of vanilla and cinnamon.

Next morning, the sun rose over the city, and although it brought another dose of worries for her, Freya pulled herself from her bed, and got ready with her head stuck in a pothole overflowing with random thoughts. Around twelve in the noon, a message from Pranay arrived, which notified her to be ready to welcome him two hours later.

For some unknown reason, she felt slight jitters at the thought of his arrival. Discarding them as random nervousness, she got ready, donning a long, modest burgundy dress. Later, she went down to inform her parents about him, but before she could approach them, she saw them neck deep in a serious conversation. Once she heard her name being mentioned in the interaction, she couldn't help but be gravitated toward the ongoing discussion. Her mother was still pondering over the safety issues regarding her probable residence at Pranay's. Finally partaking in the ongoing exchange, she uttered, "Mom, you can put a rest to your doubts and confusion, because Pranay would be here in around two hours. Tension doesn't go well with your radiant face." Walking up to her, she hugged both her parents and insisted on making the lunch while they got ready. Although indecision still floated in their eyes, they agreed to her urging.

In the kitchen, Freya started working on her favorite coconut lentil curry along with some breads and brown rice. She also decided to prepare a simple batch of walnut cookies, just for the sake of having something to call a dessert. She realized that someone as used to living a luxurious life as Pranay must always have a dessert with all his meals. She was never one to feel any sort of inferiority complex in from of the more affluent population, but for some reason, the manner in which Pranay carried himself made her a bit too conscious of herself.

It was exactly at two that her doorbell rang, and she nervously walked over to greet Pranay. As soon as the door flew open, she was mesmerized by how simple yet lavish he looked. He had donned a simple brown satin shirt with the sleeves rolled up, along with a pair of stone black pants. Stray strands of hair were flowing over his forehead in waves, and she was glad he hadn't gelled it up. For some reason, she couldn't stand the sight of gelled hair. They just felt too forced, as if the person was trying hard enough to fit into the parameters of being labeled as cool or charming. Welcoming him inside, she called out to her parents who came into the room almost immediately, and Pranay bent down to touch their feet.

Her parents guided him to the living room, and before long, they were engaged in the discussion slowly gravitating toward the topic of Freya's accommodation. Hesitantly, her mother asked, "Dear, I hope you are not uncomfortable with Freya sharing the same space as you. She told us about your offer." Pranay chucked, and then said, his voice full of authority yet care, "Mam, sir, I just want to ensure to both of you that I am an honorable man. I have a spacious home, and as my parents live back in Lucknow, I have a lot of rooms that are spare and not used as often. Having Freya over there though, isn't an option for occupying a room and sucking money in the form of rent out of her. She can stay without any payment. I regard her as a friend, and even if she might not consider me to be one just yet, I feel we can make our friendship grow. And as far as your concern about me using her in any way or troubling her are concerned, you need to believe me when I say that the city where I came from, we are taught that modesty and manners are of utmost importance. So, you don't have to worry about that."

Both her parents looked quite impressed, and it was not only because of the speech that they had heard, but also by the respectful look in Pranay's eyes. Her father said, "Son, I feel you are a nice, honest and sensible human. It is just that we are leaving our only daughter for the first time, completely alone in a city. Therefore, if you don't have a problem, can we please see the house once?" Pranay smiled. He knew it was coming. "Why not, sir. You have the right to do so. You can drop by whenever you like, I shall forward my address to Freya." He looked over at her, and she softly smiled back.

"But now, I am feeling a little hungry, as I haven't had anything since the morning. Can I please have something?" Pranay asked politely. To this, Freya's mother urged him to come to the dining area, where the dishes prepared by Freya sat on the table. As soon as she opened the lids, strong, enticing aromas of spices wafted in the air and Pranay was delighted. "I haven't had food cooked at home by someone in the longest time, since I live alone. Who made all of this?"

"I did," Freya answered, appearing in the room. A look of shock registered on his face, and he appreciated her for the culinary skills she possessed. Little did he know, his mind was about to be blown away by the flavors that would burst on his tastebuds.

After everyone was served, they all began with the meal. The first dish to be tasted by Pranay was the lentil curry, along with a generous helping of the brown rice. Although it was a simple concoction, the warmth and spices made him melt into the seat. "This is almost as amazing as the food at the restaurant, and that is made by trained chefs. Freya should probably change her mind and start working as a sous-chef at the hotel. We would become millionaires in no time." He said, which made everyone around him smile. Lastly, when he tasted the cookies, he enquired Freya about the recipe and secret ingredients, to which she laughed and said that she added a bowl of sea salt and melted brown butter to the dough just before putting it up in the oven. This helped the flavors to spread and not get settled in one place, while the brown butter prevented the charring of the crust and made it a bit pillowy. He pretended to note it on his phone and promised to tell it to the bakers of the hotel.

Soon, two hours had passed, and it was time for him to leave. Just as Freya was seeing him off, he leaned in a little closer and spoke, his voice a bit husky, giving rise to a rush of goosebumps on her skin, "I think I should have said it earlier, but you look like an absolute dream in this dress. It looks way better than the one you wore the first time at the hotel. Then again, you look flawless in any outfit, as your heart is radiant.

I do hope your parents agree to the proposition. It would be a delight to have you over." With this, he was off, leaving Freya's heart and insides in a fluffy mess.

By nightfall, she had received a message from Pranay, stating the location of his house. She informed her parents, and they were a bit perplexed, as his house was in Golf Links, one of the most posh and affluent areas of Delhi. Anyways, they decided to visit the place the next day, and Freya informed him the same.

Next morning, after helping her parents with the packing up of various items in the kitchen, Freya decided to take a bath and get ready to visit the potential house where she'd be living. Her parents got ready too, and in about an hour, they were at Pranay's place.

The sheer size of the two storied house was intimidating. It boasted of a lush garden in the front, with cobblestones lining the path to the door. The entire structure was painted in a cerulean paint, with rich cedarwood paneling. It was geometrically aesthetic, with each side forming a peak of a triangle. Marble in the same blue shade formed a few stairs that were the gateway to inside.

If she thought the outside was beautiful, Freya was about to be blown off proportions by the insides. The blue traded its lightness with depth, changing into a calm cobalt. The entire hall was lined by the same shade of linen curtains, parted slightly. A huge sectional sofa adorned one side, while in stark contrast, an ivory coffee table occupied the center. A humongous deep empire lamp was placed at another corner, while the flooring of the entire place seemed to be wooden.

Two cylindrical vases were present at two corners, made out of stained glass.

Overall, the place screamed rich, and Freya and her parents were yet to see most of it. Pranay noticed their hesitation and calmly said, "I think you all should sit down. I shall bring out some tea." But Freya's father kindly asked him to show the rest of the house, to which he obliged.

While touring the house, Freya noticed that no personal photographs were up at the wall but decided against asking about it. 'He may not be fond of such things.' She thought.

Once they were inside the room that would be hers, she noticed that although the wall shades were still dark, the overall décor of the room was lighter, majorly composed of glass and ceramics. A queen-sized bed was placed in the middle, with the windows here covering the entire wall.

Satisfied with the place and the vibe it offered, her parents finally agreed to let her live at Pranay's home, of course after a major discussion about the expenses and related topics. Delight filled her veins, and although it stung a bit that her parents were going to be away from her, she decided to look toward the brighter side of things.

Finally, the day her parents had to move out arrived, and the night before, all the three of them had a small party, reminiscing the memories they had made and relished in the walls of the house. With the help of a self-timer camera, they took a last photograph at the place. Freya sat in the middle, on the floor. Her mother's chin was supported by her head while her father stood above both of them, a bright smile on his lips. All three of them were yellow, Freya's favorite, and the color seemed to brighten up their hearts. The train by which her parents had to leave was due to arrive in the evening, and the whole morning was spent shifting her materials to Pranay's house, who was there at the receiving end to see to the unloading of the boxes.

Soon, it was around five in the evening, and with the train approaching, Freya drove with her parents to the station by a taxi, where her tears finally came out. It was as if a sprinkler had turned on, and her mother tried to comfort her, while her father hugged her back. He bought her an ice cream in the wake of her childhood, and with a teary laugh, she waved them bye.

Finally stepping out of the station, she hauled a taxi and asked the driver to take her to Pranay's, her new home. It took some time due to the unending traffic, but soon enough she was there. On ringing the doorbell, Pranay opened the door, and welcomed her inside, offering her a cup of coffee.

Once she was settled, he asked her to sleep for the night and start the unpacking tomorrow. Gratitude overflowed in her veins, as she nodded her head weakly. 'He seems to possess such a natural charm.' She thought. Too tired to say or think much, she climbed the stairs and dove straight into the bed, the gnawing drowsiness finally spreading its wings over her consciousness.

The next morning, she woke up feeling quite well rested, courtesy of the memory foam mattress. Dragging herself out of bed felt like a herculean task, and the first thing she did was to call her parents up. As soon as her mother picked up, she exclaimed, "Freya dear! How are you? Both of us were worried sick about you being alone. Were you able to sleep comfortably?" Freya giggled, her mothers' worry seeming unnaturally proportioned. "Of course, mom, I slept well. I have just woken up. I think yesterday's tiredness caught up with me. I just dozed out the moment my head hit the pillows. Now that I am awake, I think I should start getting ready." "Sure thing. I will inform your father. He is busy right now. Take care." With that, the call ended.

Pulling her feet across the wooden floor, she reached a box marked 'Toiletries.' She ripped the tape across it and took out the items inside. Pretty soon, the racks on the bathroom wall were covered with two bodywashes, one scented with the essence of vanilla and the other of freesia, a few soaps, a cardamom perfume infused shampoo and loofas. Next, she proceeded to select out some basic clothing items and finally went to have a bath.

The warm water cascaded down her shoulders and eased the deltoids, biceps, and triceps, which felt cramped because of the work done yesterday. While scrubbing her body, a small grin spread on her wet lips as she felt extremely gratified toward Pranay for letting her live in his apartment. Even though he had said that he was absolutely fine with her living just like that, but her conscience told her that a minimum sum of money must be paid to him. He was, however, nice, an acquaintance, and not someone she would regard as a close ally so soon. She had discussed the matter with her parents, and they were of the same opinion.

Drowning in these thoughts, she made her way outside the bathroom, and brushing her wet hair slightly, walked out of the room. As it was still relatively early, she made out that Pranay was still asleep. His room was on the ground floor, with three spare rooms remaining in the home after her occupancy. Deciding upon exploring her new apartment a bit, she walked around the halls, her eyes trained on the frames of certificates pinned to the wall, signifying Pranay's myriad achievements. Although, she couldn't help but yet again notice that there were no family photos to personalize the home. The first décor she had put up in her room was a photo frame of her family, which was why she found the lack of these captured moments of beauty awkward. She dismissed the finding as the fact that he was a private person and had pulled them off because she was going to live with him now.

As she reached the stairs, her eyes fell on the modular kitchen and she settled on making a breakfast for the two of them, as a token of gratitude. With this plan in mind, she strolled into the area and although it took her quite some time to find the ingredients, she eventually started with the process of making tomato upma.

While she was chopping up the tomatoes, a husky voice caused her to almost drop the knife. "What are you making? I smell frying onions." Pranay said, as he came out rubbing his eyes. "Goodness, you almost scared me. Well, I am making breakfast. I hope you don't have a problem with me using your kitchen." Freya replied.

Suddenly, Pranay took three large strides toward her, and when he was directly in front of her, he noticed how her head reached just above his shoulder. "Well, if we are going to live together, I suppose we would have to share a few items and spaces." He tipped his head to the side, and taking a step back, asked what they were having. After she replied, he turned on his heels, and ruffling up his fluffy hair, put up a smile. Just like that, he was back in his room.

Half chopped vegetables were calling out to her, and she finally gave them the attention they deserved. Before long, the tangy smell of fried tomatoes and onions filled the entire dining area, as Freya and Pranay sat opposite to each other, relishing in the warm hug that they felt with each bite. "My offer for a position as a chef in the hotel still stands, darling." Pranay said, while downing another spoonful of the dish. "Honestly, it is one of the best offers I have received in quite a while, but I would like to still keep hunting for the one I dreamed. I can be a chef at the house though because I love cooking as a hobby." Freya laughed, ignoring the slight quiver of her palms due to the endearment so casually used by him.

"Suit yourself. Would you be heading out somewhere? Because I would be leaving for the hotel in about an hour." Pranay inquired. To this, Freya replied in the negative, stating that she had to unpack a lot of things in two days, after which she would resume attending the online university she had joined.

Pranay nodded, thanked her for the decadent meal once again and left to get ready. On the other hand, Freya left for the kitchen to wash off the dishes. A short while later, she heard the main door close and assumed that Pranay had left for work.

Bone breaking work ensued, as many more boxes were unpacked, some of clothes, some of books and various other items. Arranging them was another big task. For a few hours, it felt as if a hurricane had crossed over the room, but by evening, the area was quite arranged and neat.

Finally satisfied with the way it looked, Freya left the place and walked out of the main door and into the small garden. The first plants she came across were clematis, spread around the grounds and splashing the provided earth with a shade of ocean. They were followed by golden pansies fluttering in the evening breeze. After a patch of verdant grass, her eyes landed on flamingo tinted hollyhocks, standing proudly against the backdrop of violet cosmos flowers which stretched out to merge into alabaster camellia. All of this created a vast place filled with naturally soothing aromas.

But one last smell remained, which was emanating from a canopy of burgundy wisterias forming an arc in the backside of the garden. The fragrance was so musky that it almost felt seductive to stand under them.

Freya had been sitting on a chair under the canopy for about twenty minutes when she heard the honk of a car. She walked up to the door to see Pranay engaged in what seemed to be a growing heated discussion about something. "I have told you a hundred times to place the goddamn pots on the sidewalk. But an uneducated person you would never understand. Maybe that's why you are like this. I should-" His sentence was left mid-air as his eyes landed on Freya, her own smoked with confusion.

"I would talk to you later." He huffed toward the man standing near the car, his face smeared with sweat and now, tears. He looked toward the destroyed, wet pots and then at his hands that were callused due to working on the potters' wheel. Freya took one last look at him before Pranay dragged her inside.

"Don't talk to him even if he tries to, Freya. He is a lunatic who makes useless clay pots all day long. He has caused this trouble two times before too. Anyways, what do we have for dinner?" He said, his whole persona shifting from fluttering anger to sprawling calmness. If Freya was to be honest with herself, she felt a little concerned, but she tried to shake it off.

Walking up to the kitchen, she said softly that she didn't have the time to make dinner as the whole day was spent trying to organize her room. Pranay waltzed into the kitchen and announced, "Then I think you should rest for some time. I shall too, and then I can make dinner for the both of us. It is about time you saw what sort of cooking skills I possess."

Hesitantly, Freya walked away into her room while Pranay hung his coat over a shoulder and smiled widely.

Meanwhile, after entering her room, which now smelled of bergamot and potpourri thanks to the room freshener she used, Freya closed the door. Sighing, she walked to a chair and sat down, wondering if she had been right in agreeing to stay with Pranay. Of course, she knew that it was a decision made in haste and that under no other circumstances would she have agreed to do so, provided she had some other shelter to look forward to and her parents weren't leaving. But, as it had to happen, now she was living here, in one of the finest houses of Golf Links, and yet a part of her felt kind of unsafe.

It wasn't about the fact that she didn't want to trust Pranay because he had been nothing but nice and warm to her, but it had been two times she had seen her character completely shift from being charming and alluring to downright terrifying, the kind that put everyone down. She tried to dismiss it as the pressure of work catching up on him, but it still kept looming in the back of her head.

Finally getting up from the chair, she picked up her phone and decided to call her father. Merely two rings had passed when he picked up, delight dripping from his voice. "Hello, dear. It has just been a few hours, yet it feels I haven't spoken to my best pal in years. How are you? How is Pranay? Are you two getting along?" A weak laughter escaped her lips as she summarized the day's events to him, carefully skipping out the detail about Pranay's encounter with the potter. Her father seemed relieved that his daughter had found a nice place to live, and she wanted to keep it that way.

Eventually, she heard Pranay calling her over for dinner, and she bid her father adieu.

Upon coming downstairs, she encountered the smell of herbs and bell peppers, roasted to perfection, and wondered what dish was prepared. Soon, she heard Pranay's voice, "Welcome. I hope you enjoy the dish I like the most and have been complimented for on more than one occasion. I present to you, falafel stuffed bell peppers."

A smile formed on Freya's lips as she entered the dining area to see a pan full of bell peppers, green and red, served along with two glasses of guava juice. As she sat down, he waved a hand and spoke, "You first." As she picked up one pepper and placed a slice in her mouth, she realized why he was praised for the dish. It was a concoction of sweetness and a slight grassy note, along with the earthy, herbaceous flavors of falafel. It simply melted in her mouth.

After finishing the first slice, she looked up at Pranay who was searching her eyes for a response. "Would it be appreciative enough to say that even though I absolutely despise bell peppers with every fiber in my being, I can't seem to get enough if this dish?" Satisfaction spread over his heart, and he agreed to it.

Soon, both of them had finished their meals and thanking him once again for the delectable preparation that made her eat bell peppers, Freya retired to her room.

Back there, she texted her mother about the dish made by Pranay, then dozed off to sleep.

The next three weeks were a beautiful, slow yet steady paced blur, being filled with siestas in the garden, reading up books she bought but couldn't pick up earlier, preparing files and documents, attending the university, having meals with Pranay and getting to know him more.

Although, the highlight of her week had been getting accepted as a trainee in the special market training wing of the online university portal. This had been a moment of immense pride and joy for her and her parents, and when she had told Pranay about the same, he had brought home food from a Chinese restaurant to celebrate the cause.

Over these weeks, she had seen the sunny side of Pranay, although the ugly, cloudy side had made its appearance once, when she had heard him shout and holler terribly at an employee in his department over the phone, going to the extent to say that he didn't deserve to be in the hotel.

Timidly, she had tried to ask him about the situation the next day, which he had clarified as it being the mistake of the very staff in mixing up the raw materials required for the hotel's main courses. He justified his frustration as being poured out due to earlier having to bear the brunt of his boss. This calmed her down, as she thought that if she were in his shoes, she would have probably done the same thing. This was just a fabricated lie, though. She knew all too well that she would never have shouted at another employee like he did.

Other than that, they were completely fine, and although the red flags had started posting themselves more firmly, she had not much choice but to ignore them.

It was the day when Freya completed thirty days at Pranay's. and he had insisted on taking her out to some café, because a hotel was way too formal. This was why she found herself sitting by the window of a bistro built around the cottage core aesthetic, sipping on a virgin mojito.

She was donning a black maxi dress covered with white houndstooth print, her mocha hair loosely tied in a braid. Pranay himself looked quite striking, dressed in an all-black three-piece suit accentuated by the crisp white shirt beneath.

Both of them had enjoyed their time there, talking about odds and ends, bonding over their mutual love for plants. Just as Pranay parked the car outside his house, he practically ran over to the gated and closed them behind him once he was inside. It was quite odd for Freya, because she was expecting him to open the door of the car for her.

Anyways, she got out and walked down to the entrance. The moment she stepped inside, she was met with a purple carpet lining the wood, leading up to the hall. Quite surprised, she followed the path which led her to the large room, bathed in yellow and mauve lights emanating from crystal chandeliers.

The smell of potpourri suffused in the room, and in the center stood Pranay, his hands holding a bunch of peonies. His face looked as if he was a second away from losing his lunch, and Freya immediately made out the situation.

"Freya. I know that I am bad at it, in fact I am horrible, but I think I should just say it. When I met you, I didn't feel anything different or distinguishing. You were a pretty girl, but that was that. But then, over the course of meeting you again and again, learning the little details about you, coming to know your preferences and dislikes, I learned to fall in love with the beauty and vulnerability of how perfectly imperfect you are. From your preference of violin over piano, which is a stark contrast to mine, to the fact that you know how to put me at ease, I think it is reason enough for me to confess that I am falling in love with you. And I swear to God, I am exhilarated to be able to live in this experience. I am well aware of the fact that you may not feel the same, and I am fine with that. But can you let me love you?"

Slight tears formed near the corners of Freya's eyes, and as she wiped them with the back of her palms, she nodded aggressively and ran up to hug him. For a split second, she thought she saw him smirk, but all of that was forgotten the moment he wrapped his arms around her.

"It would be an honor to be loved by the man who allowed me to live with him so willingly, and who is so much more than he shows." Freya said, her voice slightly shaky due to the emotionally overcharged situation. Little did she know, how true her last sentence was, only in a slightly different frame of context. Pranay was pernicious, and the effects of the drug prepared out of his thoughts would soon follow.

"Thanks a lot, angel." Pranay said. She felt his lips stretch in a cold grin near her neck, but the tears got the better of her and she closed her eyes, letting them fall on the shoulder pad on Pranay's coat.

Chapter 12
ONSRA

About a month had passed since Pranay's confession and Freya couldn't have asked for a more perfect boyfriend. Every night, he used to massage her scalp gently, releasing the tensed knots formed due to the day's work. He used to cook for the both of them occasionally, and she would eagerly wait for the moments when he sat her down in his lap and whispered words of reassurance in her ears, repeating the fact that she was as if tailor made specially for him, consolidating the fact that he would never let her go.

This tugged the strings of Freya's heart, who took whatever affection she was served on a silver platter from him. But she was too naïve to realize that silver wasn't only used to make platters.

Around this time, she received an offer from her university portal, carefully curated for the top six students who were under the special training wing, which encompassed and elaborate trip spanning the duration of twenty days. It stated that this group of six bright minds, which included Freya, were invited to a firm of their desired business product, which was growing its wings and strengthening their hold in the current economy. This would give them the opportunity to study market trends regarding various lines of production and hone their prediction skills about the direction they would expand in.

Excitement soared in her heart as she informed Pranay about the trip. She had expected him to be overjoyed, just like her, to congratulate her. What she had not expected was for him to suddenly become weirdly overprotective of her, refuting the idea of her traveling to some other city for a few days.

The first emotion that came over her mind was of affection, over the fact that her boyfriend did not want her to be alone in a new city. But having been traveling around the country for most of her life, she was quite confident in herself, in being able to adjust properly.

But then, his overprotectiveness turned into indignation, and this started infuriating her. "You are not to go anywhere until I allow you to do so!" Pranay exclaimed. "Allow? Who are you to allow me? You aren't my father, you aren't funding my education, you have just given me a shelter. And to remind you, I am paying the rent. It isn't like I am hogging all the resources for free. Moreover, I have earned a spot in the top six students by merit. So, like it or not, Pranay, I am going. And if you have a problem with it, we can call off whatever we have, and I would gladly move somewhere else. I would rather go back to my parents. The choice is yours. Remember, though, that I am my own person first, and not someone you can control and play with."

With this, she left for her room. A door banged down below, and she realized Pranay had gone outside. She didn't want to dwell on it, but the incident had made her extremely morose and a tad bit terrified. Was this going to become something bigger? Something so sinister that she would eventually have to give up? She didn't want to think about it, and with a sigh, she began the process of compiling her documents into one folder.

Morning came, and when Freya got up, she realized that she had slept for about seven hours. Well rested, she dragged herself up and decided to take a refreshing shower, before beginning with the further packing. She had received an email last night regarding the dates and necessities of the trip. She had also been provided with ten options she could select from, regarding the industry she was interested in. She had shortlisted it down to two, one being food and beverages and the other, fragrances. Both the companies that were open for the trip were extremely conducive and modern, but after much thought, she decided upon the food and beverages one, considering the fact that she would be more involved in the entire process.

Now, after cleaning up, she opened up the laptop to see two new mails in her inbox. Upon opening the first, she saw that it was from the university which applauded her on selecting a wonderful niche and informed her that one more student, Vipul, would be joining with her. The next email was from the company she had selected, called Sesquia, which was hugely famous for its energy drinks, but also for other health friendly options of bars and compound meals. She was being sent to the headquarters, located in Jaipur.

Delighted, she got up to inform Pranay, but her steps stopped short as she realized that they weren't on speaking terms. Last night, she hadn't even heard him come back. A tired sigh escaped her as she rubbed her forehead. Placing the laptop back on the table, she began with the remaining packing.

About twenty minutes later, she heard the door of her room open and found Pranay standing there. Before she could say anything, he began, "Listen Freya, I am extremely sorry for the way I had reacted yesterday. I was a terrible spoilsport. I have absolutely no right to tell you what to do and what to refrain from. I dint know why I got so protective. I think I just saw that you might not be able to live comfortably, but it is more of the fact that I don't think I would take the emptiness quite well. You are a ray of positivity and enthusiasm, and it is as if I have forgotten how to live alone. Regardless of it, I would like to apologize for my behavior. I wish you the best of luck for the trip."

Just as he turned around to leave, Freya caught him by the arm and said, "I will not say that it didn't hurt or shock me. But I appreciate the apology. I do know that you only have my best interests at heart. I am old enough to live on my own though. But I still need your love and support. They mean a lot to me. Of course, I felt a bit guilty yesterday after our fight. I don't want it to happen ever again."

"I promise honey, it won't. I will support every big and small dream of yours." With this, Pranay let her snuggle up in his neck, and while she closed her eyes, his face on top of hers, buckled into a baleful smirk.

Three days later, Freya was all ready to leave for Jaipur. Vipul had called her to inform that he would be reaching the next day, so she could make herself comfortable in the hotel room provided by the university.

At the airport, Pranay had come to see her off. She hugged him, and as he rubbed soothing circles on her back, he suddenly remembered something. "I had this especially packaged for you." He took out a casserole filled with the butternut squash lasagna and handed it to her. She squealed, and looping her arms around him once more, allowed him to life her off the ground.

Soon, the time for the flight neared, and he bid her goodbye.

It took Freya about one hour to reach the pink city. Although she was tired, she couldn't help but notice the vastly spread beauty of the place. Within twenty minutes, she was inside her hotel room, an aesthetically furnished, color blocked space in shades of marigold and sapphire.

After placing the required items in the cupboard, she informed her parents and Pranay about her arrival.

"How is the place? Is it comfortable?" He asked. "Of course, it is. I am just so tired; I think I will just have the lasagna and sleep for a few hours." A lazy smile spread over her face as she dropped the phone to her side. Picking up the casserole, she undid the lid and began chowing down the delicacy inside. After having to her heart's fill, she washed everything up and slumped down on the bed for some much-needed sleep.

The rest of the day was spent gathering information about the company she was going to work with, and how it managed its resources. She knew not to rely on the online sources regarding the production process of the goods, so she skipped those articles.

Next day, she was greeted by Vipul, who had called to inform her about his arrival. She went downstairs and was elated to meet him. He was tall and tanned, with a unilateral dimple on his left cheek.

Not long after, they had consumed the breakfast and were headed to the office of Sesquia, Inc. for their first day of training.

On the way, both of them got to know a few things about each other. Freya already knew that he was from Bhopal, but she also got to know that he was a trained flute player, and also a big consumer of the company they were headed toward.

The office building was huge, being connected to the production unit on the backside. Inside, they were directed to the office of the Chief Commercial Officer, Mr. Sanjay Sen, who seemed like a jolly man. He familiarized both of them to the functioning ethics and market influences of the company. This took about an hour, and after that, they were assigned to another man who took them to the production unit for a tour.

Here, they saw how the raw materials were being used to create beverages and food products. One giant machine was churning out energy bars, other was filling up cans of energy drinks and rest of the sites were packaging the compound meals.

Three groups of people were spread out around the floor too, placing all the products int definite cartons according to flavors.

The man showed them around each machine and briefly explained the products to them.

Both of them had quite a few questions regarding the production process, which were answered satisfactorily by him.

Later, when they went back to the building, they met up with the marketing team of the company. All of the members were very welcoming and helped the two newcomers get comfortable with the place.

With all of this, the first day came to an end. Both Vipul and Freya drove back to the hotel, where they shared their views and opinions about the company. After that, both of them went to bed, tiredness and slumber taking over him.

Since the next day, the real work began. Both of them had to attend meetings which discussed the performances of various products, and which variant was the most popular among the people. They also discussed promotions on social media and how they could expand into other domains.

During the first few meetings, Freya had just been listening to the ongoing discussion, but after it had been five days, she decided to voice one of her opinions regarding the marketing strategy she had thought of. She stood up and asked for permission before beginning the proposal, "Sir, after having been seeing the market trends for drinks a few times before starting this degree, I have observed that people have always been keen to diverge toward flavors that are more seasonal, purely because of their limited timespan. Consumers are aware that flavors like chocolate, banana, etc. are perennial and can be availed at any time. This is what all other beverage companies are doing. To make a slight difference, we need to curate drinks which have a seasonal fruit punch, which would be available in a particular season. Of course, the star players would still be the top tastes, which is chocolate and malt, but these variants would attract more people toward trying these limited editions, for example redcurrants."

This was quite a long speech for her, and after speaking, her palms started trembling slightly, from all the eyes looking in her direction. Instantly, the feeling of having exceeded her limits clouded her mind. She opened her mouth to apologize when a clap resounded in the room. It was Mr. Sanjay, who seemed to be super proud. He spoke, "We were really in need of upgrading our beverages game. Thanks a lot, Freya, for this incredible idea of seasonal flavors. You may take your seat."

Her face lit up due to the effect of a smile, while Vipul patted her back, congratulating her on the feat. After that, both of them redirected their attention toward the meeting again.

In the same fashion, running errands, visiting the production sites, and acquiring more valuable information from the marketing team, Freya and Vipul were able to learn a lot. Hands on information, Freya felt, was way more valuable than all the bookish one she had gathered. Obviously, it was the basis of the practicality, but on-site work was a whole another competition.

She had also called Pranay and her parents regularly, informing them about the details of the project. Her parents had felt absolutely elated at the news of their daughter performing excellently at the job, but Pranay was a different case. When she had first informed him that the company had complimented her on the ingenious idea, his voice reflected the amount of pride he had felt. But as the days dragged on, she started feeling as if he was less and less interested in how her training went.

Once, when she was unwinding while telling him about the day's events, she shared that Vipul had taken her out to a roadside shack that served traditional Rajasthani food. Just as she was relishing the taste of the ghevar she totally devoured, Pranay stopped her midway and spoke in a cold, detached tone, "I see you are enjoying your time in Jaipur. Remember though, don't go about idling with Vipul. You are there to do your job, Freya, and you better focus on that. I dint want you going out with random strangers." Saying so, he cut the call, not bothering to hear what she had to say.

This dispirited Freya, who placed the phone on the nightstand and crawled under the covers to sleep.

Finally, with one day remaining for their training to end, Mr. Sanjay summoned both Vipul and Freya into his office. In front of him, two certificates and medals were placed.

Once they were inside, Mr. Sanjay stood up and called them nearby. With pride gleaming in his eyes, he picked up the certificates. "Vipul and Freya, to have you at our company has been an honor. Such talented people deserve every bit of success. I would like to present both of you with these medals and certificates to mark the successful completion of your tenure."

Firstly, he walked up to Freya and giving her the items, embraced her in a light hug and said, "Your idea had been one of the most diverse yet sustainable ones we have received, and as you might be aware of, five seasonal fruits belonging to this time of the year are already being processed into energy drinks. So, thanks a lot. Here." With a toothy smile tugging at her lips, Freya accepted the representations of the accolades she had been provided with.

Then, he moved on to Vipul, and patted his back and beamed, "Vipul, your packaging idea regarding the energy bars had been showing such a progress that I am totally shocked. People usually berate these things as superficial, but you were clever enough to study the trends and use them wisely. Here you go." Vipul grinned, and as both of them turned around to leave, Mr. Sanjay informed them that there would be a party the next day to celebrate their time at the company. Both of them were pleasantly surprised and thanked him again before leaving.

Back at the hotel, both of them excitedly hugged each other and complimented the other on the efforts put in. Finally, after having a decent dinner, they retired to their rooms.

The next day was a Saturday, which meant it was a half day. Once inside her room, Freya called her parents as usual, informing them about the medals and certificates. Her parents blessed her heartily and asked her to forward the same to Vipul.

Then, she opened her suitcase and pulled out an astoundingly beautiful dress. It was powder blue in color, with a sleek belt in the same color running across the waist. The neck was quite elegant, with a slightly deep triangular shape conferred to it. The sleeves, though, were breathtaking. They were puffed, but not too much to make her look like a snob. They exuded elegance and bunched up neatly around her wrists. The fall of the ensemble was superb, and the clean ruched bunching to one side of the neck gave the whole outfit a sleek contour.

In short, it was perfect. Satisfied, she hung it up in the cupboard after ironing it properly. Then, she sprawled down on the bed making herself comfortable before ringing Pranay up. After a few seconds of the dial tone blaring in her ears, he picked up. She thought he sounded exhausted, but if so, he masked it well. She informed him about the party, the medal and the certificate and he seemed genuinely happy for her. She asked him if he had had his dinner, but when he said that he was still at the office, she was stunned. It was almost eleven in the night, and she immediately asked him about his health. He brushed her concerns off, saying that the suppliers of the raw products had messed-up the deliveries and some breads and vegetables weren't supplied. Now, he was having trouble communicating with them. He was trying his best, though. She wished to be with him at the moment because he sounded too tired, but all she could do was advise him to take it easy and sleep as soon as possible. He promised to do so and disconnected the call.

The next day, the party was one of the most lavish events Freya had ever witnessed. The company had booked a restaurant, and although only the employees were invited, everything was still arranged to the tee.

Smiles were engraved into both Freya and Vipul's faces as they entered the area to loud cheers. All the employees greeted and congratulated them one by one, and not only on their work performance. Both of them looked phenomenal, with Freya donning her dress and Vipul fitted in black pants, alabaster turtleneck and a hickory trench coat.

Once they were seated on a table, Vipul leaned down and complimented Freya on her attire. Chuckling, she reciprocated the same, because honestly, he was looking like a dream. After having something to eat, Vipul suggested they go take a few photos, and Freya didn't need to be asked twice. In a flash, they were clicking selfies and posing for the camera.

Freya felt light as a feather in the whole atmosphere, surrounded by people who appreciated her, and a friend who was quite literally the gentlest yet the most interesting and diversely intelligent person she had met.

Dinner time arrived soon, and she felt herself gravitating toward the malai kofta booth. Taking a generous helping of the same, she sat back and enjoyed the rest of her time.

The next morning, she had her flight back to Delhi and she wanted to enjoy the remaining amount of time she had.

The night was spent talking about odds and ends. Both her and Vipul returned to the hotel around twelve in the night, and she hugged him, saying that she had one of the best times in her life working at the company. She asked if they could just spend some time out near the swimming pool, and he agreed to come after changing into something comfortable.

In about twenty minutes, both of them were out, dangling their feet in the refreshing pool water. Talking about their life, both of them discovered their common penchant for books. Vipul was quite an avid reader, while it was still a developing hobby for Freya. He gladly suggested her a few interesting books for beginners, and she was thankful.

The sky was slightly cloudy, but a few stars were still scattered on the inky blanket. Freya sighed, then proceeded to ask, "Vipul, can you give me one life advice that you have learned throughout your life? It can be anything. Consider it a parting gift for me. You just seem so much wiser for your years; I couldn't help but ask." He thanked her for the compliment, thought for a minute, and then, with a sweet smile curling his lips, he said, "Freya, life is a carousel. Sometimes, you go up. That is your family and friends appreciating you on your successes and achievements. That is, you feeling satisfied, gratified and blessed. Others are the lows. The high of rising up is so intoxicating that we forget that the lows are next. But they are relished, too. Not by us, but by those who feed on our soul. Those who are ready to strike the first chance they get. The high is love; the low is pain. I just want to remind you that there's barely enough time to love in a lifetime. Please don't give it all away to pain. It will come on its own accord if it has to. No point dwelling over past and giving away our happiness as a debt to it."

Freya went silent, the words ringing something inside her. She looked back up, and a confident smile plastering her expressions, said, "I won't let that happen."

"Now, you need to give me some advice too." Vipul playfully nudged her.

"Forgiveness is a commonly spoken about virtue. But, as humans, we don't allow it to spread out. We don't forgive others easily, even if we speak otherwise. We bury the ugly hatred deep inside. But what we don't realize is that this turmoil doesn't only bitter our relationships with others, it binds us to heaviness. We let our ego come in between our apologies or those of others, and this hinders everything. Forgiveness gives you freedom. And sometimes, you just need to let go, not because you feel the other is persistent, but because your mental health is more precious." She spoke.

"Well, you do sure seem the forgiving type." Vipul commented. At this, she burst out laughing and he followed. Soon, they retired to their rooms, and Freya placed all her luggage near the door and went to sleep.

The following morning, she got up early and dressed herself up in some comfortable clothes for the journey. Then, she knocked of Vipul's door. Immediately, he opened it and she saw two suitcases spread on the floor. "Packing?" she asked. He replied in the affirmative, stating that his flight was in the evening. Then, she hugged him, and he patted her head gently. Promising to keep in touch, she left the hotel for the airport.

Once inside the airplane, she texted Pranay and her parents about it. The whole flight, she swiped through the various photos and videos she had stored in her phone, revisiting the days that had just passed.

Within one hour, she was at the Delhi airport, where Pranay was present to receive her. As soon as he met her, he tightly hugged her and directed her toward the car parked outside.

It was the kind of day when you are about seventy percent sure that it is going to rain because clouds had gathered up on the hem of the sky and they were rolling about, announcing the imminent downpour.

Within half an hour, both of them were inside the house, and Pranay asked her to go freshen up while he prepared tea. After cleaning up and changing into the softest flannel pajamas the world had ever seen, Freya walked down the stairs and noticed a casserole of warm potato and cauliflower curry along with another one of breads waiting at the table.

She sat herself on one of the chairs and opened the lid to be warmed up by the aroma. Pranay's voice resounded in the hall as he entered, "I hope you like simple meals, too." She replied in the affirmative, bringing a small grin to his face, and both of them began with the meal.

"This is absolutely delectable. I have had some amazing curries made by my mom, but this one surpasses all." Freya commented, once the dishes had been done.

As it was a Sunday, Freya strolled into the garden to sit by the pansies and camellia, and this time, Pranay was with her.

Sitting near the shrubs, Freya started showing the photos and videos she had captured during her trip. Initially, Pranay seemed quite enthusiastic. But, after about twenty photos, his zeal dimmed, and it was replaced by a very uncanny expression. Although, Freya was unaware of these changes as she was buried inside her phone.

The final straw snapped when they were browsing among the photos of the party, where in one particular picture, Pranay noticed that Vipul seemed to be dancing with her in a silly manner. "You shouldn't be so close with other men when you have a boyfriend, Freya." His voice came from above her head and when she turned around, for a split second she was unnerved by the stoic expression.

Composing herself, she said that it was a game where two people had to partner up and both of them decided to form a pair as they knew each other the best.

She rubbed his arm and tried to let his mind off the incident. Although she wanted to feel kind of cheerful that she had a protective boyfriend, a bigger part was still shocked by the steely face she had seen.

Half an hour passed by, and after talking some more, they returned inside the home. Freya want upstairs, while Pranay entered his room.

'This can't be happening all over again. Gia can't happen again. I can't go through the cycle of losing someone again.' He banged his fist over the wooden table, and although it hurt, he was feeling a boiling sensation in his chest. 'The person who caused this shift to happen can't be reformed in this shape. I need to get things in control, fast.'

He drank a glass of water and sat down on the floor to take deep breaths. A few minutes passed by, and he felt a lot calmer than he did while banging his fists.

Coolly, he put on a sweatshirt, slipped on a pair of sneakers, and exited the house. He got into the car and drove around aimlessly, and after some considerable time, he realized that he was in Patel Nagar, and all the memories came rushing back to him. The broken chair, the blood, the plates, everything.

Too shaken up to spend another minute, he immediately drove away.

Finally at home, he sat back in his bed and switched the television on to pass some time. It was around half past nine when he left his room, and the smell of sweet potatoes greeted his senses. He stalked into the kitchen to see Freya laying out a batch of breads into a casserole, while a bowl contained the curry.

She looked up at him and smiled, "Welcome. The dinner is ready." He mustered a smile too and went to sit at the table.

Soon enough, they were digging into the dish. Honestly, Pranay felt his tastebuds explode with flavor. "You haven't accepted the offer, right?" Numbness froze her spine. "What offer?" she asked. "About being the sous-chef." "Oh." She eased out a little. "I can be your personal sous-chef. Hotels aren't my comfort zone. Too many judging tongues and eyes." She said truthfully. "Well, no problem. I am honored to have my own chef right here."

Pranay held her hands and pressed gently on them. A smile bloomed on her lips as she said, "I only love you, dear. Vipul or anyone else is just a friend. I chose you, so no one ever compares." He slumped his shoulders and nodded, saying, "I guess I just become overprotective at times."

Both of them smiled, and Pranay went over to the coffee table to pick up a letter. "This is an invitation for the opening of another branch of our hotel in Greater Kailash. I would love if you attended it with me. It is on Saturday." Freya immediately agreed, and Pranay hugged her tightly.

The rest of the week was spent busily, with Pranay buried neck deep in his work and Freya working on finishing the reports to be submitted regarding the trip. She had talked to Vipul about three times regarding the same but decided against telling Pranay about it as she wanted to relish the calm. Moreover, whoever she talked to was her business, not Pranay's.

In the blink of an eye, the day of the party arrived. Freya had just completed an assignment she had received. Now, she jumped up on her bed and closed her eyes, drifting off to sleep in record time.

It was two hours later that she woke up. Looking up at the watch, she made out that it was half past six. She got up and decided to start getting ready. Greater Kailash wasn't that far away, only a ten-minute drive, so she was good.

After applying a subtle amount of makeup and curling her hair a little, which she admitted was difficult, she finally stepped into the simple but elegantly eye-catching jumpsuit she had picked out. It was a stark emerald in color, with buttons going up to the collar. Streaks of gold fibers softly ran down one side in an oblique manner, while the other side was plain. The whole look was tied together by a belt that came along. She left the upper two buttons undone. She had always hated it when all of them were closed. It made her feel suffocated and stifled.

Stepping into her heels, she waited for Pranay. But she was lucky, because only five minutes later, the doorbell rang, and he walked in. His steps halted midway to admire the absolute vision Freya was, and he kissed her lightly on the cheeks. If she had forgotten to apply any rouge, he had helped.

Within minutes, he was ready, too, wearing a dark green shirt underneath the suit to match to her, and they both drove off.

Once in the gathering, Freya tried to let herself relax. She wasn't necessarily a party girl, courtesy of which she had met Pranay, and she wanted to change that, but it was not possible to transform one's demeanor so quickly. She wanted to be able to meet people easily, which was why she urged Pranay to sit at a crowded table.

He more than obliged, putting on the best smile and strode off into the distance. She followed, and although she hated nothing more than being an arm candy, she pushed the thought away and made an effort to warm up to the people.

After about an hour, Freya realized that being extroverted wasn't her forte. Although she was elated to see Pranay in a light-hearted mood, all she wanted now, was to go back. Carefully approaching him when the crowd was dispersed, she tapped him on the shoulder. He turned around and smiled. She said, "I think I am not feeling quite well, as parties, especially those where I don't know anyone, aren't my cup of tea. Can we head home, please?" In an instant, Pranay's smile dropped. A scowl decorated his usually charming features as he retorted, "You had a lot of fun with your 'friend' in the party at your workplace, didn't you? I have the rights to do so too, Freya. I can let loose with my peers too. You can sit in the dining area if you want, though."

Freya was slightly taken aback. She hadn't expected his response to be so blunt. She admitted she had fun at the gathering back in Jaipur, but it was because it was much smaller, and she knew the people. Hurt and despondency flashed on her face, but she didn't let anyone take notice of it. Anyways, she shrugged and walked back into the dining area, which was empty, to relax.

She was sipping on some mojito for about half an hour when people started coming in for enjoying the dinner. She spotted Pranay with a few people, and before heading over to her, he hugged the women he was with. She excitedly got up and after he diverted the attention to her, he asked her to eat something. Both of them proceeded to collect a few food items on their plates and after they sat back down, Pranay asked, "So, you had fun?" Freya could almost hear the taunt laced in it, but she chose to ignore it. "Yeah. Very." She replied back, hoping to get the message of the exact opposite through his brain. He looked up at her, and she nonchalantly drank some juice. After having dinner in silence, both of them got up to bid goodbyes and leave.

Once inside the house, Pranay held her back and apologized for his rather cold demeanor toward her. She shrugged and getting on her toes, booped his nose with hers. "I don't want to impede your flow of meeting new people. I just wish you saw how left out I felt." After that, she went inside her room to get changed and rest.

"She is comparatively easier than Gia. I can see flickers of flames, though. I hope they remain flickers only." He murmured and stalked off into his own room.

The next day was quite hectic for her, as the joint reports regarding the trip were to be submitted on the same day. She had talked to Vipul earlier, and after having resolved the minor issues, had submitted it from their side.

A portion of her grades depended on it, and she didn't want to mess anything up.

Next, she had to talk to one of the professors on video call regarding the trip and explain the things she couldn't go through in the reports. It was supposed to be a conference call between her, Vipul, and the professor.

It was around one in the afternoon when the call started. The professor was friendly and asked both of them about their personal experiences regarding the trip, and not only the office. They also talked about work ethic and market expansions. All this discussion took about two hours, and it was around quarter past three that the call ended.

During the call, she had received Pranay's messages, asking her if she wanted a takeout for dinner. However, she couldn't respond due to the ongoing meeting.

Once the call had ended, she texted him about wanting to eat something middle eastern. After that, she called her mother and they chatted for some time.

In the evening, around seven, Pranay entered the house with a large packet. He placed them on the rack and asked Freya, who was standing near him to serve it while he changed.

She opened the box to find Lebanese lentil soup along with some flatbread. In another, smaller container was some black bean hummus. She transferred them on one big plate and waited for Pranay.

In a short while, he came and sat next to her, and they both feasted on the delicious food. Soon, the night came to an end, and both of them went to sleep.

In the coming few days, Pranay got busier with the work, and it left Freya a bit solitary. One day, while sitting idle, she opened up an online shopping site. Scrolling randomly, her eyes halted on a bottle of red liquid lipstick. She had many colors, like peach, burgundy and rose, but for some reason, she never owned the blood red one. She always felt the color to be too bold for her personality. However, now that she looked at the image, she wanted to try it for once.

Therefore, without giving much thought to it, she pressed the option for buying it and made the necessary payments.

Then, she put her phone down and began with other tasks.

A few days passed, and Pranay had been extremely caring and supportive. On a Thursday, he asked her to drop by the hotel, just to have lunch with him. Excited, she obliged. After finishing her classes, she cleaned her room a bit and picked out some clothes to put on.

She wore a blush corset top with long white puff sleeves, along with a pair of simple black stone washed jeans. While combing her luscious mocha hair, she caught sight of the lipstick she had ordered. She picked it up, and after hesitating for a while, applied a layer. This instantly added volume to her look. She loved it, and not wanting to go too overboard, left it at that.

Twenty minutes later, she was at the hotel, and as soon as she saw her boyfriend, her eyes lit up.

She hurried over, but as soon as he saw her, his lips thinned into a line. 'Red lipstick.' He thought. Nevertheless, he hugged her, and asked her to come over to his cabin.

The two of them sat, and while the food was being prepared, Pranay commented, "You know, you look different today." Freya smiled widely, happy that he noticed the difference. "The lipstick is nice, but you should take it off." This wasn't what she was expecting to hear. "Why?" she asked. "Because it is provocative, and I don't want you to wear it." Pranay calmly replied.

She was aghast. "The fact that I am wearing a red lipstick shouldn't be provocative. Yes, red is a bold color, it catches attention. But if people prey on me and label me as a skank or a nympho because of it, it is entirely their problem. They are the ones who have been brought up in a disturbingly tainted and adulterated environment to sexualize a color. It is a shade, just like mauve or green or black. You mean to say, if I wear black lipstick, I am a goth? No, this is my choice. And my choice of clothes or accessories doesn't mean I am asking for it. If I truly wear something suggestive, it is okay for you to call me out, but not based off of some lipstick shade."

She got up to leave, but Pranay held her back. "I didn't mean to say anything to upset you, Freya. I just wanted you to see what other people see" His gaze flickered down to the floor. "I am sorry."

"Yeah, well. You should be." She slightly shrugged as she sat back down, not engaging in any further conversation. The food came and she ate it, after which she left. She wanted to speak a few words to him, at least bid him a bye, but she refrained from doing so. She wanted to get her message and disappointment conveyed, and not engaging in a conversation was a strong medium.

It was an upsetting event, but Pranay had something sinister lurking in his brain that Freya's outburst wouldn't be able to tackle, and she would soon encounter it.

About three weeks later, Freya prepared the living room for a movie night with Pranay. She had known for some time that he liked psychological drama films, and had picked out one of the best, for the same, 'Whiplash.' She had also prepared some snacks, and overall, she was pretty satisfied with everything.

The drama that ensued the lipstick incident was a tad bit overwhelming for her, but she was past it now, having resolved it over a serving of spinach lasagna.

In the evening, when Pranay came home, he was surprised to see the living room modified into a small movie hall, just more comfortable with throw pillows and blankets. Just then, Freya came from behind him, and closing his eyes, whispered in his ears, "A movie night is perfect for unwinding, love." He grabbed her hands and turned around. She had expected him to look surprised, but he looked rather tired and irritated, though he managed a smile.

"You didn't have to do it at all." Freya smiled, acknowledging his humility. "I am anyways too tired. You should have asked me." This was a blow to her heart. How could she possibly ask for his advice, when she wanted to surprise him? She didn't expect some grand gesture, just a warm hug and soft 'thanks' would do.

Nevertheless, Pranay plopped down on the sofa and patted the place beside him, asking her to sit down. Freya took her place, and both of them started the movie.

Freya had to admit, she had chosen a great one. Even Pranay agreed, though he didn't say anything to her.

Some time had passed, and suddenly, she felt some weight on her head. She tapped his head, saying, "Wake up. You can't sleep. The interesting part is here."

Pranay jerked up, and instead of focusing on the movie, spoke in a dry tone, "It wouldn't have been a disappointment if you had spared the efforts."

Without waiting to hear to her side, he got up and walked away into the room, slamming the door shut. Freya sat there, the movie still playing, but she felt tears sting the back of her eyes, and she knew they wouldn't be withheld. Eventually, they became a cascade and dropped down the rocks of her cheeks like gushes of mountain water, and although she tried to explain to herself that it was Pranay who could have behaved like a more mature person and tried to put in some more effort, another, more persuasive part overtook her. 'He has been out in the office, toiling. You were in the comfort of his home. He provided you with a place to live. He has the upper hand here. He was right in leaving, you were being a nagging child. Remember the party? You wanted to leave then too. Stop opposing. He is right, you just need to become a bit more understanding.'

Although she felt as if it was akin to becoming a submissive, she couldn't help but feel the rush of emotions inside her.

Eventually, she got up to leave, shutting the television down. As she laid down on her bed, her cheeks itched from the brine. However, she was too tired to get up. Moreover, although she had tried to weigh it down, the feeling that she was in the wrong was overpowering. She was reminded of Pranay's eyes, and she thought for a fleeting moment she saw a wave of guilt in there, but it had soon disappeared. Too exhausted to let her brain ponder any more, she closed her eyes and soon fell asleep.

The next morning, she woke up early to prepare a breakfast which she wanted to take to Pranay. Her brain refused to perform so, but she decided to pay heed to her heart and go with the flow. She had heard about breakfast in bed and wanted to try it out for herself.

Therefore, she pulled on an apron and began with a simple yet filling repast, composed of two pita sandwiches, some fresh fruits, and a glass of pomegranate juice.

Placing all of them on a tray, she carried it to Pranay's room which was unlocked, to her luck. She didn't want to spoil the surprise.

She shook him, dragging the duvet down, exposing his eyes. He softly retorted, but after a few attempts, he woke up, ruffling his hair. Although she didn't mention, she thought he looked adorable. He was about to question her, but the sight of the aesthetically decorated tray halted him.

Freya cheerfully said, "Good morning, dear. I made up something for you. I hope you like it." She brightly placed the tray beside him.

This was new to him: care. He was used to doing things, not the other way round. Therefore, he smiled, and turning to the bathroom, said that he would come out in a minute after brushing.

Inside, as he looked at himself in the mirror, a sigh escaped his lips as he leaned back against the wall. He whispered, "She is making it more difficult. I am so foreign to it that I can't accept it. Breakfast in bed? That is a part of my strategy, not the other way round."

Struggling to place his emotions, he pushed himself off the wall and walked back out, putting on one of the most charming smiles the world had known.

He hugged Freya and kissed her on the cheek, thanking her for the breakfast. Then he urged her to eat along with him.

She picked up the bowl of fruits and started chewing on them. Yesterday's thoughts clashed in her brain, and as she looked at his face, she placed the negative ones to bay.

Although a little part in her heart wanted to talk about yesterday, she decided to cherish the current love floating in the atmosphere.

She would later realize; it wasn't love but lingering control and irreparable damage spreading their ominous wings.

Chapter 13
ABSQUATULATE

The next two months were blissful for Freya and Pranay as a couple. They started taking part in more healthy conversations, started engaging themselves in gardening and plantation every weekend and began cooking alternatively for each other.

Pranay also regularly asked her updates about the marketing research course, and she was more than willing to share small details of the subjects.

In short, both of them were in a content space in their lives. Everything was mellow, except for the fact that Pranay almost never talked about his parents.

All Freya knew about them was that they lived in Lucknow and his mother made the most delectable green chili pickle. Other than that, nothing. She didn't mean to be nosy, though, therefore she avoided the topic.

She had been talking to her parents one day and had almost broken down in tears after realizing the span of time that had passed without her having hugged them. But she had rarely ever seen Pranay talking to his mother or father.

Whenever on call, he was either talking to his colleagues or friends.

One day, Pranay turned up at home quite worn-out, his eyes sporting dark circles underneath them, whole his skin seemed unusually dull.

Freya helped him change back into some comfortable clothes and tucked him inside his bed. Then, she disappeared into the kitchen to make some warm chickpea soup.

When she came in, Pranay was staring at the wall. She placed the bowl on the nightstand and ran her fingers through his hair. He closed his eyes at the sensation.

"Have some soup, dear. It will make you feel better." With that, she left. She wanted to stay, but something inside told her that he wanted to be left alone. He didn't even say anything all the while.

The next day, she let him sleep in for extra thirty minutes, as she considered his state earlier. When he woke up, she asked him how he felt, to which he responded monotonously that he felt better.

Then, he went into the bathroom, got ready for work, and left.

Freya had also been busy the past week, with her upcoming completion of first semester, and everyone had decided to host a grand party. Not only the students and teachers, but also the family members were invited. This upped the visiting scale to about two hundred and fifty people, as the course had enrollment capacity of 100 students. It was scheduled three weeks later. It was anticipated that the whole celebration would be lavish, and every student was buzzing with excitement at the prospect of meeting their batch mates in person.

When she received the invitation, she gladly sent a copy to her parents, asking them to join her. She had been lucky as being in the capital of the country, the party was being in Delhi, so she didn't have to travel.

She also sent a copy of it to Pranay, who responded enthusiastically.

Three days passed, and in the meantime, Freya had ordered a dress from an online site for the event, after meticulously sorting and sifting through thousands of options for hours

It was on Friday, three days after the day Pranay returned haggard, that she decided to surprise him in the hotel. She had caught a whiff of how strenuous the past few days had been on him, and she wanted to have lunch with him to make him feel appreciated.

This was why she made some fried, seasoned cauliflower, a batch of chickpea curry, some breads and placed them in a large four tier Tupperware lunch box. In the last container, she added some store-bought semolina pudding.

Then, she hired a cab and went over to Tastel hotel.

When she reached the hotel, she ringed her boyfriend, who didn't answer. Assuming that he might be in a meeting, she informed the receptionist that she was willing to wait, only if she could send over a message to him, to which she complied.

Freya had expected to wait thirty minutes at the maximum, but it was close to an hour, and lunch time was almost over. She was beginning to get exasperated, and finally, she decided to make her way to his room. Once on front of it, she knocked on Pranay's door.

A moment later it opened, revealing Pranay, two women and a man inside. A variety of delicacies were spread out on the table, and they all seemed to have just finished their lunch.

"Didn't you get the message?" Freya asked, trying not to show how hurt she felt. "Oh, I did. You see, I was in a meeting." Pranay chucked as he waved at the other people.

Something bubbled up inside Freya, as she calmly said, in a voice which gave shivers to all the other three people, "Can we take this outside?" "Sure." He said and followed her outside.

"What happened?" he nonchalantly enquired. "Well, for starters, you didn't pick up my call. The, I got the message sent, but you blatantly chose to ignore it. Do you know how humiliating it was to sit in the reception area as some desperate teenage girl who wants to please her boyfriend? For your information, I hold some respect too. You could have simply sent back a message, but you didn't. And must I say, I though you knew how to write." Freya said, in the same unmoving yet dangerously calm voice.

"You are blowing this out of proportion." Pranay sighed loudly. "Yeah, I didn't respond. Big deal. I was with my colleagues, Freya. I wouldn't have just gotten up. Stop being so sensitive over trivial things."

"Yeah. You wouldn't have. Maybe, if someday you come to meet me and I dismiss you like trash, you would celebrate pompously. Right?" He opened his mouth to answer, but Freya stopped him. A teary voice left her, "I wouldn't ever do that. Sometimes, I think you are a heartless debauchee. Maybe, you choose to keep things from me more than I can imagine." With that, she picked up the lunch box and made her exit.

Back home, she opened the boxes stacked together and placed all the contents in a large plate. All the while, tears streamed down her face and neck. They weren't due to the cold personality Pranay had shown off, but rather of the abasement she had to face, sitting alone at the reception. Eventually, they dried up, and she washed her face with cool water to let off some steam.

Tying her hair up, she hastily went to meet the potter, whom Pranay had belittled months ago, and asked him to come inside. He was still sitting by the roadside, tending to his creations. She politely welcomed him and offered him the food. He was shellshocked, never having seen such a large amount of delectable, warm food in his life.

Tears sprang in his eyes, as he thanked her again and again. He requested her to pack the food because his daughter absolutely loved cauliflowers. A genuine smile sprang up on Freya's face, and she put them all in a container and gave it to him, all the while feeling light as a feather. He blessed her hundreds of times before departing, ruffling up her hair slightly.

In the evening, Pranay came back home from work. He knew he had to get the situation under control. For two months, his acting skills had been immaculate. But he had to do some serious damage repair to mask the truth now.

He opened the refrigerator to see a casserole filled with some cauliflower dish. He devoured them, and therefore, he thought about the incident today. It wasn't like he spared another thought to Freya, but he decided to apologize for the sake of it.

Softly, he walked up to her room, only to find her listening to some music on her headphones. Gently, he tapped her head and she put the headphones down, turning to him. Her face was virtually expressionless.

"I am so sorry, Freya. I know I was wrong. I just wanted to discuss something with my colleagues, and I know that it doesn't excuse anything, but just inform me beforehand next time, okay?" he said.

"Do you understand what a surprise is?" she calmly said, which only riled him further. But the point right now was damage control. So, he nodded lightly and hugged her, saying, "This won't happen again, dear. Just stay put, and we can have all the meals you make. What happened to the food, by the way?"

"I gave it to the neighbor's kids, because I noticed they were playing outside, and I didn't want the meal to go waste. They enjoyed a small feast." She said, promptly avoiding the real information, and went back to placing the headphones over her ears.

Pranay smiled and left, closing the door behind himself. "Well, at least she isn't trying to lie to my face. Or is she?" he mused, and trailed back into his room, getting ready to get some sleep.

On the other hand, Frey was extremely excited for the night of the party. She was determined to not let the unfortunate event with Pranay dampen her enthusiasm.

Two remaining weeks were spent compiling all her assignments and reports in a document, talking to her parents, and living a rather peaceful life at home. She half expected something to happen again, but she wasn't aware of the fact that the onyx wings were about to be unfurled completely, too soon for her liking.

The party was on a Saturday night, which had finally arrived. Although, Freya still roamed about in her pajamas. The reason for it was her dilemma. Her mother had called her three days ago to inform her that they wouldn't be able to make it, because her father was down with high fever, which the doctors predicted to be a mild case of pneumonia. It had probably occurred because he had gotten drenched in the downpour when he forgot his raincoat and had to get out of his car on a rainy night to see why it had suddenly stopped.

This was why her mother had to stay back. Although Freya was upset, she knew both of them had no choice. Her father's health obviously mattered more, and she promised to send pictures of the party to both of them.

With her parents out of option, she only had Pranay to rely on. She had told him about the party, and he had readily agreed, promising to make it in time.

It was still half past five in the evening, and Freya sat down on the sofa to quickly watch an episode of her favorite drama series. It was extraordinarily interesting, and she had to peel herself off the room to go get ready.

She put her hair up and applied some light makeup, nothing to make her stand out but just enough to highlight her features. Then, she put on the dress, a sepia fit, with netted sleeves dropping to the level of her shoulders and extending all the way to her wrists. It had a square neckline, which accentuated her collarbones. This one was rather short, ending just above her knees. Finally, she pulled her hair down, and combed it until all the strands were separate and flowy.

Then, she proceeded to place two simple, long hairclips on one side, securing the hair there neatly. Against her mocha hair, they shone brightly. Admiring the final look, she placed her feet in her heels and walked down the stairs.

It was around quarter past seven when Pranay entered the house, with a small bouquet of peonies in his hands. He almost tripped over the rug upon seeing his girlfriend, looking absolutely ravishing and stunning. She asked, "How do I look?" And all he was able to say was, "Like a dream." Freya smiled and asked him to get ready too, while thanking him for the flowers and placing them in a vase.

Once he was ready, both of them got in his car and drove to the venue, which was twenty minutes away. Pranay was relishing the fact that Freya looked like a Greek goddess reincarnated, but the darker part was soon overtaking him.

If she looked attractive, it meant everyone would think the same. This mere thought gave birth to a whirlwind of negatively charged emotions in his chest, and he tried to put them at bay.

Soon, they were in the designated venue, and the place was marvelous and blindingly bright. Spider palms lined the entrance while the inside was whole another story.

A large, rather humongous hall stretched in front of them, peachy in tone, with purple and yellow lights twinned together to create the effect of an aurora. Round, polished tables were set at some distance from each other, surrounded by chairs.

One whole wall was covered by fairy lights, arranged symmetrically to produce a calming effect.

Up further, a large poster was placed which boasted the name of her university and the course.

The smell of dark chocolate lingered in the atmosphere, which made it all the more comfortable and welcoming.

A man, probably in his mid-forties, suddenly called out to her. When both Freya and Pranay turned around, her face morphed into a huge smile when she recognized one of her professors, Mr. Nawaz.

She immediately walked to him, followed by Pranay who seemed a bit out of place and context. After exchanging pleasantries, Mr. Nawaz asked Freya about him.

"Well, he is-" "Your boyfriend, right?" Mr. Nawaz chuckled, and she followed suit. "Yeah, he is." She then briefly introduced him, and they shook hands.

Soon, many other people entered, and Freya saw Vipul among them. She was about to walk over to him, when a group of people called out to her, and she had to postpone meeting him.

Pranay, however, didn't fail to notice the glint of happiness in her eyes when she saw Vipul, and it ticked something off inside him.

People came and went by, hugging Freya, asking about random topics and if course regarding Pranay, who stood by her side, coiffed and elegant. She was evidently enjoying the gathering, her eyes reflecting her enthusiasm, while someone was getting impatient and irritated.

After another thirty minutes, Freya finally got to meet Vipul, and her elation reflected in the way she high fived him.

"You look gorgeous." Vipul commented, winking. Freya retorted, "You don't look so bad yourself." She called Pranay over, and after having introduced both of them, Vipul said, "You must be extremely lucky, Pranay. She is a really caring and intelligent woman." Bile rose in Pranay's throat, more so when he saw her smiling at him.

He bit back a scowl and nodded; the fakest smile plastered on his charming face.

Before long, the dance arena opened, and although Freya wasn't much of a dancer, she was urged by her colleagues and professors to join them. Finally, she sighed and turned toward Pranay, "You coming?"

He shook his head while sipping on some lemonade and she got up, stroked his cheek, and assured that she would be back in a few minutes. As soon as she stepped on the stage, many people surrounded her, and one group sucked her into itself, and she let herself feel the beat seep into her bones.

Five minutes later, Pranay's eyes trailed up on the stage again, and what he saw rubbed flint stones in his gut. Vipul was striding over to Freya. Pranay almost got up to grab her by the arm and leave, but he saw him crossing her and going over to some professor.

He let his muscles relax and stretched back on the chair. He waited for another fifteen minutes, and while Freya was enjoying her time, he clearly was getting bored out of his brains. This was why he decided to walk out into the parking lot for some time.

On the other hand, Freya was dancing away with a group of people on the stage and was too preoccupied to take note of the sudden disappearance of her boyfriend.

About fifteen minutes later, she found herself sitting by the rooftop pool, her feet dangling in the water, with Vipul on one side and another student, Neha, on the other.

All of them were talking about odds and ends, about how difficult they felt the course was going to become in the next semester, and what their future expectations were.

Just then, someone called Neha, and she got up to leave, hugging Freya once more.

Vipul slumped back a little, and after taking a sip of his mojito, asked, "So, how is Pranay? Is he nice? I mean, it is obvious that he is attractive, but how it the nature?"

Freya thought for a moment but deciding upon keeping the more distorted part to herself, she said, "He is charming, that is how I would describe him. He has this way around words that I can't stay mad at him."

"That's nice. But is he thoughtful of your emotions and feelings? I am, in no way, trying to paint a picture or imposing any opinion. I am just asking how he is, on the inside." Vipul clarified.

"I would never get angry at you, Vipul. You are like a friend to me, and I know you have my best interests at heart. To question that would be wrong." After a pause, she continued, "Well, you see, he is very considerate and almost too virtuous at times, you know? Like the hard to believe type. But, on other, less frequent occasions, he seems quite aloof and unapproachable. In those moments, it is as if his whole personality shifts for five minutes and then comes back. Moreover, even though I want to remain angry at him, it just becomes impossible with his naturally persuasive and attractive demeanor. I don't know what else to say."

"Try to talk to him, dear. It may be that it is a part of his personality, but you can at least get to know him better if you communicate." After a pause, Vipul continued, "Freya, you need to learn to be unapologetic for the times you are right. You've got to realize al you're worthy of and all you can accomplish, whether or not anyone approves or supports you. Come here." He said, and patted her head, ruffling up the hair.

Just then, she felt a hand holding her arm. "Get up, Freya. We need to leave." Pranay's voice boomed over her head, with Vipul's hand still over it. A lethally deceptive smile spread over his lips as he tightened his grip slightly, and Freya got up instantly. She bid goodnight to Vipul, wore her heels, and made her way out.

She wanted to ask what had come up, so urgent they had to leave like they did. But she acknowledged the time and noticed it was eleven. As she was beginning to get tired, she slid it off.

Once they were home, Freya opened the door and went in. She refrained from switching on a lot of lights, as it was unnecessary. Placing the keys on the table and wishing Pranay good night, she started walking up the stairs.

She had merely taken two steps when Pranay took hold of her forearm and dragged her down. She almost tumbled, her heels scraping the lower step.

"What the-" Freya was astounded, as Pranay had never dealt with her in such a harsh, raw, physical way.

He pinned her against the wall forcefully, with so much vigor she felt the impact in her sacrum and coccyx.

He had always been a tad bit mercurial, but the situation was becoming perilously untamed at an alarming rate.

When she opened her eyes, pain reflected through them clearly, and if Pranay saw it, he chose to blatantly ignore it.

"I see what you are doing, Freya. And I don't like it." He snarled. "Do you know what you have done?" Trembles cover her body, and she was unable to react.

"Answer. Me. Right. Now."

A whimpering 'no' left her mouth.

"There, we have out preciously innocent Freya back. It truly amazes me at times, how fricking gullible you can act. But you know what, it isn't cute. It is terribly pathetic."

Before she could stabilize herself, he fisted her hair, and turned her around, pulling on them with all his might. Her back arched, and the rawest, most infiltrating pain invaded her senses. He pulled on the bundle in his hands like a harness, and hauled her close to his mouth, as her back was now facing him. In the same lethal voice, he had used at the pool, he uttered, "Well, do you know what sort of people I like?" She shook her head in no. "I assumed so. Well, you know something about me. Let's start with that. You know I like my bread buttered on one side. You know I like my cufflinks polished to perfection. You are also aware that I like my coffee as latte the best. Isn't it so?" Freya nodded.

"Words." He ordered, his voice turning authoritative. "Yes." She stuttered and winced when he tugged at her chestnut lengths again. "Amazing. Now is the time to find out how I like my people. I would love to let you know that I like only one trait. I like them obedient and meek. Got it?"

"Yes."

"Excellent. So now that you clearly broke this mold I set for my people, and considering that you are 'currently' an important part of my life, I think you deserve some sort of punishment, don't you?"

If Freya was scared earlier, she was totally paralyzed and crippled by the fear now. She felt his free hand taking strides up her back and in a flash, it was wrapped around her throat.

His thumb pushed on the jugular vein, and a choked cough left her. "I think you like it, right? Choking? I presume so. If yes, you will absolutely admire this. I just suggest you to not move, as it can cause some unwanted pain."

With that, he turned her around, and halted for a moment. Freya wanted to scream, to break the windows, to escape. This wasn't her or Pranay. She wasn't the one to bear abuse, and he wasn't an abuser. Clearly something was taken in the wrong context. But the horror she was feeling, it crippled all sense and rationality.

She was dazed, and the thought process was broken by a sound. And a sensation. A painful one.

She felt burns on her cheek. For a split second, she was shell shocked, and then her brain officially entered panic mode. She started cowering behind the sofas, but Pranay held her by the arm and dragged her out. "I hope it doesn't hurt much. It was a starting representation, dear. A depiction of all the frustration you have caused to me."

With that, he dragged her down to the kitchen aisle, and practically threw her on the marble slab. He purposefully pushed her off to hit the corner, and a weak, piercing cry left her mouth as she sank to the ground.

She didn't even have any energy left to get up, and she just lifted her head to look at the counter. Memories of them making lunches and dinners invaded her brain, and a tear slipped out on her cheek.

"Oh goodness. Don't cry, dear. I thought you were strong." Pranay cooed, as he tried to wipe the brine off. Instinctively, Freya backed off, and this riled him up.

He grabbed her neck and forcefully dragged his hand all over her face. She cried out, but there wasn't anyone to listen to her, except Pranay. Well, the information wasn't of much help. The irascible side of him once again overpowered his brain, and darkness visibly loomed over the room.

Another resounding slap reverberated in the entirety of the house, and this had a heightened effect, as her cheek was still crimson from the previous one. Despite trying to suppress it, a sob tore out from Freya's chest, and the sound of it didn't please the man in front of her.

"You have absolutely no right over here to play the victim, okay? I am the person who has been suffering from your unfaithful ways." Pranay shouted. "Unfaithful?" she asked, although she had no sensibility left inside after bearing the two blows. She was almost half sprawled on the floor, her heart simultaneously feeling as if it was going to burst out of her chest, and also that it had ceased to function.

But Pranay was far from over. The side of him that he had buried down for so long was now out in all its ugliness, and she was alone to bear the brunt of it.

"Of course, Freya. Who had gone out to another city with a man she knew nothing about? Who was dangling their feet in the pool with him like he was the best man in the world? Who danced with others while her boyfriend sat alone? You." He breathed down her neck, and the room fell into the most disturbingly horrid silence ever.

Thirty seconds passed, and just as her heart rate started to normalize a bit, Pranay got up and swirled her around, so her cheek was pressed against the cold countertop.

The cool feeling didn't soothe her, rather, it sliced through her like a javelin. Before she could move a limb, she felt something cold pour down her hair and face.

Water splashed all over her head, and some of it entered her airways, causing a coughing fit to spring into action. Pranay held a half-filled jug of water over her head, crushing her temporal region under the weight of it.

Something broke inside Freya. She absolutely lost control of herself, but even that wasn't allowed under the searing gaze of her supposed boyfriend.

He picked her up by the hair instantly and splashed the remaining amount of water directly on her face, after which he threw the jug away. With a loud thud, it landed in some corner of the room.

Going limp, Freya's entire body swayed like a drunkard's while she held his wrist to try to reason with him. For a single second, both of them looked into each other's eyes, and Freya silently pleaded him to stop with this insanity.

But whatever flicker had lit itself up, was blown away by the malignant forces of his darker part. Before she could process anything, the most painful sensation erupted on her left shoulder, as he practically dug his fingers on her skin. He remained like that for a good forty seconds, his face contorting into the most dreadful grin she had ever seen.

Although she tried to cry out, it was as if her shoulder didn't exist to her. All that existed in the moment was her ripped, slashed heart covered by the ominous charcoal darkness of the man in front of her.

Once more, skin met skin, heated against feverish, but although it sounds lovely and romantic, none of it was. It reeked of toxicity, of illegitimate possessiveness. This one was particularly more painful as her cheeks were still soaking from the water.

As soon as this happened, Pranay left her and strode back inside his room. "I hope you learn from your mistakes." He whispered in her ears before slamming the door shut.

Just like that, it was over. The darkness had entirely consumed them, and although Freya was the embodiment of positivity, she felt like the bleakest gloom in the world at the moment.

She wanted to run, but her muscles and joints had given up.

She wanted to breathe, but her lungs were filled with water, quite literally.

She wanted to speak, but it was as if her vocal cords had been dissolved.

One step at a time, she walked up the stairs and into her room. The whole process took her ten minutes. One look at the window, and all she wanted was to jump off. But she tamed her thoughts. She sat down by her bed and closed her eyes. But she couldn't remain so, because flashes of the ghastly night made her gasp and open them. Tears flowed down her cheeks, some sliding down her ears and some falling onto her chest.

She turned slightly, but that caused her left shoulder to meet the wooden board, and she had to place a hand over her mouth to prevent any sounds from escaping.

Slowly, although it felt impossible, she drifted off to sleep, water staining her cheeks, bruises on her shoulder and her scalp hurting immensely, while her head met the floor.

Morning came, and although the world went out and about, children jumping and studying, office workers buried neck deep in files and housewives maintaining their abodes, the universe had shifted in a house in Golf Links.

No lights were turned on, and although Pranay was awake, he didn't have the guts or courage to leave his room. He knew full well that what he had done was animalistic. Hell, even animals were more humane than he was. But he reminded himself, 'She had this coming. Cheating is always wrong, that is what we have always been told. What goes around, comes around.'

With that, he opened his door and walked down the hall. He sat there for about an hour, brooding nothing in particular. One person was on his mind, Gia. Had she never been there, he would have been better. Normal.

Just then, Freya's door opened, and she walked out like a corpse. No expressions appeared on her face as she stepped down the stairs, but as soon as her eyes fell on the man, her feet halted and breathing shallowed.

She forced herself to move again, and she did. She walked up to the kitchen aisle, and although tears and shivers appeared on her skin reminiscing about the indescribable things that had occurred there not a long while ago, she pulled out a glass and poured herself some water.

The fluid felt like elixir, and she relished in the calm it provided to her body.

Finally placing it down, she walked back inside her room, where she found her phone buzzing. She took a look at it and saw that it was her mother. Her fingers couldn't even move forward to pick it up, and the call ended.

She just crawled back inside the covers and tried to release the unsurmountable ache inside her heart, and this time, no tears fell. They had dried up, and she felt relief. No point wasting them over a heartless, animalistic, predatory, and insanely controlling person.

The whole day passed by this, and she couldn't even begin to describe the amount of hurt she felt flowing down her vessels when Pranay didn't even as much try to come and check on her, not that she expected him to. She couldn't believe that he might be in his office, laughing over silly jokes and attending meetings, after having stained her soul permanently.

Hunger gripped her insides though, and she carefully opened the door again, not at all willing to meet him. His name turned bitter on her tongue, and it made her gag.

Finally making it to the kitchen, she managed to open the fridge, but only after she had rested her forehead against it for a good minute.

Slowly, she took out a few fruits from inside. Then, she turned toward the jug usually placed on the slab. Bad move.

As soon as she turned, her blood ran cold in her vessels, and she almost had a brain freeze.

Water. Down her face. Into her ears. Her lungs. Instantly, she started feeling suffocated again. Hyperventilation almost knocked the wind out of her system, but she somehow managed to curb it. She filled up a glass and left for her room.

Feeding herself felt so strangely herculean, that she felt bile rise in her throat. These fruits came from the money Pranay had earned. And right now, she didn't want the shadow of his name on the surface of her brain, much less ingest anything he had laid his hands on.

But, realizing that she had started feeling unnaturally weak, she forced the food down her throat, although its taste turned to sawdust.

Just then, she felt the buzz of her cell phone in her ears, and weakly reached out to take it. She saw that it was Vipul.

Hesitantly, she answered him. His excited voice indicated something big had occurred. Suddenly, a hiss escaped her mouth as the cool glass of the device touched the finger imprints on her face. Instantly, Vipul quietened down. He had been telling her about how their joint report had been placed in the first position, which was something she felt momentarily proud about.

But the pain inflicted on her cheek had been elevated due to the phone, and Vipul now asked her, "Hey, why didn't you attend the classes today? Are you sick?"

There it was. The unbridled cascade of saltwater running down her face and neck, smearing not only her skin but also her heart in renewed, freshly opened wounds. Trying to keep her voice as steady as possible, she coughed out and informed him that everything was fine, that she was just feeling a little under the weather, probably because she had eaten a few kebabs that could have had soybeans in them. She said that she was extremely allergic to soybeans and had started breaking out in hives on her back and mild fever.

Vipul asked her how she felt now, and she responded that it was better with the medicines. Her heart ripped out while lying to him, but she had no other option.

Before keeping the call, Vipul softly said, "Remember my advice Freya. You are an amazing woman, which is why you deserve someone equally competent. Never exchange company for self-respect. Take care."

As she closed her eyes, Vipul's words rang out in her ears:

'Freya, life is a carousel. Sometimes, you go up. That is your family and friends appreciating you on your successes and achievements. That is, you feeling satisfied, gratified and blessed. Others are the lows. The high of rising up is so intoxicating that we forget that the lows are next. But they are relished, too. Not by us, but by those who feed on our soul. Those who are ready to strike the first chance they get. The high is love; the low is pain. I just want to remind you that there's barely enough time to love in a lifetime. Please don't give it all away to pain. It will come on its own accord if it has

to. No point dwelling over past and giving away our happiness as a debt to it.'

Freya was able to visualize Pranay so clearly in the people who prey on others that it scared her. There is barely any time in life to love completely, and she wasn't ready to give it all to pain.

Although she didn't have any will or voice left to speak to the monstrosity that shared the house with her, she could still convey her message by writing a letter.

This was why she sat down, and with great difficulty, started the process of tracing letters on a blank page.

Once finished, she decided to slide the letter below Pranay's room the next day while he was away, as she didn't want to see his face at the moment. Mentally exhausted, she decided to just go to sleep after applying some ointments to her injuries, as nothing could be more reassuring than escaping the real world.

The next day, when she was sure Pranay had left for the hotel, she tiptoed to his room and slid the letter underneath it. As she turned around to leave, she was reminded of the time she had brought him breakfast in bed. She tried to smile, but all that rolled out was a broken whimper.

She immediately grabbed a packet of soup and prepared it hastily. There was no reason to hurry, but it was as if every time she looked toward the door, her body underwent a bout of tachycardia, and before anything adverse could occur, she decided to take her bowl and leave.

Drinking the soup provided her some sense of relief, but unbeknownst to her, she should have consumed something more solid and filling, for what was about to come.

In the evening, Pranay returned home in a rather cheerful mood, solely because he had received a raise. The fact that he deserved to be raised on a pole and be pierced through and through didn't occur to him.

Entering his room, he placed his shoe on something, causing him to slip off. He stabilized himself and saw that it was a yellow envelope. Curiosity got the better of him as he opened it.

He sat down on his bed while reading it, but each word felt like pure venom dripping on his heart, and by the end of it, his hands were trembling from unfurled fury. His dominant, irrational and possessively animalistic was taking over, and he was relishing it.

The ends of the paper crumpled in his hold, as he took one last look at it.

'*Pranay,*

I have loved you with everything in me. I have tried to give all of myself to this relationship. And I believe you have too.

But what I experienced with you two days ago was traumatizing, and it is a good way to place it. My bones are cracking, not under pressure, but fear.

I have never experienced something so deeply unnerving. Although we haven't spoken about it, we don't need to. It is a nightmare come true.

The worst part is that you aren't going to ever talk about it. You are going to pretend you are right. I am not a toy or doll or clay for you to mold me, and I don't think we should live or be together.

Think about it.

Freya.'

"Bullshit! I need to go see her right now." He stormed up the stairs, each step like the rolling clap of an imminent tsunami.

He barged through her room, only to find her sitting by the window, her leaden eyes overlooking the road. She turned her head, her pupils visible dilating.

"Escaping me isn't an option, Freya. Understanding your fault and being punished for it is, though." Pranay spoke in an eerily haunting voice, as he slammed the door shut and locked it from the outside.

"No! Pranay! Open the door! I am sorry! I just wanted to give you some space! You can't lock me in here! No! Pranay!" Freya screamed and rushed with the speed of light, but the door had long been slammed in her face.

Her form crumbled against the stiles of the door, as her entire body as if convulsed with each breath. She felt practicality and energy escaping her body like wispy smoke, and she was covered in sweat and helplessness.

Pranay, on the other hand, felt a sense of relief wash over his heart, like a balm and he ignored her hoarse cries and walked off into his room.

Inside, Freya's situation became static, her eyes focused on nothingness, as shallow breaths left her, constricting her lungs painfully. Her shoulder still pained, and the muscles strained tremendously, but she was past caring, at least for the moment.

She drowned into the chaos because that is where the most incredibly pristine flowers grew.

Morning came, and Freya was still in the same position, although she had shifted a little to allow her shoulder to relax.

Finally, she stirred, and the moment she moved her neck, she felt her head was going to fall off of it. Intolerable throbbing consumed her, and she got up while holding her shoulder.

In a flash, she was grasping her phone and trying to call her father. She had been foolish in not telling him everything, but firstly, she was traumatized and then, she didn't want her parents to file some police case, although Pranay could easily have been arrested for the stunt he had pulled off.

But the sight that greeted her was of something conspired devilishly in hell. There was no cell service on her phone. She couldn't believe it.

She was confident in the fact that Pranay had something to do with it. Her eyes closed on their own accord, as she visualized her parents smiling toward her, ruffling her hair up.

Without a moment's hesitation, she entered the bathroom and turned the shower on, and sat below it. The cool, relaxing water poured on her head, down to her shoulders and feet, as if cleansing off any bleak ideas in the process.

Each droplet was such a stark contrast, soothing her body and yet burning right through it with the force of a thousand arrows. She wanted to erase his imprints from her body, to forget that the atrocious night ever occurred. The water didn't reach her brain though, and for some twisted reason, she liked that she remembered every inch of his actions.

After what seemed like an hour, she finally got out and dried herself off. Her cheeks were slightly red, and she walked up to the door and kicked it so harshly that the hinges shivered. All her pent-up fury was being unleashed, and in a flash, she threw a bottle of some ointment at the window, which then landed with a thud on the floor.

She ran up to it, and removed the curtains form the glass. What greeted her was unimaginably horrific and alarming. Three large wooden bars were nailed across the glass, and the view was blocked.

She knew, though, that it wasn't the view that Pranay wanted to block, but her escape. Her unbridled rush of anger didn't allow any tears to form, though. She just placed a palm over it and tried to let whatever warmth she could find, soak her skin in. For a few minutes, she stood like that, staring at the skin of her palm. Then, later on, she returned to her bed, and as if nothing had happened, picked up a book and began reading it.

The only thing worse than feeling pain was feeling absolutely nothing, and Freya was dangerously close to crossing the line over and delving into irreparable damage.

It was close to nightfall, and Freya was fast asleep in her bed, tiredness overpowering her. She was woken up by the sounds of something dropping on the floor downstairs, and although panic kicked in, she held her palms together and got out of bed, standing near her table.

As she had expected, the door opened, and although all she wanted was to throw a book at Pranay and run for dear life, she remained calm, but refused to look him in the eye.

"Here, have some food. It is Chinese, one of your favorites." Pranay said as he waited for a moment for her to say anything. When she didn't, he sighed and held her elbow, making every bone in her body quiver in fear, "I am doing this for us. You will understand it later, but you will surely thank me, dear." With that, he locked the door and went away.

She couldn't believe what her ears had just heard. There was no 'us' between them since the moment he decided to push her up against that wall. That 'us' died the moment he grabbed her by the hair. Now, all that remained was a parched, dead atmosphere.

The hunger was overpowering, and Freya took out a box of spring rolls and another one of fried rice, scarfing them down within fifteen minutes. Pranay could have very well added a sedative in it, but she didn't care. Starvation does that to a person.

After feeling like her insides had rejuvenated once again, Freya threw the boxes in the dustbin and looked toward her phone. She didn't know if her parents had called her, which she was sure they had. Tears formed on the brink of her eyes, but she wiped them off instantly.

After washing her face and arranging her bed, she decided to read for some time and soon fell asleep, thanks to her now full stomach.

The next day, while bathing, a perilously insane and dangerous idea came to Freya's mind. She couldn't believe she hadn't noticed it before. Sure, what she thought was crazily harmful, but she was beginning to sink into madness, and an escape was necessary.

There was an awning window at the very top, as was a custom have it to let out moisture. Pranay had surely put wooden bars on her main windows, but this one seemed untouched. Pranay, she knew, liked living lavishly, which was why he made it large enough and had even covered it with vines on the outside to provide it an aesthetic look.

But before getting her hopes high, looking at the situation dead in the eye, she decided to check if the window actually opened. Therefore, she made a makeshift staircase out of a tub, a bucket, and a small stool, and after getting on her tiptoes, she was able to reach it. With trembling hands, she held the knob and closed her eyes. Praying to God that it was not jammed, she put all her strength into turning it. She had half expected it to be stuck, but it opened with a swoosh, letting in a fresh gush of wind. The pleasure was so indescribably ineffable that Freya almost topped down the structure she had created. Hastily closing it, she made her way down and placed everything back where it was supposed to be.

But her smile couldn't be contained. It grew even wider when she remembered that she had an old rope somewhere in the back of her cupboard which was used during her shift to this hellhole.

The natural color that returned to her cheeks was marvelously ethereal, and she took one of the longest showers she had in a long time.

The moment her feet landed outside, she hastily wore her clothes and comber her hair. After sitting down for a few minutes, opened her almirah. Removing contents from the lowermost compartment for about five minutes, she was greeted by the sight of the rope. In the moment, it looked like it would help her ascend to heaven, which in a way it would. She took it out and placed it inside the bathroom. Then, she began moving rapidly, placing her things that were in the cupboard into her suitcases. Her clothes, books, laptop, blankets, everything was placed into three suitcases. By five in the evening, all of her almirah had been packed into those three large bags.

She kept quite minimal number of things in her table, as she felt it always crowded up the spaces. She decided to put aside a bag for it and left the things outside remain untouched. She felt so lightheaded that her insides almost bubbled up, the view of the world outside clouding her senses. But she put up a sad persona, which was actually very present, and hopped on her bed.

Later, around eight in the evening, Pranay returned home. Although Freya felt all giddy inside, she tried to calm down her nerves. "This will hopefully be the last time you see his treacherous, monstrous, lying face." She reminded herself and sat down on her bed, waiting for the lock to click open.

"Freya? Here you go. Some food. You must have been hungry." Pranay said in a singsong voice, as if his house had been all sunshine and roses lately. This time, he didn't even wait for a response and strode off, locking the door away.

Freya picked up the packet and saw that it was box that contained some palak paneer and some breads. Although she didn't want to eat anything he brought, she decided to be wise and have the food, because she would require all the energy she could muster for the escape.

After consuming the products, she threw the box away, and once she had confirmed that Pranay had left for his room, which was around eleven in the night, she stealthily got up and locked her door from the inside too, so that he couldn't come barging in.

Then, she collected everything lying on her table and put it into the bag, leaving no trace in her wake. She could have easily escaped alone, but the thought of her things left behind in the abomination of a place she currently resided in repulsed her.

Then, she carefully placed her wallet in the bag too, after triple checking it to contain all her documents.

After that, she went to sleep for some time, but not before placing an alarm for three in the night. She made sure to keep the volume at a minimum, so that only she could hear it and it wouldn't reverberate through the whole house.

The night was slightly warm, and Freya looked up at the ceiling, remembering all the events that took place in this house. However, her head soon hurt, and she closed her eyes.

At three a.m, the alarm softly rang in her room, and she immediately woke up to dismiss it, hoping Pranay hadn't heard the blare. Without wasting any time, she changed into some jeans and a hoodie, put on some sneakers, and pulled off her bedsheet and pillow covers. Stuffing the covers and clothes into one of the suitcases, she dragged all of them into the bathroom, where she looked up at the window. She went back in the room and removed the photo frame from the wall and placed it in one of the bags. Tears formed in her eyes, and she gathered all her bathroom supplies too, shoving them down her backpack. Again, she didn't want any of her things to remain in this inferno.

Then, she tied up her bedsheet to one end of the rope. Constructing the makeshift staircase again, she securely wrapped the end on the rope to the handle of the window. Then, she dropped the entire thing outside.

When she looked down, a smirk formed on her face to see that it reached the ground. Frisson bubbled up in her brain, and she almost felt heady from the sensation.

She had put her foot out to start climbing down, but then turned back to her backpack, took out a pen and some notebook, and wrote down furiously on it what was a supposed letter to Pranay. Placing it on the table, she put the notebook back inside and decided to throw the backpack down first, because it wouldn't make much noise. Once it was down, she looked back to check if any motion was heard in the house. Nothing. She sighed in relief.

Then came the difficult part. Each of the suitcases were heavy, and she had some real struggle moving them up. Once she was at the top, she pushed it down, hoping it wouldn't stir up too much disturbance.

Obviously, it did make louder clamor than the backpack, but the shrubs lining the house covered it up. Moreover, everyone was asleep, and if she barely heard the rustle, it was highly unlikely anyone else had.

In the same fashion, she threw the other two bags too, all landing on the ground. The last one did make some noise, and for a moment her heart stopped, but she forced herself to trust the process and immediately ran back inside the room to check if anything else remained. After scanning thoroughly, she unlocked to door and slid down the rope and bedsheet and placed everything around her. With some difficulty, she crossed the low masonry fences of the house and walked away into the night.

Her heart was shattering like shards of glass with each step, but it felt manically liberating. It was at this moment that she realized why peace and piece were pronounced alike. In order to make peace with your soul, it is mandatory for you to be able to discard a few burdensome, dark pieces from your life and glue the bright ones together.

Without a second thought, she presented at the police station, and everyone around was shocked to see a woman with loads upon loads of luggage appear at the door at four in the morning. The attending officer rushed over to her and asked her to sit down.

He brought out a glass of water and asked her to drink it. Once she had emptied it, the man asked her if she wanted to call someone. She immediately responded, "My parents." He gave her his cell phone, using which she called her mother. After four rings, she picked up. "Who is this?" she asked in a sleepy voice. Fresh brine stained her face as she uttered, "Mon, it's me." "Freya? Oh, my goodness. Do you know how many times we had tried to call you? The rings weren't ever answered. Where are you? How are you? Whose number is this?" she asked in a panic laced voice.

"I am at the police station, mom. You shall be informed about everything once you come here. Can you please come?" A broken voice left Freya.

"Of course, dear! The first things we do now is to catch a flight or train to Delhi. Don't worry. Is Pranay there?" her mother asked, obviously unaware of anything.

"N-no. He isn't. Just please come fast." Freya almost broke down further at the mention of his name, but the police officer rubbed her shoulder gently.

After placing the phone down, she rested her head in her palms. The man let her accommodate and relax. After about ten minutes, she raised her head up and said, "Do you have some time, officer? Because this is going to be long."

Curiosity and suspicion clouded his features while he nodded.

That was when all the incidents flowed out like a brook, which turned into a stream and finally a river. The police officer sat stunned at the thought of the extreme torment the girl in front of him had gone through, which included verbal, mental and extreme physical abuse.

When she showed him the scars on her shoulder and various other areas, some of which had turned purple, his eyes widened to the size of saucers.

He immediately sprang into action and called a doctor, while simultaneously providing her something to eat.

It was one in the afternoon and Freya's parents were sitting in a couch in a hospital, while she had her head placed in her mother's lap. Her father was sitting like a stone while rivers of tears ran down her mother's face, a few drops landing the side of Freya's face too.

"I am so sorry, dear! I should have forced you to come with me. You are never to leave my side again, do you listen?" Her mother said, while placing a hand on her shoulder, to which she winced. Instantly, she pulled it away and whispered a sorry to her.

Just then, the police officer who had come in, sat down, and said that they had sent a search group to check the outskirts of Pranay's house, while they were still waiting for him to show up. They said that they had found the rope and bedsheet tied together, probably left unnoticed by him as the bathroom faced to a side and not the front.

After that, he left.

Silence engulfed the entire atmosphere as everyone drowned in their own thoughts, while Freya fell quiet on her mother's lap, too exhausted from the cruelty the world had imposed on her.

As her eyelids turned leaden over the field of her vision, she realized one thing.

Attachment is the senile feeling of being taken by someone, so foreign and yet so singularly bound to you that you drown in the most they create around you, breathe in the air the exhale and slowly let the possessiveness envelop you from inside out, creeping over you like a poison ivy, spreading itself, and although it snatches away the oxygen from your lungs, you have grown way too pliable by that time that you feel high on deliverance and not asphyxiated by the loss of life from inside you.

She knows it was a late realization, but it made her somewhat content that the knowledge finally bloomed inside her. It was the last thought on her mind as her eyelids blocked her vision, and she fell into the dark pit of sleep.

Chapter 14
CINGULOMANIA

BACK TO PRESENT

"After I had been checked for other major injuries and received the green signal to leave, all three of us rented a room in the government guest house for a few days, until we heard something about the proceedings of the case." Freya said, rubbing her palm over her neck.

"Later we got to know something none of us could have imagined. I was sitting by the swings in the garden of the guest house when I heard a familiar voice behind me. When I turned around, I was met with Ishan, one of Pranay's friends whom I had met in some of the parties I had attended. I almost dropped out of my chair, but he held me and made me regain my calm. After asking for permission, he sat down in one of the other chairs and said something so unbelievable I felt my world shake. He told my why Pranay behaved the way he did, and what was the trigger for it."

After a long pause, she continued, "he told me that Pranay had been suffering from anti-social personality disorder, commonly called sociopathy since the past two years. He had been hiding it well, and I had absolutely no clue about it. How could I, until a long time had passed? Sociopaths have the cunning ability to appear extremely charming and approachable, which makes it impossible to tell them apart from normal people. Ishan told me that before meeting me, Pranay had a girlfriend named Gia while they were in college. She was a very caring girl, and always tried to put her best foot forward. At that time, Pranay too was quite naïve. But then, something happened that changed everything."

"Both of them used to live in Patel Nagar at that time, and it had been three months into their relationship. Everything was rosy, but then one day, Pranay came back quite late, because of some college work. He didn't want to worry Gia further, who had already been troubled since he hadn't picked her calls. When he came back, he was greeted not by water or food, but by a hoard of questions shouted at him and accusations of cheating. This was the first of many events to come. Then, it increased in intensity. Each time, Pranay tried to dodge her, but things escalated quickly when Gia broke three ceramic plates consecutively on his back. This was a turning point. After that, Pranay's behavior started changing. Every time Gia asked him for forgiveness and demanded a conversation, he would just look blankly at her, and would successfully manipulate the situation into blaming her. It was her fault, but she had a condition she kept hidden, because she felt mental health was a stigma, which it shouldn't be. She suffered from Intermittent Explosive Disorder. After the episode of the plates, Pranay started molding her into a frame bit by bit, without her noticing it. Soon, her anger was directed toward herself, and she almost slit her wrist once. To the world, Pranay became the outgoing, successful person, while on the inside, his soul had started rotting. He transformed into a versatile manipulator, with deceit flowing in his veins. I guess it was just bad luck I ran into him, ever. It was when he had closed me in the room that I had the first bout of chest pain. Last I heard of him, he was in some facility receiving treatment."

A sigh escaped her lips, as she whispered, "One thing I learned that time, though, is still imprinted in my brain: Destruction almost always comes immaculately disguised under the pretense of perfection."

A minute of silence passed before she resumed, "I had to undergo four and a half months of therapy to be able to rise a little above the trauma Vihaan. The bad part is that it still looms inside me. The good part is that the cracks inside me allow the light to shine through them."

Fiddling with her fingers, she closed her eyes as a whispery voice escaped her, "Pain is such a small, flimsy word. Four letters. People say that they are in pain all the time. Physically, mentally, socially. But what is real pain? Real pain isn't felt at all. In fact, it numbs all sensations. It makes you believe that the source of warmth has long been lost, that the cold, biting darkness is your abode now, and that is all you deserve. It eats you from within, like a moth. Pain makes you realize that all you have ever experienced was hollow happiness. Happiness can never be felt on its own. That is the drawback of that emotion. Some form of pain, some sadness is always attached to it. But the beauty of pain is that it can be whole. It can completely consume you, and there wouldn't be any space left for happiness. You can truly only wallow in sorrow. With shock comes surprise, with happiness comes suspicion, and with success comes fall. But with pain? Nothing. It comes alone. It is like that flower in the forest that blooms on its own, cracking up the stones in the process. It doesn't with easily, rather multiplies endlessly, until it has completely devoured the surface of the stones. And all that is left in the end is the root of misery, gripping the stone of life inside, not letting it receive the light, it is as if it is enough. It is truly the most diabolical feeling."

With that, Freya closed her eyes and laid back, and Vihaan held her hand. He couldn't even count the number of times he had cried with her, imagining everything she had gone through. Even greater to imagine was the volume of pain she had been harboring inside her cheerful exterior, just to hide away the broken pieces of herself she was too scared to let out in the open, just to be stepped on again. He couldn't imagine the number of nights she had to wake up in a cold sweat because of it.

A tear slid down her cheek and dropped down her neck, as she whispered, her voice a broken sob, "Now, I am afraid of the sound of locks clicking in, Vihaan. I am terrified. The moment I hear it, unbearable panic sets in motion inside me. I physically feel the air evacuating my lungs. I don't want to be like this. I want to be unafraid. I just- I feel bound and locked in this derogatory mindset at times and I can't help it."

She wiped the brine off her cheek and sighed deeply.

Vihaan's palms trembled heavily. He placed his hand next to hers.

"I am not going to say that you would outgrow it in a jiffy. You don't outgrow trauma that easily, Freya. You were terribly battered, and no amount sugar-coated words could ever soothe the open wound. The brain is a crazily complex system. It induces such deep-set fear based on the distorted past that it seems as though there isn't ever any escape possible. It cages you in the most unbelievable ways. But I have to say two things: one, you are the bravest person I have ever met, and two, you have me till the end of the universe. Even after that. Also, although I pray it never happens in a lifetime, but if someone remotely tries to harm you, I want you to call me and let me see how you demolish them, you strong woman." Tears pooled in the most enchanting pair of gray eyes Freya had ever peered into, and her arms moved to hug Vihaan, who didn't waste a second in scooping her up. A laughter escaped her, and Vihaan almost lost his heart. It was simply the purest thing he had heard in his entire life, and he despised the figure who made it dimmer. He hadn't met Pranay Shukla, and he never wanted to. He understood the struggles of suffering from a mental illness, but one look at Freya's face and all of that washed away into liquid gold, shimmering its way down them. After that, he put her back on the bed, and stroked her head, while she fell into sleep.

Walking out of her room, he slowly made his way to his own, which luckily wasn't too far away. He should have been here two hours ago, because Dr. Nitin had said so. Anyways, he was now. He saw a patient's uniform placed on the bed, and as soon as he moved toward it, a nurse entered the room.

"Nice to see you, Mr. Vihaan. You can change into the clothes while I bring out a few papers for you to sign. After that, we can take a round of tests."

Vihaan nodded and while the nurse walked out, he changed into the light green wear.

After that, he washed his face and lied down on the bed. He was deep in thought when the nurse entered along with Dr. Nitin and his parents, all of them forming a circle around him.

Dr. Nitin asked him to relax and produced a file which had a few papers he had to sign. After the procedure was completed, he directed him outside, to one of the elevators which took them to the second floor which had the labs.

On his way, Vihaan passed Freya's room and her calm sleeping face brought a smile on his own.

Once the tests were complete, he was directed back to his room, where he was placed on a simple oxygen mask. Slumber soon took over him, and he rolled off into deep sleep, one where Freya was elated, and no worries could ever touch her, where they were happy and content together.

Chapter 15
AUBADE

The next day, Dr. Nitin came in Vihaan's room almost waltzing around, while he placed a stack of reports and scans on the table.

"I have been able to study the tumor further, dear. Now, I am here to ask you to start breathing deep and easily, because your lung lobectomy will be a sure shot success, thanks to yours truly." He said, excitement pouring out of each cell in his body.

An honest laugh escaped Vihaan, as he spread his arms into which Dr. Nitin walked and patted his head. His parents had been sitting on the chairs, and as soon as they heard this, they hugged each other and thanked the Gods repeatedly.

Dr. Nitin took in the atmosphere of the room, and then turned around to face his patient. Vihaan's face was the epitome of the conflict brewing inside him, and it didn't go unnoticed by the man standing beside him.

"What happened, Vihaan? You suddenly seem a tad bit distraught. Are you fine?" Dr. Nitin asked. Vihaan looked at his palms, and tracing the lines etched along them, whispered, "Will I make through it? Will I be able to go out of this room, doctor?" Affection floated in the elder man's eyes as he placed a hand on Vihaan's shoulder, "I have been in this field for quite some time. I have seen a lot of patients get cured, and a lot of them succumb to the disease. I am in no way saying this to scare you, though. What I have experienced is what I want to share. Every person is in a fight, be it internal battles or the ones with others. We all are in a constant turmoil. And it is human nature to try to win. But some of us take the wrong path. We trick and deceive in order to succeed. What I have seen is that today, it isn't necessary for only the righteous to win. It is the resourceful that wins. We are all starring in a drama of the survival of the fittest, and our end goal is to thrive. It is correct, too. It is when we give in to our unending desire that we become blind. The human desire to survive is the death of all. Of humanity, of rationality. Don't ever let the question of survival trouble you, not in its positive aspect, and certainly not in its negative one. You are one great person, and every ounce worthy of survival. Cheer up because you are soon going to be out of this place."

The doctor smiled and left the room. Vihaan reclined back on the bed and felt his father's hand caress his forehead.

After a few moments, he received a call from Freya, over which he told her everything.

"I am so happy for you, sunshine! I can't even put in words the excitement I have for you getting all hale and hearty again." Vihaan thanked her and asked how she felt, to which she replied in the positive. Both their surgeries had been planned on the same day, two days later, and it was as much of a relief as it was a worry.

After placing the call back down, Vihaan turned to his parents and asked for some food. His father gladly made his way out, while his mother started talking to him.

After ten minutes or so, the door opened, and in walked Dr. Dev and Jatin. In an instant, Jatin rushed over to hug his best friend, while Dr. Dev said, "I just met Mr. Jatin downstairs, and decided to accompany him here. I must say, he is an extremely interesting person. So, how are you, Vihaan?"

Vihaan smiled and replied in the positive to which Dr. Dev excitedly said, "I am so glad to hear that. I am sure you will be fine in no time." With that, he took his leave.

Vihaan and Jatin resumed their conversation, and his father returned too, with a plate of porridge and a bowl of soup. He handed them over to his son, who didn't look too impressed, but finished the meal anyways.

The rest of the day was spent talking to his best friend, his parents, watching some television and reading a book he had brought along.

The next day was quite uneventful, except for the hour-long video call Vihaan had with Freya. They had been talking about plants and books, when Vihaan had asked her, "What is your secret wish, Snowflake?" Freya was a bit taken aback by the question, but continued, "I have always wanted to visit Venice. I have also read a lot and seen videos about it. Doge's palace, Saint Mark's Basilica, the Grand Canal, Piazza San

Marco, and the most beautiful, Bridge of Sighs. It is said that the prisoners would sigh at their final view of beautiful Venice through the window before being taken down to their cells. Also, it is a belief that if you have the chance to pass from below the bridge along with your partner even once in a lifetime, you are bound together for ages."

Vihaan listened to her as he smiled and then added, "We will go there, snowflake, and change your wish into reality. Do you even have any idea how much I love you? I love you in a way that if someone as much as whispers your name over my dying figure, life would flood into each cell of mine instantly."

He expected Freya to smile, not to frown. She furrowed her eyebrows and commanded, "Take the last sentence back right this instant. No health hazards around here on my watch, Mr. Vihaan."

Vihaan laughed as did she, and once it had subsided, she asked, "Will you take me to Venice?" Vihaan breathed in deeply, "You are Venice, Freya." After a pause, he continued, "Venice is the epitome of artistry and beauty. So are you, Snowflake. You are delicate art incarnate. Venice is the symbol of love, and you are the source of it. You fill me with light and love, and that is why you are my Venice."

"I love you." Was all Freya could say before the waterworks started, and Vihaan shushed her down, saying soothing words to her, praising her for all she was.

"I love you too, dear. You are buried deep inside my soul, wrapped around my bones, and pouring out through every cell of mine. Now, I want you to cut the call and sleep, because you need to preserve energy, not waste it by crying on some gray eyed boy who maybe loves you way beyond the moon. And God bless my heart, your eyes are so damn perfect, it drives me crazy. They are like luscious dark chocolate with a dusting of powdered sugar, decadent and sinful, yet ever so tempting." Vihaan said, and although Freya was still crying, she closed her carob eyes, the coffee that Vihaan liked the most in all of Café Athena, the one and only citron smoke that he wanted to fill his lungs and the only breath he would ever exchange against a lifetime of riches.

After placing the phone down, he switched the lights off and turned over to sleep, while his lungs almost rejoiced at the prospect of healing soon.

The next day, after having eaten the most monotonous meal of his entire lifetime, which consisted of a plate of papayas, which he absolutely abhorred and a bowl of plain oatmeal, Vihaan received a video call form Freya.

Upon answering, he heard an ear-splitting shriek, followed by a string of repeated thanks. He laughed, as he saw his girlfriend bury her face in the most gigantic bouquet he had ever seen.

Last night, he had asked Mr. Naqvi to prepare a collection of the flowers he liked the most. After the blooms had been arranged, Mr. Naqvi had called him back to inform so, after which he had been asked to tie them up together and arrange a water sponge beneath them, well-hidden of course, so that they didn't wilt. What he didn't know was that Mr.

Naqvi was an excellent flower arranger, having trained under a Japanese expert for a year, due to which he had learned the skill of 'Ikebana,' or flower arranging.

He had full and well exceeded his expectations and what had presented itself in front of Freya, was obviously a larger than life and breathtakingly delicate display of blooms.

"Do you want to know what all of them symbolize?" Vihaan asked, to which she eagerly nodded. Studying about flowers was his passion, and although he was an engineer, the enormity of artwork and hues God was the creator of never failed to befuddle him.

"The yellow ones you see at the bottom are azaleas, and they are the symbol of beauty and self-care." He said, as Freya ran her fingertips over them.

He continued, "The white ones are gardenias, and I must tell you that their zesty yet flowery smell if to die for. They symbolize gentleness and purity." The smile on her face widened.

"The pink ones forming a bridge, right in the middle, are called Ranunculi. These are one of the prettiest flowers I have ever come across. These body the idea of attractiveness and charm." A hand brushed over the blush petals.

"The ones interwoven with them are-" "Rhododendrons. You gave them to me." Freya completed for him. "They symbolize.... strength and beauty, I think." "Absolutely right! I see you learn quickly." Vihaan applauded her, before continuing.

"The ones behind them that look like two triangles meshed together, are amaryllis. They are the epitome of strength and determination." He felt something like pride suffuse in those hickory eyes.

"The bright scarlet ones behind them are gazanias, and I honestly don't know at this point, how the bouquet is holding together." He said, resulting in a chucked escaping both of them. "They exemplify wealth, fortune and riches."

And the ones standing atop all of them are anthuriums. I gave these to you, too." He spoke. "Right! They are still present on the entrance walkway of the café. These are a symbol of hospitality." Freya concluded.

Vihaan nodded, and then continued, "Now, the most important part. Do you see the scarlet, almost sangria masterpiece at the bottom? That's a blood red rose, as you know. This is the most crucial, Freya. This is the largest epitome of undying, unremitting love. My love. You can't even imagine the fear I wallowed in when I saw you in that motionless, almost quiescent state. More than that, though, even I can't fathom to imagine the number of times you have overwhelmed me by each word of yours, each twinkle in your eyes. Thank you for just existing and choosing to share this lifetime with me. Just imagining spending, it with you makes me heady, my palms sweaty, and my pulse rate accelerate, and although all of them seem like symptoms of some grave medical condition, they aren't. It is the most delicious side effect of being by your side, and if it means having a little bit of trouble thinking straight, so be it."

The most pleasingly garish smile formed on Freya's lips, and Vihaan had the urge to capture it in a glass pot and bathe himself with it.

"Wait a second, don't move." He said and captured a screenshot of the moment. "Just saved the best thing that ever happened to me."

"Do you want to know the best thing that ever happened to me?" Freya aske. He nodded, eagerness coursing its way all inside him.

"There was once a boy that came to my café. When I saw him, he was holding one of my all-time favorite books in his hands. On our first meeting, he seemed to be a bit reserved, but I was glad he opened up to me about liking the book I suggested him. Then, slowly but surely, our friendship grew, nestled in the walls of the café, but our topics of discussion were way beyond that range.

Over the course of time, I saw something in him that I hadn't in a long time. I saw a bewitching gunmetal charm in his eyes, which were determined like the unwavering steel one moment and fragile like cinders stirred up on the wind the next. Yet, there was something other than gray in those eyes. There were specks of white and silver, and though it may seem unnatural and uncanny, it was the most magnetizing thing I had ever seen.

But the charisma doesn't end here. This was until I had seen him smile. And when I saw, it was a heartstopper for me. That smile alone could burn me to ashes and resurrect me like an elixir. The real baffling thing, though, were his eyes, yet again, which turned into two crescents when the laughter escaped him, never failing to let a stampede begin in my belly.

His eyes were so much like the Saturn that I felt drawn toward them just like Titan and Tethys, with specks of white circling it whenever he was brooding. I never thought I would fall in love again, much less alone due to a pair of eyes. When I look into his eyes, I am bound to believe anything and everything. Pain turning into peace, the molten feeling of despair turning into a cascade of pleasure, rivers of tears being frozen over by the cold touch of relief. Want to know why? Because he is my universe. And the universe is ever so unraveled, just like his irises.

The real deal came out when his personality opened up to me. His heart was the purest I had ever met, and at times I felt disgusted to be with him, tainting his immaculate soul with mine. But, even without knowing anything, he stuck with me through thick and thin, cried with me, and made it sure to write the most heart-warming letter I have ever received, only because he felt intimidated at the thought of verbally expressing his feelings.

All of this, combined with his par excellence knowledge of plants and an interest in literature was like a recipe for attraction. I knew it could be dangerous to let myself out in the open again, but he made it sure to put his best foot forward, and never ceased praising me for the most mundane things.

This man, may I say, is extremely gorgeous too, with jet black hair falling in his eyes, his nose upright like the mountains. His chin is like the plateau made of raw earth and mud. His hands are the embodiment of his credence, a bit callused, which expresses his belief in hardships, yet soft to the touch, indicating his luminous and unblemished personality on the inside. I had never encountered anything so larger than life, and it made me equal parts drawn to him and terrified to poison his life. But I tried to trust the process, and I am beyond glad it led me to this point, to us.

There was something else, too. I could feel it. His zinc eyes were caged with metal doors, pleading to be opened, but the keys were yet to be discovered, resting in some unknown place. I hope I have found them, though. Even if I haven't reached the depths of different aspects of his life, I want nothing more than to explore them.

Lastly, but this is the most cardinal point, this man made me fall in love with not only himself but love too. The process of falling in love and embracing it. Letting it settle deep in you, claiming every cell of yours. Falling in love is scary because we are unaware of what awaits us. I am deeply and forever thankful to this man to make the fall feel like flying.

You are the wishes I scattered all over in my backyard, forgetting all about them as I grew up. But not all scattered things decay. I may have lost the track of their progress over time, but that didn't hamper them from turning themselves into such an undeniably perfect yet rightly humane form.

I love you, for all you are worth, from every atom in my body, and I believe in you, because you have proven time and again that you are the pillar, I can succor myself on. All I want for you is success and love, sunshine."

Vihaan was dazed, while Freya gulped down a few sips of water. "Whew, what was quite a speech. The longest I have spoken in a long time. So, did you like it?" she asked.

"Freya, I.... I didn't know you felt so deeply for me. I thought it was only me. Thank you, a thousand times, for sharing your thoughts with me. All I want now is to hug you, but sadly, that will have to wait. I am beyond in love with you, and I am enjoying every second of it." Vihaan breathed out, tears threatening to spill out of his eyes.

Suddenly, he shook his head to one side, and then looked back up, a fuzzy smile formed on his face. "Did you just yeet away your tears?" Freya asked, obviously shocked.

"I did, didn't want my cheeks getting wet. Cool, isn't it?" Vihaan asked, seeming impressed with himself. "I must say, it is very effective in preventing your makeup from getting ruined. I shall try that sometime." Freya retorted. Both of them laughed out about it, after which tiredness started overtaking them, so they cut the call and curled-up in their blankets to sleep.

The day the surgeries had to be performed finally dawned. Vihaan's hands were trembling slightly, while Freya seemed to have forgotten what speaking meant, as she called for Dr. Kriti the second time. Upon her arrival, Freya almost got out of bed, but composing herself, asked, "I know I shouldn't be troubling you like this, mam. But it is just that my nerves won't calm down, and all these negative thoughts are invading my mind. I will get well, right?"

"It is normal, dear. I can't imagine being under the scalpel and trust me when I say it is like taking a leap of faith, believing that there is someone above all of us, much more knowledgeable and powerful, the one who looks over everything we do, and He will never let anything happen to you. It is all about faith, so keep a strong bond with Him." Dr. Kriti said, patting Freya's head.

"When exactly is my surgery?" Freya asked. "If the operation theater gets free according to schedule, we should be good to go at four in the evening." She informed, smiling softly as she headed out.

Dr. Nitin, on the other hand, was playing a game of carrom with Vihaan, as he proclaimed it was his self-sought way of distracting his patients from the stress of the impending future.

His method had worked, and Vihaan was now watching some Australian web series, his anxiety seeming to have reduced. He had been informed that he would be taken into the operation theater around half past four in the evening. There were three hours to it, which he could spend doing whatever he liked.

Soon enough, it was half past three. Thirty more minutes till Freya would forever be free of the obstruction and pain she felt collapsing her chest, almost tiring her to the brink of a severe blackout. She would be able to run freely and strain her body, not crumbling under the fear that her heart might give up on her.

Surprisingly, she felt comparatively relaxed. The jitters were very much present, but a thrill, though it sounded weird in her head, was overtaking the charged cells of her body.

She grabbed her phone and dialed Vihaan's number, who picked up after three rings. "Feeling scared, sunshine?" Freya asked, anticipating something along the lines of 'we will be okay' or 'we have each other forever.' But what he said was far more soothing, and she fell in awe once again at how eloquent he was.

"I am feeing nothing and everything at the same time, snowflake, as if all the questions bubbling up in my mind are threatening to present themselves soon. I am trying to be calm, but it is difficult. However, I am confident that you must be more composed than me."

"A snowflake is quite fragile, Vihaan. How do you expect me to be level-headed? My father has been stressing out more than me, though. Anyhow, I haven't called you to increase any of the anxiety or stress. I have another thing to say."

"And what might that be?"

"I have never truly gotten the chance to appreciate our nicknames. I know you have explained the reasoning behind calling me snowflake, but I want you to know why I love to call you sunshine."

"Go ahead, snowflake."

Ignoring the splash of unrivaled euphoria the name left her with, she spoke, "The sunshine is the source of life to the entire earth. It nurtures everything it grazes; its touch is vital. When you wove yourself into the messed-up yarn of my life, I felt my insides light up with your positivity. You filled me with a baffling luminosity. Looking at you, I could only remember the sunshine, hence the nickname. However, I now view our nicknames in a different light. A snowflake and sunshine are the polar opposites, they almost can't survive together. Sunshine is warmth, while a snowflake is iciness. But, over the course of time, I have realized that the sunshine doesn't always mean warmth, it also means glow. It produces the most pristine reflections. Therefore, I want to thank you, my sunshine, to let me, a snowflake, bathe in all your splendor and glamour. Thanks for everything, sunshine."

Her words held so much substance that Vihaan was taken aback. That she thought so deeply and was attached to the nicknames was astounding and endearing.

"Well, I, as the sunshine, am the one who should be honored to be able to shine over such a symmetrically phenomenal snowflake. So, thanks to you too." Vihaan concluded.

They talked for some more time, building up each other's confidence, and although the red mass of muscles in their chests was trembling, there were the lungs to stabilize them, much like they had each other.

As she lay sprawled on the operation table, a million thoughts were speeding through Freya's brain, but she let them pass, except for the pictures of Vihaan and her parents behind her closed eyes.

Warmth bloomed in her body, and when Dr. Kriti asked her if she was prepared, she nodded and closed her eyes in a silent prayer to God, the one and only creator, the source of everything, and most importantly, the personification of love.

Patient: Freya Gupta

Surgery: Coronary artery bypass graft

Time: 4:02 PM

Attending surgeon: Dr. Kriti Desai

"Success."

Another operation theater was occupied, too.

Patient: Vihaan Sharma

Surgery: Lung lobectomy

Time: 4:35 PM

Attending surgeon: Dr. Nitin Tripathi

When he is six, Vihaan falls, tripping over a rock on the road. A sob tears through his chest, but no one comes to help him until fifteen minutes later.

When he is sixteen, he falls, slipping over the mud and into a construction tunnel, because his friend had accidently pushed him. By the time he is out, blood is oozing from his arm, and yet again help arrives late.

When he is twenty-four, Vihaan falls. Falls for the cascade of brunette hair flowing down her back. Falls for the chestnut of the eyes, which widen whenever anything entices her. Falls for the books and bindings which she adores. Falls for every leaf and bloom she smells. Falls for the coffee she finds delectable. Falls for the butterflies escaping in his stomach whenever he caught sight of her. Falls for all Freya is, all she comes with, and all she upholds. He falls through centuries of centuries, until he forgets he is falling, and the fall starts feeling like flying. He falls in love with Freya, and his soul soars.

But this time when he falls, she would be right there to catch hold of him.

"Success."

EPILOGUE: CWTCH

Vihaan walked ahead, strolling through the busy Piazza San Marco, while Freya gobbled up another bruschetta, whining about going back to the shop for some more.

They had been in the city for three days, and this was the fourth. Freya was already planning on buying a house there.

"You have already bought five of them, snowflake. Leave some space for the caprese salad, please." Vihaan tried to reason with her, while she frowned, trying to appear furious, but it only added to the already overflowing beauty she held.

Anyways, she agreed, and they walked forwards, gearing up to visit Doge's palace. The Venetian gothic architecture was a class apart, and the opulent interior immediately enthralled both of them.

Three months had passed since the surgeries, and both of them had been advised with ample of rest for about a month. This had helped their bodies regain some strength and had made them feel more complete, renewed, and rejuvenated.

Life had been going on and about for the world, but their worlds had shifted, and both of them couldn't have been more grateful for it.

After exiting the palace, they strolled some more, and while the sun set over the water, Vihaan and Freya filled themselves up with a generous helping of caprese salad and corn cannelloni.

"Do you ever go back to the time when we met, and well, things before that?" Vihaan enquired, feeling slightly uncomfortable, but had this question in his mind for a while now, and wanted to let it all out.

Freya smiled and rubbed her palm over his arm. "You don't have to be uncomfortable in the slightest. It is a genuine question. As far as the answer goes, it is a yes to both of them. I do think about my rather… unpleasant time with Pranay. It surely was devastating, but I did learn a few extremely valuable lessons from it. However painful it was, it is over and, in the past now, and it is the best if it remains that way. And of course, I remember the first time I met you, and how far we have come. I can't believe you could be so naïve to think I would ever forget even a single detail about it. So, yeah, I remember everything, and I have made peace with my past and fallen in love with my present. "

The same charming, relaxed smile spread over Vihaan's face, as his eyes closed into the most precious crescents. Having finished their dinner, they paid on their way out and strolled back to their hotel.

The next day, as the water turned glossy with the sun peering into its reflection and grazing it with warmth to relieve it from the cold night, Vihaan and Freya sauntered down the cobblestone pathways.

They had planned to cover the Grand Canal today, and the idea of riding a vaporetto was supremely exciting to both of them. Once on it, both of them had to admit that it was the most spectacular boat they had ever gotten on. The glass windows allowed them to gaze at the precisely symmetrical and intricate Venetian architectural beauty, and it was breathtaking in the least.

After covering the waterways, they walked over the Rialto bridge, where Vihaan suddenly went rambunctious and almost threw himself into the water from below the arches. Later on, they paid a visit to Scala Contarini de Bovolo, a small palazzo known for its multi-arch spiral staircase, the Teatro La Fenice, a humongous opera, and the Santa Maria Della Salute, a Roman catholic church with an impressive dome.

All of them were competing with each other in grandeur, elegance and individuality.

Although, by four in the afternoon, they were famished, and with it being in their second last day, Freya was both glad and gloomy. She was excited to be going back home, but a part of her was filled with sadness over having to leave this magical place behind.

They were feasting on some pasta primavera in an outdoors café, when Vihaan suddenly received a call from his office, and he excused himself to pick it up, busking away into the crowd to search for a rather quiet place, promising Freya to be back soon.

She was about to take another bite, when a voice arose from behind her, resulting in shudders running through her entire spine. "Never thought I would meet you here, Freya."

She turned around, and she saw the sight that made her eyes bulge out, her breathing to turn irregular, and her hands to shake so much that she the fork almost fell.

Appalled.

Alarmed.

Enraged.

Perplexed.

Still as charming, and maybe still as difficult.

With great struggle, she placed the fork back on the plate and stood up, eyeing the man up and down. "Wish I could say the same about you, Pranay." Her eyes raked him from head to toe, and although she was in a jam-packed place, she still felt his aura trying to overpower her.

Pranay noticed her discomfort, and immediately spoke, though not taking any steps toward her, "You have nothing to be afraid of. I know the words may seem hollow, and that you may never want to see me or think of my condition, but I just saw you here and thought of saying hello."

This relaxed her nerves a bit, and although she prayed Vihaan to come back soon, she also wanted to stand up to her fears. "Well, it was really nice seeing you. I don't really want to ask, but you may sit down, if you want to." She pointed to a chair beside the one occupied by Vihaan.

He contemplated for a moment, and then gave in, sitting down with a sigh. "So, how have you been?" He asked.

"It has been rather difficult, as you may be aware of." Freya narrowed her eyes, and Pranay shifted slightly. She sighed and continued, "I am not holding any grudges anymore, Pranay. I just want to clarify that. I would never deny that I was scared and hurt, both mentally and physically and almost destroyed completely, while I was with you. But so were you. You did something awful, but it isn't completely your fault, as you weren't exactly in control. Even so, I am not horrible enough to wish anything bad upon you. I know you too aren't."

She felt his legs tremble but didn't point that out. Before anything could be said, Vihaan appeared back, saying that he was extremely apologetic for leaving her alone, but his sentence was left mid-air as a look of confusion crossed his features.

"I am assuming this is your boyfriend, right?" Pranay asked her, and she nodded proudly, her eyes shining with love and adoration toward a still befuddled Vihaan. "Take a seat, sunshine. I want you to meet someone I know." Freya said, and from the corner of her eyes, she saw hurt, but something else, something like happiness flash in Pranay's eyes.

"This is Pranay." Freya said, completely ready for Vihaan to get enraged, although it was rare, or to him start asking her to leave, which was more likely. What she didn't expect him to say, though, was, "Your loss." This had been said so calmly, it was almost disconcerting.

An unnerving smile bloomed on his lips, and what chilled the atmosphere was that it didn't reach his eyes. "I am Vihaan. It is a pleasure to meet you, Pranay." He said, while sliding the plate of pasta toward him, "Care for some?"

Pranay hesitantly shook his head in refusal, and Vihaan settled down comfortably.

Freya spoke, trying to defuse the tension that lay over them like a blanket, "So, Ishan had come to meet me once and had told me you were in a 'better place' than when you were, well, with me. How come you are here?" "That is what I told him to tell everybody. I didn't want anyone finding out I left the facility, because no one would believe me when I would say that I had been officially released from there. That was why I only informed my parents, and now I have been here for the past few months." He informed.

"How were things at the facility?" Freya asked. "To be honest, when you left, it was so unbearably enraging for my brain to have lost control over someone, and I almost committed suicide. In the first few weeks of being admitted, I clearly was the most troublesome person in the whole place. But, in about a month, I began realizing that throwing tantrums would only land me in more trouble. Slowly, I started talking to a few people, asking them about their struggles. It was difficult, trying to understand their emotions, because my brain wasn't accustomed anymore for it. My parents had been immediately informed, obviously, and they were very supportive. They came to visit me frequently. I talked to a therapist daily, and also befriended the psychiatrists there. It was slow, weird at first, and somewhat painful, but I began thinking about all the horrible things I had done, and when I finally realized the magnitude of it, I almost killed myself over there, by slitting my wrist. Thankfully, the nurses stopped me in time. Eventually, the conversations, environment and medicines worked, and I got significantly better. When I was finally released, with a very mild dose of two medications still continuing, I decided to turn over a complete leaf. I figured out it was time to change my surroundings for some time, and although my mother was initially not quite sure, she gave in after much persuasion. I think I needed it Freya, because now I am in a much better place, and have opened a restaurant just near the Bridge of Sighs, and it had been flourishing quite well by the grace of God. And although I know there is no forgiveness or redemption for what I have made you go through, I would still apologize to you a thousand times, and thank you, for being so understanding at that time. You are a gem, and Vihaan is lucky to have you."

Freya looked up at Vihaan, who was staring right into Pranay's soul. "You are a nice man, Pranay. Sure, you made some terrible decisions, but it was your brain and not entirely you. If Freya is ready to forgive you, consider your redemption arc completed. Also, I apologize for my cold behavior earlier, it was not intentional, just came out of remembrance of Freya's past." He spoke.

"It is fine, Vihaan. If I were you, I would have probably flipped off the table by now. Thanks for listening. I hope you both find all the happiness in the world." Pranay smiled. Just then, a message chimed on his cell phone.

"Something came up at the restaurant, and I would have to leave. It was extremely relieving meeting you and confessing everything, Freya. Hope you live a fantastic life ahead. This is my card, and I would be pleased to see you at the place if you feel comfortable." He said, while getting up and sliding a yellow visiting card on the table.

"Sure. We will." Freya smiled slightly, and he walked off, while she released a breath, she didn't know she had been holding.

"How are you feeling?" Vihaan asked, wrapping an arm around her shoulders. "Free, elated, and secure. Free, because I finally have the closure I always wanted, and I guess Pranay too had been searching for that. Elated, because I now know that he is in a much better place than three years ago. He is visibly healthier, and I am glad he got the help when it was crucial. But above all, I feel secure because I have you, Vihaan. I have the most precious and amazing person in the world by my side, who will protect me no matter what, and will love me beyond the stars and till the end of time. And for that, I feel blessed." Freya concluded, and Vihaan wrapped his arms around her in a tight hug, while smelling the signature vanilla and cinnamon smell.

After that, they decided it was best they go back to their hotel and rest. Freya gleefully agreed, buying another bag of bruschetta on their way back, while Vihaan agreed to give her a piggyback ride.

The next morning was pristine, and Freya woke up in a cheerful mood. The breeze was cool, and the sun shone softly upon the streets and waters of the place. After having some breakfast at the hotel, she decided to pack up a few things in advance for their impending flight in the night, so as to avoid any last-minute hassle.

By the time they were on the streets, it was one in the afternoon, and the only thing to do that day was to ride a gondola from below the Bridge of Sighs. Freya had insisted on saving it for the last, because she wanted it to be imprinted in their minds for a long time.

But before that, they had to visit Pranay at his restaurant. It was convenient due it its close proximity to the bridge. This was why they found themselves sitting on the comfortable and plush chairs of 'Nuvola,' one of the most enchanting and highly rated restaurants in the city. They had been sitting for a minute, when Pranay appeared in front of them, dressed in a powder blue two-piece suit and a white dress shirt. Smiling down at them, he asked what they would like to have. Both of them decided they wanted him to order whatever he considered was the best, and he assured them that what would come would be delectable.

After about ten minutes, on their table were ravioli with coconut milk and lemongrass, bruschetta topped with grilled vegetables and feta, and some black bean and corn quesadillas, along with two flutes of champagne.

"Hope you like it." The waiter said, while disappearing into the crowd.

They more than liked it. It was the best food they had consumed in Venice, and it was saying something as all the dishes they had had were mind blowing. After having finished the food, they waited for the bill. None arrived, rather Pranay came back. "How was the food?" He asked. "Beyond delectable. It was ineffably delicious. I am not surprised by the crowd you gather." Vihaan commented.

A laugh left him, "I have seen to your bill, and it is on the house. Before any of you object, I should clarify that I am not going to listen. I still am apologizing, and it is a part of it."

Freya smiled, while she said, "Thanks a lot, Pranay. I truly only wish the best for you too. I hope you find both success and love. We would love to keep in contact. Would it be possible to exchange phone numbers?" "Sure." He said while pulling out his cell phone. He exchanged contacts with both Vihaan and Freya and bid them goodbye soon.

Now that the meal was over, they had only one place on mind. The Bridge of Sighs. Walking hand in hand, they reached over to Doge's place, where they paid the fees to join a group of tourists to enter inside it.

Once they reached the beginning of the bridge, Freya held Vihaan's hands tightly as excitement poured over her in waves. The guide told them about the importance of the bridge. The arched structure wasn't made to be open air and possessed only two windows to look out at the city. The name came from the sighs of prisoners who crossed the bridge on their way to their prison cells or execution chamber, catching their last glimpse of sophisticated beauty of Venice through the small windows. It was more mind blowing than both Freya and Vihaan had imagined it to be, and when they peeked through the small windows, they were able to see the expanse of water and the overlying bridges crossing over the canals like interwoven yarn against them.

Finally, when the tour was over, they descended down to wait for their gondola, and they were fortunate that it arrived within five minutes. It was copper and indigo in color, with plush navy seats and small roses covering the expanse of the floor.

With each step on it, the gondola shook a little and the boat rower helped both of them on board. Freya bent down a little, and something dangled from her neck. Vihaan has noticed earlier that it was a silver chain, which looked heavenly on her. But what he saw now knocked the breath from his lungs.

The pendant. His memories rushed back to the Christmas they had spent together. "The serotonin pendant." He whispered.

Freya turned to him and placed a palm om his cheek. "Remember you had said it is the happy hormone? I found my happiness in you, Sunshine, and this is the most precious expression of the feeling. She held his hand as both of them stood on the boat, and Vihaan felt his heart swell with admiration for the woman in front of him.

Once aboard safely, both of them sat facing each other on a seat, boring into the others eyes, and copper clashed with zinc, forming the most spellbinding gateways, which opened into the vastness and wilderness that passion and love were, into the never-ending waters of dissolving so wholly into the other that you felt reformed into an entirely new being, into a comfortable night that held secrets of affection and buzzed with songs of admiration.

The gondola neared the bridge, and the rower pointed that out softly. Both of them looked up, the under surface of the bridge coming into view gradually. Just as the boat came closer to the masterpiece, both of their heartbeats soared a mile a minute. The tip of the gondola crossed the bridge, and Vihaan pulled Freya by the arm.

It was within a split second that he gently placed his lips over hers, and Freya felt an entire zoo go rampant in her stomach. It wasn't much different for Vihaan. He felt his insides turn into silver, and with each heartbeat, the moment grew more beautiful.

There was nothing slovenly about the kiss, it was pristine and simply the most divine moment both of them had ever experienced. It was like tiptoeing over the edges of stars, burning in their ferocious glare, yet in your heart of hearts, you know that the burn is the ultimate soothing sensation creeping up your spine, because gases are not what stars are made of. They are made of undying hopes and wishes, the desire to find that one lone person who will look past your skin and into your heart. The stars are plasma, glowing incandescently, letting the plasma in your body course its way through you, to make you feel alive. Just like her lips did to him. It was fulfilling, just like both of them suffused inside each other, and even though it had barely been twenty seconds, they parted, and immediately longed for the moment to come back.

"I am beyond in love with you, Freya. I am mesmerized and infatuated, and a lot more that I can't express. This was just a physical demonstration, but my feelings runway deeper than something superficial. I want to be with you, and I promise to give you all the contentment, acknowledgment, desire and value you are worthy of. You are my Venice and my Paris, my sin, and the redemption for it. You are all the music I want to listen to, all the directions I want to traverse. You are the catharsis to pain inflicted over millions of years. You let my soul grow on your soil of vastness, of abundance, of madness, of euphoria. You are the destination I long for and the longing my destination glorifies. You are the carmine of my blood, the alabaster of my bones and the ash of my eyes. You are the needle to my flesh broken over the pain of loneliness. You are the rain that pours over the sea; you mix into the water itself, yet you are a thousandfold more riveting to watch than the drops falling on concrete, only to evaporate. I was never prepared to fall so infinitely deep into you, but now that it seems I have fallen, I never want the process to cease. You are home, and I would rather live inside of you than to experience all the glory the world has to offer, because you are the flow of the universe, Freya."

He leaned in and kissed her forehead, letting another batch of butterflies roam about unbridled in her body. They had turned around and were headed back, with the bridge approaching again.

A lazy, dazed, alluring smile warmed up on Freya's lips, the kind that was worth a thousand sunrays and that could make anybody drunk on her.

"You are everything I have ever desired, Vihaan. You are the dust over the moon that every poet longs for. You are the glow of the fireflies that illuminate the caves with a soft luminescence." The bridge neared. "You are mine. You are the desired silence amidst the clamor of the race to be on top. On the other hand, I am the struggle of the fish flowing against the current of the river. I belong to you just as much as the fish's efforts ultimately blend into the crystal water, for that is where they belong. You made me fall in love with yourself, myself, and love again. But above all, you are the one who made the fall feel like flying."

The bridge closed in on them again, and she leaned in, with Vihaan holding her above him by her waist, to seal their lives together with a kiss made of melting passion and searing determination, which ignited them into the blazes of each other, and none would ever complain.

www.ingramcontent.com/pod-product-compliance
Lightning Source LLC
LaVergne TN
LVHW041151150826
845673LV00001B/129

9798892779470